# SAMANTHA SUTTON

AND

## THE WINTER OF THE WARRIOR QUEEN

4 —

ART
395

# SAMANTHA SUTTON

### AND

## THE WINTER OF THE WARRIOR QUEEN

### JORDAN JACOBS

Published by Sourcebooks Jabberwocky, an imprint of Sourcebooks, Inc.
P.O. Box 4410, Naperville, Illinois 60567-4410
(630) 961-3900
Fax: (630) 961-2168
www.jabberwockykids.com

Library of Congress Cataloging-in-Publication data is on file with the publisher.

Source of Production: Versa Press, East Peoria, Illinois
Date of Production: November 2013
Run Number: 21854

Printed and bound in the United States of America.
VP 10 9 8 7 6 5 4 3 2 1

For Linz

**Site Name**

Wardy Hill, Cambridgeshire, UK (WH)

**Unit/Level**

N/A (received in Palo Alto, CA, by rush mail, from Ministry of Culture, Lima, Peru)

**Find #**

SSFNb2

**Object Type**

Notebook (fragmentary)

**Measurements**

24cm x 18cm x 4cm

**Material**

Paper; aluminum; long piece of nylon string (knotted)

**Description**

Reporter-style field notebook in very poor condition. Cover (front and back) not present.
Water damage, mildew, mold, some soil (and blood?) staining throughout.
Loose inserts between some pages (see also SSFNb1).

**Context/Associations**

~~The object's recipient knows it to be the "field" notebook of Samantha Isis Sutton~~
~~from her excavation of Wardy Hill, Cambridgeshire in the winter of~~

Please see attached document for detailed contextual information.

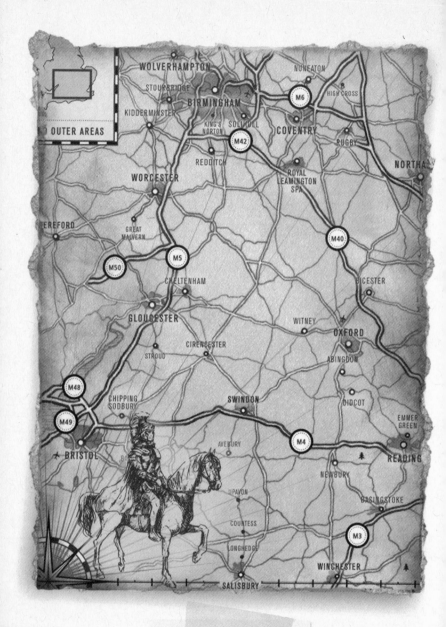

SSFNb2-[Loose Page] 20b

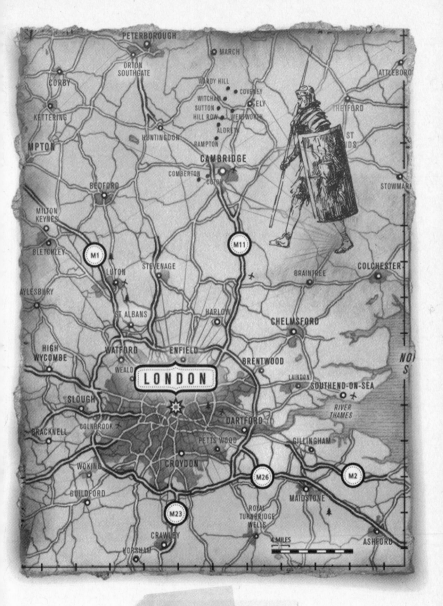

# PROLOGUE

England. Samantha Sutton risked a glance through the train window and up at the overcast sky. In the panic of her escape, she hadn't factored in the early northern sunset. Now, in midwinter, it was dark by five most evenings, and on a day like today, the covering of clouds could snuff out the sun as much as an hour before.

There were maybe fifteen minutes left of daylight, she figured, and still forty miles between her and the great cathedral city to the south. All of her journey would be in the dark. And most would be at a run.

She took a long, deep breath as the train ground to a stop and held it until the doors groaned open. Could he have followed her here? Would he be waiting, just outside? She put her head through the open door for a look up and down the platform, and for a second—then two, then three—she was exposed to all who passed by. But a chime and a recorded voice warned her of the train's immediate departure, and she had no choice but to step outside.

She felt her muscles clench, ready for hands to close around her throat or to rip her precious backpack from her shoulders. But nothing happened. No one even turned to look at her. The thin crowd just pushed by, indifferent. Threading between the last of the passengers and through the station of glass and steel, she allowed herself a little hope. Maybe she'd lost him, after all.

She stepped out into the January evening as gloomy Swindon began its slow shuffle home. Her fear could keep the cold away, but not the wet. The snow that showed in the light of the streetlamps had an intensity that surprised her, until she realized that her royal blue raincoat was already flecked with white, and melting snow was seeping through her jeans. She reached behind her to make sure the backpack was cinched all the way closed. The bag was so streaked in mud that the stripes and bars of its Union Jack design were only barely discernible—the red, white, and blue merged to mottled dun. But tacky as it was, the backpack was well made and would shield the object it contained during the long night's journey ahead. She pulled the bag higher on her shoulders and hurried into the shadowy city streets.

She knew she couldn't afford to look lost. A disoriented twelve-year-old girl—especially one of her small stature—would attract concerned attention, questions she couldn't answer, long-distance calls to her parents in California, and the involvement of police. Any delay would be catastrophic. No one would be able to protect her from the man who hunted her now.

The first close call came only minutes into her journey. She passed a pub, bustling with evening commuters, and the burly clientele who had spilled out onto the sidewalk to smoke. Samantha shouldered her way through and all fell silent, their eyes pinned on her backpack.

And no wonder. The bag would have been noticeably heavy to anyone who saw it, the way it arched her back and slowed her pace. But it was what pressed outward through the bag's dirty canvas that attracted the men's attention. The light streaming from the pub drew out the contours so anyone could guess at what she carried. There were the big ears, there the professorial brow, and there the sharp Roman nose. A close look would have even revealed the loops of hair, cropped short, as slight ridges beneath the fabric. It was, essentially, just what it looked like: a severed human head.

"Oi!" cried someone through the pooling cigarette smoke. "What's that you've got there?"

Samantha flinched.

"Didn't you hear me, love? I asked you a question."

But she just pulled the straps tighter and increased her pace, her heartbeat thudding behind her eyes.

She did not slow until she was free of the city center, when the clusters of grim apartment towers gave way to open parkland. The snow had eased enough to make out the motorway in front of her—the M4—and just beyond it the moonlit fields of Wiltshire. Here, at last, she could pause to orient herself.

She fished her notebook out from beneath her jacket, where it hung from her neck by its knotted length of twine. The map she'd torn from the atlas told her to go almost directly south—through Wiltshire's fields and downs and its ancient, sacred groves. She would pass through villages with storybook names like Upavon, Countess, and Longhedge—names that on any other journey would conjure a smile to her face and a desperate need to rush to the library and research their origins. But not tonight. While she may have lost her pursuer in London some hours before, he had surely guessed her destination and was likely racing to intercept her somewhere ahead.

Still—she tried to convince herself—that was tomorrow's concern.

An overpass spanned the motorway ahead of her. She hurried toward it.

"Excuse us."

"Miss?"

The voices startled her so much that the backpack slid from her shoulders. Two figures emerged from the shadows some feet away. They were police officers—one man, one woman—each garbed in a fluorescent yellow vest. Part of her wanted to turn to them, confess everything, and beg for their help. But there was too much at stake. And they wouldn't be able to protect her, even if they tried.

She was about to break into a run when they caught up with her, flanking her one on each side. As innocently as she could, Samantha shielded the backpack with her body.

"What are you doing out here?" the female officer asked. "Not a nice night for a walk."

Samantha knew not to say anything. Her pale freckled skin, slight elfin features, and dark brown braids were not out of place in this part of the world, but her accent would immediately identify her as a foreigner.

"Miss?" the man said, taking off his cap. "Are you lost?"

"Come on, then," said the woman, stooping to Samantha's level. "It's cold tonight, and more snow is on its way. Can't we give you a lift?"

Samantha forced a smile. She knew she would have to respond.

"Oh, I can make it on my own," she began, trying to avoid any telltale American "*r*'s." "I'll be okay."

The officers looked at each other. It hadn't worked.

"Sounds like you might be very far from home, indeed," said the man.

He turned to his partner.

"Better call this in."

But just as the policeman unclipped his radio, and just as the policewoman reached out to comfort her, something stopped them short. Pounding footsteps, at a run.

Samantha felt the evening's chill. So he had found her, after all. He had tracked her like an animal all the way from Cambridge, across busy London, then through Swindon's darkened streets. He had stalked her all this way, waiting for her to enter the frozen countryside where she would be vulnerable and exposed. Here he would reclaim what she had stolen and exact his revenge.

"Keep her there!" came the deep, familiar American voice. "Don't let her get away!"

The moment of confusion was enough. Samantha twisted free. And then she ran, fixing her eyes on the overpass ahead, her heavy backpack slowing her steps through the deepening snow.

"Grab her!" cried the voice. "That's my niece!"

Now Samantha broke into a painful sprint, her lungs sucking in the frozen air. There were cries behind her, orders to stop, and then muffled sounds of struggle. But it wasn't until she sped up the icy ramp and reached the bridge's midpoint that she risked another look back.

From above the sparse and speeding traffic, she saw the officers writhing in the snow. With horror, she noted that her pursuer had slowed his chase. Samantha could not make out his features in the darkness, but his muscular shadow was well defined in the pool of a streetlight, black against a patch of snow. There was nothing left to stop him. Now he could take his time.

"It's hopeless, Samantha," said the voice, hoarse from yelling. "You don't have a chance."

She feared that he was right. The weight on her back now seemed impossibly heavy. She stopped, ready, almost, to hand over the bag and accept whatever retribution he had in mind.

But then something cried out from deep inside her.

*Boudica. For Boudica.*

And she began to run again despite herself, deep into the cursed English night.

...n Jay would at least tell me what kind of site we will be working on!

**BRITISH ARCHAEOLOGICAL PERIODS***
(*the dates of the different ages seem controversial)

World War 2 defenses: bunkers, *pillboxes, crashed planes

Industrial Revolution: Ironbridge

**MODERN**
1700 – now

Henry VIII: Palaces excavated: Hampton Court, Nonsuch

**1461:** Battle of Towton: mass grave, archaeology shows how people died (very painfully)

**POST-MEDIEVAL**
1500 – 1750
"Black Death" Plague Cemeteries

**SUTTON:** Hoo: Big cemetery site. "Ship-burial"—helmet, spoons, bowls, "angons." PAULOS/SAULOS

Motte and bailey

**MEDIEVAL**
1066 – 1500
Norman Conquest from France: William the Conqueror, Hastings

Crosby Garrett (Roman) Helmet: Looted (legally!!) and sold (The UK seems to have a big problem with looters)

**ANGLO-SAXON**
450-1066 Viking raids: York (Jorvick), ect

**ROMAN**
43 – 450

122 CE: Hadrian's Wall
61 CE: Under Emperor Nero, Voadicea/Boudica leads rebellion
43 CE: Emperor Claudius invades
55 BCE: Julius Caesar visits (??) Britain

**LOOK UP LATER:**
Portable Antiquity Scheme (??). Finds Liaison Officer

-DRUIDS-

"Celtic" tribes and Kingdoms

Iceni, Trinovantes, Brigantes, ect

**IRON AGE**
700 BCE – 43 CE
Bog bodies: human sacrifice, naturally preserved because low oxygen

"Beaker Culture:" similar kind of vessel, across Europe. Trade?

**BRONZE AGE**
2300 – 700 BCE

**FLAG FEN:** "Causeway" bridge with offerings left in marshes. (Water very important in religion...two worlds)

**NEOLITHIC**
4000 – 2300 BCE

Star Carr

Stonehenge Avebury

Standing stone and earthworks. Used for centuries. "Archaeo-astronomy" Ritual landscapes. Some stones from as far away o Wales. Pilgrims came from continental Europe

**MESOLITHIC**
10000 – 4000 BCE

# CHAPTER 1

Samantha recognized the truck all the way from the corner of Sycamore Lane, parked in her parents' driveway at the end of Colby Drive.

"Whose car is that?" asked Janet Pitt-Rivers, wheeling her bike to a stop.

"Yeah, whose?" asked her twin sister, Jeanette. "Did your brother get his driver's license?"

Samantha didn't answer. Normally, the sight of the truck's chipped red paint, grimy windows, and thick layer of bumper stickers would have given her a giddy feeling— the sense of an adventure about to start. But on this November day, it only brought back the dread of her horrible summer. She felt again that crawling panic, that fear of mayhem and madmen on the far side of the world.

"It's just my uncle's," she said at last. "Evan's too young to drive. He's only fourteen."

"Oh," said Janet. "I guess he just *seems* older."

"Because he's so *mature!*" said Jeanette.

"You don't know him like I do," Samantha said, then cycled down her leaf-strewn street toward home.

The summer seemed so long ago, now. Memories of Chavín de Huántar, Peru, had been swept away by the autumn winds, then layered over by the new friendships, new interests, and the weird and unfamiliar demands of junior high. It was a fresh start—one she needed badly. But her uncle's reappearance brought the undercurrent of unease again to the surface.

Of course, it wasn't Jay's fault how her summer had turned out. Not entirely, anyway. Most of the blame could be laid on the dangerous pair who were now inmates of Peru's Canto Grande prison—the same duo who had pillaged the site, kidnapped Samantha's brother, and come so close to destroying her uncle's entire career. She would never have to worry about them again, Jay had told her. And this, at least, she believed.

Samantha had made another enemy that summer, though—she and her uncle both. Adam Quint had once been her uncle's prize archaeology student at the red-roofed university on the far side of San Francisco Bay. But not anymore. It was because of Jay that Adam Quint had abandoned his research at Chavín. And it was Samantha's fault that Adam had fled from the Andes on a doomed bus, had tumbled from a cliffside road, and had been scarred for life—a grisly *X* seared forever across his throat and jaw.

In their one phone call since Peru, Jay had been infuriatingly casual in telling her that Adam had forsaken his studies and disappeared. To where? she wondered as she sat in her new classes, day after day, or tossed and turned through her wakeful nights. And now Samantha saw him everywhere, or thought she did. A man with mirrored sunglasses at the grocery store. The square-cut cap of a soldier on leave. One day, Adam would come for her and for her uncle—Samantha knew it—and he would have his revenge.

Now she wheeled into her driveway, parked her bike in the side yard, and slipped in through the back door to slink to her room unseen. But her parents caught sight of her down the hallway from the living room, and there was no escape.

"Your uncle's here," said her mother.

"Come on, Samantha," said her father. "Come and say hello."

Her parents had fully forgiven Jay now for what had happened in Peru. Or what they thought had happened. Things would be different if they knew the full story. No one did, though, outside the archaeological team. Though Jay was banned from ever working in Peru again, and barred from returning even as a tourist, he and his colleagues had reached a delicate truce with the Peruvian officials. The authorities' own embarrassment over how they had handled the looting investigation and their failure to protect the site ensured that the details would never get out.

Samantha was grateful for this. But it had been also been her uncle's job to protect her at Chavín, and he had failed.

And now here he was in her living room, as if nothing had happened. His big, brown eyes were as mischievous as ever, his grin just as big on his unshaven face. Other than some new gray strands in his dark brown hair, he was his same old self.

"Sam," he said in his warm baritone. "Just the girl I wanted to see."

She sank into a chair beside the window.

"Wait a sec, kiddo," Jay said, his wide smile fading. "Where's your notebook?"

Her hand flew up to check, forgetting for a moment that she hadn't worn it from her neck since school began.

"Oh," she said. "It's in my locker."

His grin returned.

"Don't worry, Sam, I get it. Seventh grade. New school. You might not want to be known as the Girl with the Notebook."

No, she thought. That wasn't it. What other kids said never bothered her. It was that her interest in archaeology was all confused. She didn't know whether she ever wanted to have anything to do with the science again.

"Maybe this will help." Jay said, throwing something at her with such enthusiasm that she barely had time to react.

The object she picked up from the floor was a crumpled backpack, the kind that cinched closed at its top with a cord. It was bright blue, with red and white stripes running across it at diagonals. As soon as she pulled it flat, she recognized its design as the Union Jack, the flag of the United Kingdom.

"You're going to need it, Sam. I'm going to England in December for a project, and you and Evan are coming to work with me."

She felt cold all of a sudden. The same old fear.

"We are?" she asked. It came out almost as a croak.

Did Evan know about this? He wasn't home—probably off somewhere with his latest girlfriend, Annie Cartano.

"You are," said Samantha's mother. "You'll have to miss some school, unfortunately, but your father and I agree with your uncle that it will be a net positive for your college applications."

"Sustained interests, Samantha," her father said. "Sussstaaaaaained. Remember what the college admissions counselor said?"

She did. And she remembered the counselor's bewildered tone when her parents left her alone with him and he asked why, at only twelve years old, Samantha was already preparing for college.

"It'll be real archaeology this time," said Jay. "Plain and simple. Fewer..." he looked sidelong at her parents. "...interruptions."

Everyone was silent, waiting for her consent. She looked at the backpack spread out in her lap. She knew she would be going to England whether she wanted to or not.

She gave a hesitant nod.

———

So, with weary resolve, she slipped a brand-new notebook into her brand-new backpack and returned to her old table at the Yolo County Library.

Getting started wasn't easy. Britain's past was a jumble

of invasions, and none of the books seemed to agree about where one culture ended and the next began. Her first notes were equally messy—a tangle of sketches and terms and lists of things to look up later. But as she went on she took more care, trading her old, cartoony style for something more precise.

It felt good just to be studying. There was a certain kind of magic in the smell of the books and in the studious silence of the reading room. Slowly, Samantha found herself drawn into the descriptions of mottes and baileys, torcs and loom weights, Druids and Normans and Anglo-Saxon hoards.

Soon, she was her old self again. There was nothing that couldn't be fixed with a little research—her uncle was right—and the promise of more archaeology overcame the rest of her lingering fears.

"What's this?" asked Evan that weekend, noting the tower of library books on the dining-room table. "The Archaeo Kid is back at last?"

"Don't call me that," she said.

But she knew he was right. The Archaeo Kid *had* returned, and she was ready for her next adventure.

————

By the day of their departure, Samantha's enthusiasm had rekindled. She felt its warmth growing on the way to the airport and through her parents' good-byes at the security checkpoint. It smoldered all night on their bumpy flight across Canada, Iceland, and the ice-capped North Atlantic, then blazed when the plane banked low over London, revealing its monuments under the low morning clouds. And when the woman at the Heathrow Airport immigration desk placed the stamp in her passport, Samantha almost laughed aloud, so great was the excitement within her.

"I can't believe they let you in," Evan said, as they awaited their luggage at the carousels. "I thought farm animals had to be quarantined."

But Samantha kept smiling, and smiled still all the way to Paddington on the Heathrow Express, and then to King's Cross–St. Pancras by way of the London Tube. Now, as their train sped north out of London and the vistas through the window arrayed themselves one after the other like a series of arranged scenes, her earlier reluctance seemed almost silly. She had fallen in love with the place already—exactly like Jay said she would. This was England, just as it should be, entire and whole and perfect, all mist and moss and snow-patched green.

Her brother was less impressed.

"It just looks like California," he said.

She shrugged. She had been trying not to fight with him lately. To others, Evan seemed back to his usual confident self—the ninth-grade captain of Emerson Junior High's soccer team, Spanish Club *presidente*, first-chair trumpet in band. But she knew it was more complicated than that. Her own summer had been bad enough and haunted her still, but no one could have gone through what Evan had without some lasting effects.

"Okay, fine," he said, in response to her silence. "The buildings are older than the ones back home. And there's snow."

Maintenance work on the country's railway system had redirected their train to a different route, and now all of Samantha's research about the towns they were to pass was useless. But it didn't matter. There was timeless calm to be found in the pleasant, snowy pastures and clouded hills that unfolded along the tracks. Squat, sturdy steeples rose from stone-hewn villages, and Samantha's remaining worries were lost among the shadows of the hedgerows.

A discordant melody interrupted her thoughts. It was Evan, poking at the phone their parents had given them for any emergencies that might arise.

"It *is* an emergency, Archaeo Kid," he said, reading her halfhearted glare. "Annie's going to break up with me if I don't explain what happened!"

Samantha shook her head. That one girl found her brother likable was wonder enough. But now two girls were competing for his attention, and the scandal had exploded last week to involve Emerson Junior High's entire ninth grade.

"What would you possibly say, Evan? You *did* ditch her right in the middle of the Winter Formal. I heard her crying in the girls' room. And then I saw you dancing with Wynnie Malman right after."

"But Wynnie asked me! I had promised her a dance! I was just…" Evan trailed off. "Wait, why I am talking to you about it? You spent the whole night playing basketball in the gym with the rest of the losers."

She hadn't been playing basketball. She had been reading *Britain BC*. But Evan was fiddling again with the phone.

"Evan, don't."

"Quiet, I'm dialing. Wait…country code, then area code, then the number…"

"Hang up," she said, with greater force. But he held up a hand to silence her.

The sound of ringing chimed through the receiver, followed by a bleary "hello" from seven time zones away.

"Hello, Mr. Cartano? This is Evan Sutton. Is Annie there?"

The voice on the other end rose in volume and anger.

"Do *I* know what time it is?" Evan stammered into the phone. "Why are you asking me? I'm not in Califor—"

"The time difference," Samantha whispered. But the damage was already done.

A look of horrified realization came over Evan's face.

"It's 2:37?" he spluttered. "In the morning? Um… well…is Annie still up?"

Samantha sighed, settled back in her seat, and left her brother's doomed conversation to reach its inevitable end.

———

It was just after noon when the train eased into their stop. Samantha and Evan zipped up their jackets and pulled their suitcases from the overhead rack. They moved slowly, still dazed from their long journey, and an automated voice warned, "Doors Closing," just as they wheeled their luggage free.

No one was there to greet them. They stood for a moment in the cold sunlight of the platform, scanning the few students, professors, and tourists who milled beside the tracks. Samantha checked her watch. The work on the railroad had delayed them. Had Jay already come and gone? She had not prepared for this. Jay's instructions ended after their arrival at the station. Where would they go? Would they need to enter the busy town by themselves?

And then she saw him at the far end of the platform, somehow unaware of the comings and goings of the trains. He was leaning against the wall, his back toward his niece and nephew. Only when they got closer did they see that he was not alone. Someone was pressed to him, her cheek to his in close embrace.

That someone was Dr. Clare Barrows.

"Hello?" cried Evan. "Uncle Jay, were you just going to leave us standing here?"

Jay spun around. But other than the guilty flush across his face, he seemed even happier and stronger than when Samantha saw him last. His first week in Cambridge had clearly been good to him, eliminating any lingering effect of Peru.

"Kids! You made it!" he said, hugging them both in turn. "Clare wanted to welcome you to Cambridge herself."

"Weird way to do it," Evan said. "Looks like she's still welcoming *you*."

Samantha felt her own face go red. But it was nowhere near as red as the young professor's, and Samantha tried to rescue Clare from her embarrassment with a hug.

"It's so lovely to see you!" Clare said, squeezing her hard. "You must be freezing! We have real winters here in Cambridge. Blown in straight from Siberia, or so they say. I imagine that might take some getting used to for a pair of Californians."

Samantha smiled. Clare had lost much of her color since the summer months, and it was jarring to see her in the smart clothes of a city. But she was just as unpretentious and naturally pretty as she had been in the dust and glare of the Andes. Jay's goofy grin showed that he thought so too.

"We should get going," he said. "Can't keep his lord-ship waiting!"

His niece and nephew exchanged a questioning look.

"Lordship?"

But Jay had grabbed both suitcases and was off already, striding with Clare through the turnstiles and toward the sign for the car park. Samantha and Evan straggled behind, left to wonder just what sort of lord awaited them.

## RANKS OF BRITISH NOBILITY
- Duke/Duchess
- Marquess/~~Marquessess?~~ Marchioness
- Earl/Countess
- Viscount/Viscountess
- Baron
- Baronet?

LATIN (What the Ancient Romans spoke)
**Ave, Imperator. Morituri te salutant.**
→ Hail Emperor. We who are **ABOUT TO DIE** salute you

First we met the strangest man ev
real lord! But he's not like a knigh
and a really stupid joke about Sut
of the Department. He's weird locati
and Uncle Jay says that his stud
him the **EMPEROR**. After that
in Jay's car to the site. Whe
there, though, there was a pe
detectorists. And when Emper

**PILLBOX →**
From WW2

Uncle Jay says they're
the worst thing that's
ever happened to
archaeology. (I agree.)

Edward III Groat

van **ATTACKED** him! I couldn't believe it.
ht that they might kill each other.
; what they're doing is
ously wrong,
don't think
ham knows that.
eel like I have to
ach him: what
rchaeology is and

**Phosphates at WH**
~~LOOK UP~~ Phosphates are
released into soil when organic
material decomposes.
More phosphates = More human/
animal activity.

SSFNb2-WH: 2

20

# CHAPTER 2

H e's a real lord, all right." Clare said as she drove them along the narrow streets. "Newly elevated."

Her car was a funny, hulking orange thing, with unfamiliar angles inside and out. The backseat was roomy, but somehow Evan still found a way to elbow Samantha while she did her best to focus on the conversation.

"He even wants us to call him Lord Cairn now," said Jay. "Or is it Sir Catesby? I can't seem to get it right. But either way, plain old Cairn Catesby is a thing of the past."

"Plain he never was," said Clare. "But *Sir Cairn's* new title matches his long-held view of himself."

"He's a *Sir*?" Evan asked. "Like a knight?"

"Worse," said Jay. "He's a politician. The crown, in its infinite wisdom, has placed our self-important colleague in the actual House of Lords!"

Clare's smile grew tight.

"The Lord Professor also happens to head the Archaeology Department. He's my boss. Yours too," she added, to Jay's groan, "whilst you're here."

Their uncle relented.

"I'm kidding, guys. Catesby and I go way, way back. I was his student once, back in my graduate school days when he was just a new professor. We called him the Emperor, even then. But he's harmless. You might even come to like him."

He considered this last statement for a moment.

"Well, maybe that's a stretch."

Clare took a hard right onto narrow, leafy Tennis Court Road, where the more modern buildings of the outer city gave way to the rough-hewn stone and crooked timbers of its medieval core.

"So where's the university?" asked Evan, eager for their long journey to be over.

Jay gave a wide gesture with his hand.

"All around us. The individual colleges, the different departments, the lecture halls—all spread out through town."

Another right put them onto Downing Street, a canyon of chimneys and pediments, of gateways and gables of honey-colored brick.

"Here we are," Jay said, as they slowed to a stop. "The Archaeology Department."

Beside them was a large, grand building, the triple arches of its entrance decorated with fantastical carvings of animals and gods.

"Looks like he's still in his office," Clare said, pointing to an old-fashioned car in the Department's shallow driveway. "We should hurry. He's probably furious by now from waiting."

But Jay had another idea.

"Let's have a little fun with his lordship, shall we? Evan, Samantha, there's something I want you to do…"

————

The faculty offices lay through a low, dark gallery. Glass cases on either side showed off a range of artifacts from around the region, and neat labels explained that many came from Cambridge itself—a modest collection of brooches, torcs, and curled medieval shoes. In the last case was the skeleton of a woman, poker stiff on her back, and displayed right alongside her were the bones of the rodents that had burrowed into her coffin to nibble on her heels. Samantha shuddered, her giddy nervousness shifting for a moment into something else.

They came at last to an office, its door marked in large gold letters:

LORD PROFESSOR SIR CAIRN COLIN CATESBY
BARON CATESBY OF COVENEY
MBE, PhD, FBA, FSA
PROFESSOR OF ARCHAEOLOGY/DEPARTMENT HEAD
MASTER OF PEMBROKE COLLEGE

The door itself was slightly ajar—an invitation to rival scholars to come inside and challenge him. Samantha raised a timid hand and knocked. There was no answer. They waited for a moment, then two, until Evan nudged the door inward from over her shoulder and stepped backward to let his sister enter first.

Samantha's eyes fell immediately on a bear of a man standing at a table in the middle of the room. While his body was large and ungainly, his face was slight and angular, like a statue with mismatched parts. His big ears stuck far out, and his loops of short-cropped hair hung down onto his imperial brow. A pair of round wire spectacles perched across his sharp Roman nose. Behind them, the Lord Professor's eyes were small and piggish, and seemed much too close together on his stern, serious face.

But Catesby's focus on the artifacts before him was such that he took no notice of their arrival, and Samantha watched as he selected what looked like a long iron nail from the tray and held it to the light. The intensity of his beady stare was powerful. When he at last acknowledged them, she was glad that he didn't move his eyes to meet hers.

"Well?" he said, in a languid, sleepy voice. "Who are you?"

"Sutton," Samantha replied, just as her uncle had instructed.

Still, Catesby didn't look up.

"Who?"

By now, Evan had retreated into the hallway. Samantha cleared her throat and tried again.

"Sutton."

Catesby picked another nail off the tray to study it.

"Sutton who?"

He let the silence linger for some time before removing

his glasses and finally lifting his gaze. Samantha felt herself shrink a little. His eyes were as piercing as she had feared, but they flashed with dry mischief, and at last she registered the pun. Sutton who. Sutton Hoo—one of the most famous archaeological sites in all of England. Lord Catesby had some of her uncle's sense of humor; that was for sure. This must be their standard greeting.

And just like that Jay burst into the room, releasing a built-up roar of laughter.

"Catesby," he said. "These are Samantha and Evan, my niece and nephew."

"Good God," Catesby said, eyeing them over the top of his glasses. "More Suttons."

"Be nice," said Clare from the hallway. "Not everyone appreciates your brand of humor."

"You know them, do you, Barrows? Please tell me that they're an improvement upon the Sutton we've already got."

"They are," said Jay. "By a long shot."

Catesby studied them in earnest now, his piercing gaze focused on Samantha, then Evan, then Samantha again.

"Their manners seem to be better, certainly. They speak only when spoken to, and I am sure that when *they* do, they will address me by my title. Am I right?"

Evan was the first to speak.

"Yes, your lordship."

At this, Catesby laughed—a wet, high-pitched hoot. And then more hoots tumbled forth from his small, round mouth, revealing a row of sharp little teeth.

"*Lordship*! Goodness me! At least this one's got the right idea," he said.

He took off his glasses and drew out a handkerchief to polish their lenses.

"But truth be told," he said quietly, "I can't say I'll ever be used to all this 'Lord' business. Did you hear that the students are even holding a boat race in honor of my new title? The Catesby Regatta, they're calling it, to be held in three weeks' time. You rowed at Cambridge, didn't you, Sutton? We must get you back in boatie shape."

"Whatever you say, m'lord." Jay's sarcastic tone was unmistakable now, and Catesby's smile faded, just a little.

"Again, Sutton, it's 'Lord Catesby,' if you'd like to use the honorific. 'Sir Cairn' is your other option."

"I think I may just stick with Emperor."

Catesby turned a little red.

"Remind me, Dr. Barrows. Where did you find this fellow again? His area of study is what, exactly?"

"You know the answer to that, Sir Cairn," Clare said flatly. "He was your student, after all."

"Oh-ho! A Cambridge man? A true *Cantab*? If memory serves, he spent most of his time at Cambridge *not at Cambridge*…flying off to Cuba one week, Nigeria the next."

Jay laughed.

"What, Cairn? Is my degree now in question?"

"As a qualification for being here? Yes. As well as Barrows's judgment for inviting you. This is not California, Dr. Sutton. Nor is it Peru. England's past is not simply a series of savage races, one after the other. Ours is a complex heritage and demands complex knowledge—especially given the constraints of time."

Jay's eyes narrowed as he readied a response. But Clare intercepted him.

"You lot should be off. Sir Cairn and I have things to discuss."

"Okay, okay," said Jay. "I take the hint."

Evan and Samantha headed for the door. But their uncle turned around a final time.

"*Ave, Imperator*," he said. "*Morituri te salutant.*"

And then he gave Cairn Catesby a deep, exaggerated bow.

————

By now, midday had shifted to late afternoon and the sky was a deep, dark blue. It was darker still above the forests of chimneys spewing smoke from professors' hearths. The town seemed empty, more or less, as most of the students were away for the holiday. What few people remained in the old medieval town had sought the cozy comfort of their homes. The Suttons had Cambridge all to themselves.

It was all so beautiful, Samantha thought. But it was more than that. Beneath her feelings of awe and wonder, she felt a familiar archaeological urge. She couldn't wait to peel back Cambridge's layers and plumb its ancient depths.

"Where are we going to be working, Uncle Jay?" she asked.

"Where?" he said. "Or when?"

He fished some keys out of his pocket and punched a

button on the keychain. Headlights flashed twice from an odd little car nearby.

"I'll show you."

"Right now?" said Evan. "We've been traveling forever. And it's almost dark!"

But Jay was insistent.

"The rest of the team has a two-day head start on you guys. Don't you want to catch up?"

Evan and Samantha looked at each other, sharing a fleeting smile. As usual, their uncle's enthusiasm was contagious.

"Now come on, Sam. You're sitting up front with me."

She took a few running steps toward the car.

"The other side," he corrected her, when she instinctively went around to the right-hand door. "Unless you want to drive."

She giggled and slid inside the tiny rental as Evan squeezed into the back. And soon they were flying north in the dying light of day, and deeper, deeper, deeper into Britain's distant past.

———

The car her uncle had rented was as strange to Samantha as Clare's had been. But while the English professor's had been boxy and vast, Jay's was tiny, and Samantha could feel her brother's knees pressed against her seat back.

The site was a half-hour drive north from the Cambridge city center. By the time they reached the deep countryside, an evening mist had swept in, obscuring whatever was left of the view and hastening the winter dusk. Little by little, the road began to rise until they reached a strange silent space above the soft, white mist and below the twilit clouds. Samantha heard the crunch of gravel under wheels, and Jay made a final, jolting turn before stamping down hard on the brakes. They had arrived.

She swung open her door and stepped out, feeling the sudden cold and damp like a slap across her face. Jay left the headlights on, and swirls in the white mist below showed fleeting peeks of the vast, darkening country-side all around them. She pulled on her gloves and the warm hat she'd stuffed in her pocket, tugging her braided pigtails free.

"This is it?" Evan asked.

"Sure is," said Jay.

"But it looks like an empty field."

"Sure does," Jay said, and he led them across the patchy snow.

Samantha agreed with her brother. There didn't seem to be an archaeological site here—no castle or monastery or mysterious henge of stone. In fact, other than a short concrete shack just up the slope, there seemed to be noth-ing here whatsoever. All that distinguished this spot from the miles and miles of empty farmland was the gentle bulge in the landscape on which it sat.

Samantha gave her brother a nervous look. The whole flight over, he had been talking about the Avebury level in one of his favorite video games, *Pillager of the Past III*, where the ghosts of angry druids hurled oak staffs at the Pillager as she burrowed into the chalky soil. All that was here were rabbits, hopping furtively among the scattered heaps of snow. Would this real site disappoint him—this low and barren knoll?

But Evan seemed relieved, and instantly she knew why. This was nothing like Peru. There was nowhere for danger to hide in a bleak and empty field—no underground passages in which Evan could get lost or attacked by bats, or dragged inside and drugged by a maniacal madman.

He caught her look and gave a quick, embarrassed smile. The empty field was the fresh start he needed.

"This," Jay said, "is Wardy Hill."

"Warty?" asked Evan. "Like the Archaeo Kid?"

"Wardy, kiddo. With a '*d*.' It's an old, old word, meaning 'lookout.'"

"Like *warden*," Samantha said, pulling her notebook from her backpack and beginning to write.

"Yeah, Sam," said Jay, nodding. "They have the same root. Now, you'll have to trust me on it on an evening like this, but the view from here can stretch for miles, all the way south back to Cambridge, and to the northeast, all the way out to the ocean. If you want to spot an invading army, this is the place to be."

He pointed at the lone concrete shack in the gloom, just across the road. It was an ugly, modern thing, but its design seemed to reflect a specific purpose.

"Take that, for instance. It's what they call a 'pillbox'—a

bunker from World War II. A lookout in case of a German attack."

"Cool," said Evan.

"Very," said Jay. "And it's still in good shape. We're going to be using it for our lab. Our job here is to figure out who was first to make use of this place as a *Wardy*, and what, exactly, they were trying to keep an eye out for."

Jay took a printout from his satchel. A grid was laid out on the page, with each box representing a five-meter square. Straining her eyes in the fading light, Samantha could see how some parts of the field were shaded gray and black. Her uncle was eager to explain.

"This shows the results of some of Clare's preliminary lab work. She tested for phosphates—a kind of chemical left in the soil when all the organic stuff has disappeared. They're a telltale sign of occupation. And this one…"

He pulled out a second page.

"…shows all the surface finds we've collected over a couple days of field-walking."

This map was shaded too—light gray where only a few finds had been made, darker where the artifacts had been more abundant. The two maps matched, with the darkest patches radiating out from a central core. It was where they were standing now.

Samantha looked out over the barren surface of the field and smiled. A clear research objective. A common goal that she could take part in. An opportunity for real science. Something had been here long, long ago. And it was awaiting them now, just below the surface. *This* was real archaeology, just as her uncle had promised.

But Evan wasn't smiling. His eyes were fixed on the middle distance just below them on the mist-cloaked slope, where two beams of light cut spears through the darkness and sent rabbits hopping away in fear.

"Flashlights?" she asked.

They watched a pair of figures advance on a diagonal, their beams dancing across the ground. Before long, their outlines could be seen clearly against the fog.

"Wait," Evan whispered. "Look what they're doing."

Something sneaky, Samantha agreed. Something bad.

The larger individual held the flashlight in one hand and some sort of tool in the other. It was a long wand, sweeping left and right across the ground and emitting the occasional chirp. Suddenly, there was a loud mechanical squawk, and the smaller shadow dropped to its hands and knees to burrow into the earth.

"Hello?" Jay called out.

The figures froze.

"That's a metal detector," Samantha whispered, realizing it all at once. "They're looting the site."

"Looters!" cried her brother, some buried rage unleashed within him. "Looters!"

And before Jay could stop him, Evan was charging across the field, leaping over ridges and furrows, his hands clenched in fists and ready to fight.

"Stop, Evan! Wait!"

But Jay's cries went unheeded. In the faint blue light of dusk, Samantha could barely see the scuffle that ensued. She could certainly hear it, though. There were grunts, thumps, a sharp yelp of pain, and the sound of tools and equipment being thrown to the ground.

Then there were three people coming toward her in a struggling mass. A long and lanky man gripped Evan by the neck of his jacket with one hand and pushed a second boy forward with the other. Restrained though they were, the two boys were still taking swings at each other, even as they were hauled across the ground.

"Oi!" cried the man as he approached. "You there! Your boy's attacked me son."

He was a hard-looking man and tall, made even taller by his thick rubber boots. He wore a mud-flecked vest full of pockets over his collared shirt and a flat plaid hat pulled low. His face was sharp and pitted, and his lips could barely contain a jumble of stained and crooked teeth. Nothing about him seemed clean—even from a few yards away he smelled of sweat and cigarettes. And he was fuming mad: Samantha could see steam rising from his mouth and nostrils in short, angry puffs.

"Get off of me!"

Evan's clothes were sullied from the struggle and he sported a new red scratch across his cheek, but he was otherwise unharmed. His young adversary's winter hat had been knocked askew, revealing a head of gelled blond hair. But he was also unhurt and seemed much more bewildered than angry. And his attention was still so fixed on his attacker that he hadn't even noticed Samantha or her uncle.

The man released his hold, and the boy and Evan shook themselves free to stand beside their respective guardians. Samantha studied the tall man's son and was surprised to find gentle features and kindly eyes, large and blue and searching. He wasn't quite Evan's height, but the way he put his hands on his hips and stuck out his chest made him seem much bigger.

"Cheap shot, that was," said the boy, panting still. "What did I ever do to you?"

Evan straightened his coat.

"Are you kidding me? I caught you. Red-handed." He turned to appeal to his uncle. "You saw them, right? They were digging something out of the ground!"

"I think there's been a misunderstanding…" Jay began.

For once in her life, though, Samantha was quick to defend her brother.

"I saw them too. They were digging."

By now, the man had noted their accents.

"Yanks, are you? Tourists?" he said. "This is private property, this is. You're trespassing."

Jay held up his hands, trying to calm things.

"I'm Dr. Jay Sutton, and these are my niece and nephew. I'm an archaeologist."

"Oh," said the man. "Are you, now?"

There was a long silence as the families sized each other up. They certainly didn't look very guilty about being discovered, Samantha thought. And Jay was not someone who would let a crime be committed right in front of his eyes. There must not have been anything illegal about what they had been doing, even if it was so plainly wrong.

At last the tall man wiped his palms on his trousers and broke the awkward quiet.

"Ned Aubrey," he said, and he and Jay shook hands. "And this is me son, Graham."

The boy spoke up now, rage still in his voice.

"We have permission to be here, not that it's any of your concern. It's all legal. We're not a pair of bleeding nighthawks. We're archaeologists, same as you. Just more amateur-like."

But Evan couldn't hold back.

"You? Archaeologists? Please. Where are your forms to record your finds? Where are your tape measurers and unit string and plumb bobs and screens? You're not archaeologists. You're just a couple of thieves."

Graham's large eyes narrowed, his mouth a handsome scowl.

"And who do you think are you, mate?" he asked, taking a step in Evan's direction. "I dare you to say that again!"

Samantha had had enough.

"He's Evan, and I'm Samantha. We're just here for a few weeks to help our uncle."

The boy turned to her, as if noticing her for the first time. To her surprise, his temper deflated immediately. In fact, he grew a little embarrassed and could not seem to look her in the eyes.

"Did you find something?" she asked him. "Can I see?"

Graham hesitated, then fumbled in his pocket and held out a dirt-lined palm. Samantha moved close for a better look and felt the warmth of his breath upon her cheek. He smelled nice—like lavender soap and damp earth and the wool of his jacket—and he turned his flashlight toward his open hand.

"All heads up," he said. "Lucky!"

Three coins gleamed up at her through casings of mud. Two were far too dirty to make out, but the third showed a face, head-on, with locks of hair tumbling from beneath a mighty crown. Samantha plucked it out of his palm to study it.

"Is that a queen?" she asked.

Both Aubreys laughed. But while Ned's was a cruel, hard chuckle, his son's was sweet and kind.

"A warrior and a king," he corrected her. "Edward III, that is."

She turned the coin over in her hands, marveling just as much at its beauty as the miraculous luck that had led it across her path. It had been here—right here—all through the Middle Ages, the Renaissance, and a bloody Civil War. It had been here when the Pilgrims first left Cambridge on their roundabout route for the New World, and when the American colonies had risen up in revolution. And it had been here when brave British soldiers manned the nearby pillbox, their eyes trained on the horizon for the sight of Nazi invasion. The coin had been waiting all this time, just so this boy could find it and share it with her. It felt a little like fate.

"So," she said, when her eyes had taken their fill. "Do you want to give these to us?"

Graham pulled away.

"*Give* them to you?" he asked. "Are you having a laugh?"

"Since we're archaeologists," she said, phrasing her explanation carefully. "Professionals, I mean. We'd record them, weigh them, photograph them, plot their locations."

She thought of the maps Jay had shown them a few moments before, and how the kind of amateur collecting the Aubreys were doing made this kind of analysis impossible. But it was Jay himself who cut her off.

"That's not how it works here, Sam."

Ned Aubrey gave a crooked smile.

"No, it's bloody well not. These coins belong to us."

Graham was eager to show off his own knowledge.

"Unless they're silver, of course, or gold. And then the government gives us money instead."

Evan's temper flared.

"Wait, the government *pays* you to loot sites? But what about the archaeology?"

Ned Aubrey's patience was gone.

"I've been searching these lands for decades, lad, and you're mad if you think I'm going to stop for some bunny-hugging Yanks."

He placed a hand on Graham's shoulder.

"Let's leave them to their scratching and poking, boy.

We'll come back when there's peace and quiet, and no one like to attack you."

They trudged into the darkness, their flashlights disappearing into the murk.

"*Bunny*-hugging?" Jay asked, when they were just out of earshot.

But Evan needed more than that to calm down.

"They can't be serious, can they? That's just looting!"

Jay could only shrug.

"Private land, private finds, with gold and silver artifacts going to the crown for a cash prize. Why the government even allows it to happen is beyond me. That the government *pays* for it is a disgrace. But it's tradition. And traditions don't always make sense—especially around here."

Samantha frowned in the growing darkness. Graham must not know that what he was doing was wrong. She would just have to explain it. He would understand, if she had correctly read the intelligence in his eyes.

She had really liked those eyes.

## THE COLLEGES THAT MAKE UP CAMBRIDGE UNIVERSITY

hrist's Col.
hurchill Col.
Col.
Hall
sti Col.
n Col.
ng Col.
Emmanuel Col.
Fitzwilliam Col.

Girton Col.
Gonville and Caius Col.
Homerton Col.
Hughes Hall
Jesus Col.
Lucy Cavendish Col.
King's Col.
Magdalene Col.
Murray Edwards Col.

Newnham Col.
Pembroke Col.
Peterhouse
Queen's Col.
Robinson Col.
St. Catharine's Col.
St. Edmund's Col.
St. John's Col.
Selwyn Col.
Sidney Sussex Col.

Trinity Hall
Wolfson Col.

Founded in 1350,
after the Black
Death killed
all the lawyers

GRASS UNLESS
ACCOMPANIED BY A SENIOR
MEMBER OF THE COLLEGE

there
are so many rules here.
But like Uncle Jay says,
it's just tradition, an

SSFNb2-WH: 3

# CHAPTER 3

They're turning it into a movie, you know," Evan was saying from the backseat as they careened back to Cambridge in the dark.

"*Pillager of the Past?*" said Jay. "I heard something about that. Sounded fun."

Sounded terrible, Samantha thought. She had no patience for her brother's favorite series of video games. It wasn't just the errors the programmers had committed with the archaeology of whatever country the Pillager found herself in—the cursed (Mexican) *Aztec* calendars in Peru, the angry (European) *Neanderthals* in Africa's Olduvai Gorge. It was the whole idea of it: sneaking around sites and stealing artifacts from tombs and temples, their black-market value tallied and scored at the end of every level. To her relief, Evan's handheld version was still lost in some Andean pass. But that he could bring it up now, after their encounter with the Aubreys, was a disconnect she could not understand.

The conversation continued as they sped back into

town, left the car at the Department, and headed north through the cobblestone streets. Samantha knew she would need the daylight to take in all the jutting steeples, grand arches, and great oak doorways of the medieval colleges jumbled together in the university's central core. But her long, long day was catching up with her at last, and she lagged behind her uncle and brother as they trudged along the cobbles of the King's Parade.

Finally, they turned into a narrow alley, leaving semi-darkness for something closer to black. What few lights existed here did little but turn the patchy snow an unsettling orange, and in their exhausted state Evan and Samantha stumbled on unseen bulges in the stonework. But Jay went on with confidence. He knew the route too well.

By the time they came to a stop at last beneath a modest portico, Samantha was half asleep. Still, she recognized the dour stone face beside the entrance, holding them all in its judgmental gaze. The coat of arms confirmed it—a white crescent on its side, surrounded by a black and white shield and capped with gold.

This was Jay's old college, Trinity Hall. Nowhere made him happier, he always said, than the prettiest corner of all the world.

"Just straight through here, guys. Watch your step!"

He led them into a warm, narrow room, the Porters' Lodge, which controlled all the college's traffic, in and out.

"Good evening, sir," said an older man behind the long, low desk. His graying hair was oiled flat, and the white-and-black-striped tie of the college complemented his smart black suit.

"Hello, Tom," said Jay.

"And the bags, sir? Some help for the young gentleman and lady?"

Evan seemed ready to accept the offer, but his uncle cut him off.

"They can manage, thanks. Have a good night."

"And you, sir."

They pushed through the far door and entered the college proper.

Before them was a scene Samantha knew well, lit by lamps at regular intervals along the walls. This was the college's front court: a tight grassy quadrangle crossed with pathways. She could make out the graceful buildings that framed the space and the white cupola that crowned the building opposite. From the engravings, sketches, watercolors, and photos that lined the walls of Jay's office, she knew it had looked exactly this way for centuries. And to Samantha, it already felt like home.

"Was that our butler?" Evan asked, still fixated on the conversation in the Porters' Lodge.

"No butler, kiddo. Tom's one of the porters. An officer of the college."

"What kind of *officer* carries people's bags?"

"That was a courtesy, Evan. A onetime offer. Don't get the wrong idea. It's the porters who run this place. They have a way of knowing everything."

They ducked through an archway and up a winding flight of stairs. Samantha was astonished to see that each stone step dipped in the center, eroded by the passage of thousands of students over hundreds and hundreds of years. Jay had told them that the place was empty for the holidays. But as they made their way to the very top, she could swear she heard noises through the walls and doors around them—odd creaks, muffled scrapes, and footsteps that didn't match up with their own.

It's just an old building, she told herself, as the summer's terror welled up within her. And she used a word from the summer to try to bring herself back to reason:

*Cálmate.* Calm down.

They reached the highest floor and entered the accommodations Samantha would be sharing with her brother. Inside was a small, wood-paneled sitting room—with two leather chairs, two desks, and a great marble fireplace, from when fire was needed to stave off the medieval winter's chill. An electric heater now hummed beside the entrance.

Doors led to individual bedrooms on either side. Samantha's was comfortable enough, but plain. A bed was made up for her, piled high with thick quilted blankets, and a window looked out upon the narrow street below.

"Good night, guys," Jay said, and left them for his own quarters across the landing.

Samantha placed her clothes neatly in her bureau, and her atlas and other books in a stack atop the desk. From her backpack, she drew out her trowel. It was stained and scuffed from its summer of work, and bits of Peru itself still streaked its wooden handle. She placed it on her night-stand and turned off the light.

She eyed the trowel as sleep set in. The memories it raised were scary ones. But it was her first trowel, from her first excavation, and she was determined to keep it for as long as she lived. As pitted and stained as it was, the triangular blade was sharp and shiny, and reflected the weak glow of a high English moon. But then another light joined to make the blade shine silver. She propped herself up to look out the window. She was just in time to see a flash of brilliance in the alley below, and then the hurried movement of someone reaching to turn it off. A flashlight, aimed—at least for a moment—at her.

"*Cálmate*," she said, this time aloud.

She lay back down, listening to the haunted creaks of ancient floorboards. And even when her eyes fluttered shut, she wondered if someone was watching her.

———

Jet lag woke her before dawn, programmed as she was for California time. But some half-remembered sensation from the night before—the unsettling feeling of being spied upon—kept her from going back to sleep.

Her brother's loud voice from the next room didn't help either.

"Annie, that's not what happened! I only danced with Wynnie for a single song."

She looked at her watch on the nightstand. It was 6:25 in the morning—10:25 at night back home. Evan was using the emergency phone again, but at least this time he had remembered the time difference.

"Yeah, it was a slow dance. But so what? I wouldn't care if you had done the same."

Not true, Samantha thought as she climbed out of bed. No way. She knew her brother's jealous streak far too well.

"Wait," he went on, "you're going on a date with who? Keith Barrett?"

Samantha sighed. A shift in power had occurred in the phone signals, somewhere over the Atlantic. She braided her hair into pigtails, then crept to the door to listen to her brother's love life explode.

"To a movie? Are you kidding me? That's totally different than one stupid dance!"

There was a silence so long that it seemed like the call had ended. But finally Evan spoke again, his voice low and shaky.

"I think we need to take a break, Annie. And it's not me, it's you."

Then he hung up and set the phone down hard.

This sort of thing was new to Evan. He had always been popular—an unusual thing for a smart kid at Emerson Junior High. He was handsome, mischievous, and confident. He was loved by his teachers, and had always gotten all the attention he could handle from the many girls who came to his soccer games and band concerts or even joined the Spanish Club to get to know him better.

Annie was the latest girl to try her luck, and she had not skimped on effort: organizing his locker for him, buying him gifts, bringing him junk food to complement the organic sandwiches and fruit that Ray and Phoebe Sutton insisted upon for their children's lunch. How desperate, Samantha thought. Why would a girl act like that for any boy? she wondered. That someone like Evan could have a love life seemed unfair. When would someone like her?

But there didn't seem to be anything to be jealous of now, not with Evan sniffling in the next room. She found herself feeling a little bit bad for him. It was obvious that he needed cheering up, but she knew she was not the one who could do it.

She heard a knock, the creak of the outer door, and her uncle's worried whisper.

"You okay, Ev? Sorry, but our walls are kind of thin. You sounded a little upset."

"I'm fine."

"Want to talk about it?"

But then Evan's mood turned nasty, and Samantha's feelings of sympathy dissolved.

"I don't want to talk about it with you. To be honest, Uncle Jay, you might not be the best person to give me relationship advice."

"Ouch," said their uncle. But his cheerful voice showed that he was feeling confident in that department.

"No offense," added Evan.

"None taken. But I do have some other advice for you. That's the emergency phone…"

"Why do people keep saying that? It *was* an emergency! But I won't use it again, okay? Especially not after this. Jeez. Keith Barrett? What is Annie thinking?"

"Forget Keith and forget Annie. We've got a big day. And we might as well get an early start. Go see if your sister is up."

Samantha took two tiptoed leaps back to her bed, but the creaking of the floorboards gave her away. Evan flung open her door and flipped on the light switch before she could slip beneath her covers.

"You better not have been listening."

"I wasn't," she said. "Not on purpose, anyway."

Evan turned away.

"Go ahead and laugh at me, Archaeo Kid. You'll never understand."

And in a weird way, Samantha worried he was right.

————

Making sure her field notebook was tucked safely inside her backpack, Samantha followed her uncle out into the deep cold of morning. They were greeted by the doleful sound of church bells, ringing softly from the chapels of half a dozen nearby colleges. She pulled her thick blue jacket tight and pushed her gloved hands deep into her pockets. At home, winter brought fog and wind and days of drizzling rain, but never cold like this. It wouldn't be easy to get used to.

An overnight snow had frozen to ice on the lawn of the forecourt. Evan took several crunching stomps across it.

"Get off the grass," said Jay, the force of his voice surprising her.

But Evan was enjoying himself too much.

"Sounds like I'm stomping on potsherds."

"It sounds like trouble to me, kiddo. Knock it off."

But there wasn't time. The door of the Lodge swung open, and Tom the porter strode toward them in the early morning chill.

"Sir! Keep off the grass, please! Off the grass, at once."

Samantha spied the wrinkle of irritation creasing her brother's brow. He did not like being told what to do—he was much like their uncle in that regard—and the morning's downbeat phone call had put him in a defiant mood.

"I'm not touching the grass," said Evan. "Not technically. I'm touching the snow that's on the grass."

Tom straightened, and only now did Samantha spy the tattoos that peeked up from below his collar: the point of a blue-ink dagger and in a curling script the words, *Royal Marine*.

His next words carried the force of his former career.

"Off. Now."

"Okay, okay, okay!" Evan said, moving quickly to the path. "I'm off!"

The porter did not blink, and his stare followed Evan until they were through the Porters' Lodge and out the college's main door. Jay put his hand on Evan's shoulder.

"I should have warned you. Lawns are for college fellows only."

"Seriously?" Evan grumbled, as they picked their way through the narrow passageway. "That's a stupid rule."

Jay laughed.

"It might seem stupid to you, Ev, but it's how things have always been done here, forever and always. Like I've been saying: traditions don't have to make sense. So please, kiddo, do me a favor and watch the attitude."

Evan looked at him with genuine befuddlement.

"What attitude?"

———

There could be nothing prettier, Samantha decided, than Cambridge in the snow.

"Maybe," said Jay, smiling when she shared the thought aloud. "When the snow is fresh."

But it *was* still fresh, and as they emerged from Senate House Passage onto the King's Parade, Samantha felt awake and fully alive.

They walked down the empty street between the hulking icons of the university. There was the stout steeple of Great St. Mary's on the left, the tidy edifice of the Senate House on the right, and there, farther down, King's College and the immaculate lines of its glorious chapel—its marble steeples glowing violet in the light before the dawn.

"Well?" Jay asked, an arm across her shoulder. "How do you feel?"

He wanted an opinion. Her opinion, most of all. But it was too hard to put into words. The town seemed awash in its centuries of knowledge. It was as if wisdom seeped from the stonework and ran from the gutter pipes like melted snow. Great authors, poets, and philosophers had studied here. Great archaeologists too, piecing the human world together over hundreds and hundreds of years.

So when Samantha answered her uncle at last, she chose her words carefully.

"Young."

"Don't worry, kiddo," Jay said, misunderstanding her completely. "I thought you might feel a little over your head in a university setting. But you *do* belong here. In fact, this place was built for people your age. Cambridge used to accept students as young as twelve."

He reached over to muss her hair.

"If only you were alive in the thirteenth century."

"And not a girl," said Evan.

"And not a girl," Jay agreed. "That's true, Sam. Cambridge was boys-only for its first seven hundred years."

He saw her scowl and chuckled.

"You can't let *that* bother you, Sam. Obviously, it's different now. It's just how things were done here. Tradition, remember? It doesn't have to make sense."

Her frown only deepened. This bit of trivia was like a wedge between her and the place she was beginning to love.

But her irritation faded as Jay led them down one empty

side street and then another, disorienting his niece and nephew on a rapid, rambling tour. Samantha remembered from her research that Cambridge was made up of more than thirty separate colleges, each with its own courtyards and gardens and chapel, and their own dining halls and dormitories where students made their homes.

To their right now sat ancient Peterhouse College, with its stark brickwork matching its reputation for curses, murders, and many angry ghosts. After a long, looping detour came Downing College, all columns and porticoes, evoking an era of powdered wigs and tricornered hats. Last on their route was Pembroke College, where Lord Professor Catesby lived and took his meals. To Samantha, it seemed a natural pairing. Pembroke's balustrades, buttresses, and showy coats of arms fit a man of Catesby's pompous manner.

"That's it for now, guys," Jay said, leading them toward his parked car. "To be continued."

Samantha wanted to keep going. She wanted to see all the colleges that made up Cambridge and walk its labyrinth of lanes. But it was time to go to work—twenty miles to the north and unknown centuries back in time.

———

She felt like a time traveler as they sped out of town in the gray light of morning, and the reverse arrangement of the steering wheel made Jay seem like her copilot. But being on the left side of the road played tricks on her mind. What little oncoming traffic there was seemed to be heading right at them, so with each approaching car, she found herself ducking a little in her seat, twisting a braided pigtail nervously around a finger, and bracing for an impact that never came.

As they entered the motorway, a seedling of pink appeared in the east. It blossomed to a bloom of blue by the time they reached the countryside, where the marshy landscape was blanketed with clean, white snow. After Ely, with its great stone cathedral rising above the countryside like a ship at sea, they turned onto a narrow country road—zigging and zagging through the marshy landscape, through tiny villages, and along the hard-won boundaries of ancient farmsteads.

"Not much farther, guys," said Jay, as he channeled his own impatience into the gas pedal.

He was fast, but not the fastest. As they made their gradual climb to the top of Wardy Hill, there was a roar of engines behind them, and they were flanked suddenly by a pair of white vans screaming past on each side at dangerous speeds. Jay laughed, stole a glance out both windows at his competition, and accelerated all the faster. Samantha bit her lip, gripping her seat belt tight.

But the road race ended almost as soon as it began, with the crunch of gravel and the squeal of brakes. The vans had won, and Jay jerked to a halt behind them just as their sliding doors crashed open. This, Samantha knew at once, was the excavation team. There weren't very many of them, but they were a boisterous bunch despite the early hour—laughing and shouting and wrestling one another to the ground, with no regard for the misty morning's peace.

"I'm lucky," Jay said. "It wasn't easy to find people willing to give up their winter vacations just to help me out."

"To help out Clare," said Samantha.

"Right, to help out Clare."

The British professor was there already, her funny orange car parked farther up the road. Jay took a few running steps in her direction, and there was no mistaking the joy in her eyes when she saw him coming. Whatever he said to her as he grew closer made her blush and laugh out loud.

The whole group gathered at the pillbox bunker, waiting in a small, busy mob until Clare unlocked its doors. With all the scarves, hats, and massive jackets pressed together into the tight space, Samantha couldn't pick out any familiar faces.

She was nervous who she might find among them. But he was the one who found her first.

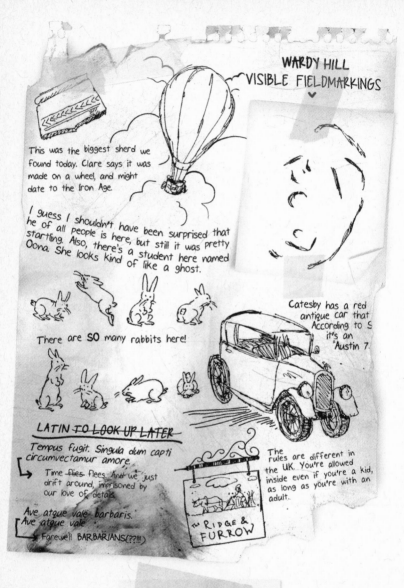

WARDY HILL
VISIBLE FIELDMARKINGS

This was the biggest sherd we found today. Clare says it was made on a wheel, and might date to the Iron Age.

I guess I shouldn't have been surprised that he of all people is here, but still it was pretty startling. Also, there's a student here named Oona. She looks kind of like a ghost.

Catesby has a red antique car that According to S it's an "Austin 7.

There are SO many rabbits here!

### LATIN TO LOOK UP LATER

Tempus fugit. Singula dum capti circumvectamur amore

↳ Time flies flees. And we just drift around, imprisoned by our love of details.

Ave atque vale barbaris.
Ave atque vale
↳ Farewell BARBARIANS(??!!!)

THE RIDGE & FURROW

The rules are different in the UK. You're allowed inside even if you're a kid, as long as you're with an adult.

# CHAPTER 4

"The Archaeo Kid in England! I never thought I'd see the day."

She knew the pleasing Scottish accent as soon as she heard it—it belonged to the one person in the world who could use her detested nickname without making her the least bit mad. Stuart Forsythe pushed through the group, and she flushed a happy and unwelcome pink.

"And I'm here too," said Evan. "Thanks for noticing."

"And you, Evan," laughed Stuart, slapping him on the back. "Hey, what's the matter? You're like a half-shut knife."

Evan shrugged.

"Ah," said Stuart. "Trouble with the missus."

"Yeah," Evan admitted, with just a touch of pride. "Well, my girlfriend, anyway."

"We'll fix that. Just you wait."

Samantha looked at the other students as they rough-housed in the cold. They were all good friends, clearly. And, she realized, almost all were male.

All but one.

A young woman stood apart from the group—apart in every way. She seemed more like a spectator than a member of the team. A coldness seemed to radiate from her—colder even than the bleak winter landscape. While her comrades wore thick nylon coats of reds and greens and yellows, and toughened, mud-streaked jeans, the young woman was clad all in black, and in clothes far too nice for the task at hand.

And she was beautiful, amazingly so, with fine, delicate features and a tiny, heart-shaped mouth. But her coloring seemed off. Her complexion was almost paper white, her tightly cinched hair a near-white blond, and the eyes that peered out from above her scarf were the iciest of blues.

"You each brought your trowels, I reckon?" Clare asked them. "I do have some spares, if you need them."

"Got mine," Samantha said, pulling it from her backpack and raising it high. But Evan had left his trowel behind in their hotel in the Andes—on purpose, Samantha thought. He took one from the pile now as a circle formed around them and Clare held up her hand.

"We'll start with a few test pits," she said. "They'll give us a sample of what's here and help us figure out what sort of excavation—if any—will be necessary in the weeks ahead."

But as Clare pointed to the field's barren surface and began to describe its various features, Samantha had no idea what she was talking about. There was no standing architecture to be found, no stone foundations, no anything, from the look of it. Only when she looked closer did she see the faint scars on the field's stubbly surface, between the patches of snow. They were clearer in some places than in others, and there was a pattern to them—slight changes in color where walls had once been thrown up, ditches dug, pathways beaten down. As Clare went on about Wardy Hill's gullies and ditches, Samantha could almost see the features she described, rising, falling, or changing course as the professor laid out her theories.

"She's in her element here, isn't she?" Jay whispered. "A natural leader. She's like a modern-day Boudica."

"A what?" asked Samantha. *Boudica.* The word seemed familiar. But Jay had already moved on to stand beside his colleague. She would have to check her notes.

"Let's get started, then," said Jay, when Clare had finished.

His colleague met his smile with a grin of her own. They seemed like a perfect partnership in every way, and Samantha was pretty sure they thought so too.

"Right," said Clare. "Let's begin."

———————

The team broke into set pairs—duos established before Evan and Samantha had arrived. So she would have to work with her brother, she realized, with some disappointment. But Evan surprised her by asking one of the students if he could work with him, and she was left to search out a partner of her own.

For a terrible instant, her eyes met the chilling stare

of the young woman across the circle. Would she have to work with her? But then Stuart came to her rescue.

"Your brother's gone and taken my partner, the scunner. So what do you say, Sam? For old time's sake?"

She moved to stand in his protective shadow, taking her field notebook from her backpack to write as Clare announced the plans for the day. The test units would be one-meter squares, just to get a sense of what could be found in the plough soil before real excavation would begin.

The team spread out to assigned spots, and Jay and Clare moved around the field with their maps, measuring tape, and "total station"—a small electronic instrument on a tall, yellow stand—which made the geometry easier with its lasers, levels, and internal compass. As she and Stuart waited for their coordinates to be mapped, Samantha gazed off into the morning landscape—where rabbits hopped in timid bunches as far as she could see. A hot-air balloon glided far to the south, its orange canopy like a second sun. The daylight was muted, and everything was still bedecked with mist, lending a somewhat creepy feel.

It was then that Samantha realized the striking young woman was not among them. She cast her eyes across the frozen landscape, made uneasy by the student's sudden disappearance.

"She's in the lab," Stuart said, guessing at Samantha's surprised expression. "Won't stoop to work with the likes of us. Beautiful, though. I'd say she's the bonniest lass at Cambridge!"

"Who is she?"

"Oona Jessel. One of the Emperor's students. She's used to working in museum galleries and libraries, not out in the mud and muck."

"Maybe she's just shy," Samantha said, noting the deep male voices that cut through the winter winds from the scattered pairs around the site.

Stuart laughed.

"Sure, Samantha. Maybe that's it. Our Oona, just a wee, delicate girl."

It took less than five minutes for the professors to plot out their unit, and soon Samantha and Stuart were kneeling on the ground, scraping away the frozen grass and brambles with their trowels. The setting was new, but the work was familiar, and Samantha felt herself give in to the comforting scrape, scrape, scrape of her blade across the soil. As the wind slackened, the sound of their work was joined by birdsong. There was the caw of crows and cry of hawks and the trills and cheeps of warblers. England was waking to greet them and to lay its secrets bare.

The first artifact popped out of the ground as soon as the vegetation was scraped free. It was a sherd of dull gray pottery, and Samantha might have missed it entirely if not for her training in Peru. Then other artifacts dislodged with each pass of her trowel. Handfuls of them. And while they wouldn't draw crowds at any museum—a few gnarled animal bones here, some plain gray potsherds there—they were enough to fire Samantha's imagination and excite her archaeological mind. Wardy Hill might have had a story to tell, after all. People—real people—had made their home here, butchering these animals and using the once-whole pottery to live their daily lives.

"Where are the screens?" Samantha asked Stuart, when she'd accumulated a pile of cold, loose earth between her knees.

"No time, Samantha. Not for the test pits. We're on someone else's schedule here."

A loud noise cut through the sounds of breeze and birdsong before she could ask what he meant. It belonged to an engine, an antique, puttering up the slope from the village of Coveney below. Samantha had seen the strange old car parked in front of the Archaeology Department, and it was clear from the hush that fell over the team that everyone knew who it belonged to.

Lord Professor Cairn Catesby. The Emperor himself.

Clare and Jay exchanged concerned glances.

"Bloomin' fantastic," said Stuart, as the car came to a stop at the edge of the field.

"I'll handle this," said Jay. "Stay focused, everyone."

But no one was eager to comply. As the team crouched once more in their units, all eyes were trained on the Lord Professor. They saw him dismount from the antique contraption and stumble awkwardly from the running board, a clump of rabbits scattering at his feet. From the alarm on the faces of the students around her, Samantha guessed that this was his first visit to the excavation in progress.

And from the smug look on the Emperor's face, it was clear that he was enjoying the worry he had caused.

"What's he doing here?" she asked. "This is Clare's project, not his."

She found herself whispering, even though the Lord Professor was too far away to hear.

"That may be," said Stuart. "But it's the Emperor who we work for, in the end."

"Because he's the head of the Department?" she asked.

Her partner set his clipboard down.

"No, Sam. Because he's the owner of the land."

"Wardy Hill belongs to Catesby?"

"To him and all the Catesbys before him." Stuart said. "But Vivant Romani will be all his."

Again, Samantha must have looked confused.

"Didn't your uncle tell you anything?" Stuart laughed. "It's the whole bloomin' reason you're here!"

No, Jay hadn't mentioned a Vivant Romani—whatever that was. But there was no time for Stuart to explain. Catesby's crossed arms and imperial stance showed that he wanted a bigger audience, and Jay and Clare waved their arms to call in the team.

No one seemed to want to get too close. But Wardy's wildlife seemed indifferent. Rabbits had already begun to congregate around the car, attracted by the warmth of its motor. Catesby shooed some away before he addressed the group.

"As of this moment, two and a half days of work have

been completed at Wardy Hill," he began in his odd, sleepy voice, forcing everyone to gather even closer. "And how have you squandered your time so far?"

There was silence. Catesby had to answer his own question.

"You spent the first day setting up a completely overblown laboratory, and the entirety of the second day fieldwalking. And for what? Some sheep bones? Three bags of coarse ceramics?"

Samantha felt the sting of his words, even though it was her first day on-site. Gone was the awkward, bumbling professor from their meeting the day before. Catesby's mild pretension had expanded into a nasty arrogance. Stuart leaned in close to whisper in her ear.

"There's no way he could know that. Not in such detail. He must have a spy."

"Archaeology takes time, Cairn," said Jay. "*Good* archaeology, anyway. And it would be easier if you didn't interrupt us in the middle of our workday."

Clare shifted uncomfortably on her feet, and Catesby gave an imperious shrug.

"*Tempus fugit*, as Virgil would say. *Singula dum capti circumvectamur amore.* Time stands still for no man, Dr. Sutton. And for no woman, Dr. Barrows. Our profession teaches us that much."

The rabbits were growing bolder. One emerged from behind the car's thin wheel to nibble at the Lord Professor's shoelace. All the students laughed—all but Oona—and

Catesby muttered something dark and angry. There were muffled boos from the group as he roughly nudged the animal away.

"I've decided to reduce your obligation here from six weeks to a more manageable four. I hope you see this as an opportunity to get things moving."

Samantha watched her uncle step forward.

"Four weeks at a site like this? With this much material coming out of the ground already? That's just not a reasonable time frame, Cairn. And I think you know it."

"Jay," Clare said. "We'll make it work."

"Yes," Catesby said. "You will. After all, professors, while life may creep in its petty pace, it really should signify *something*."

Catesby laughed his wet coughing laugh, pleased by his own turn of phrase. But his triumph was dashed when he tripped over some of the rabbits and stumbled headlong into his car.

No one laughed this time. And as he drove away the team stayed silent, their stunned eyes scanning the vast field around them, crushed by the impossible task ahead.

———————

"Ridiculous!" Jay shouted, as they sped back toward the university town. Samantha swallowed hard.

There was work to be done to accommodate the shortened schedule. The entire excavation plan needed to be rewritten, and he and Clare had ended the day early to address it—asking everyone to reassemble at their usual meeting spot in Cambridge.

"Four weeks! Has Catesby lost his mind?"

This wasn't the time to ask her uncle about Vivant Romani—whatever that was. For now, Jay seemed to be channeling his frustration into the accelerator, and Samantha braced herself against the door and dash.

"We can do it, Uncle Jay," she said, hoping to calm him down.

She should have followed Evan's lead and squeezed into one of the vans for the trip back to Cambridge. For all Jay's speed, the vans had left them far behind. So unsettled was he by Catesby's pronouncement that he took one wrong turn and then another on the gloomy Fenland lanes, cursing himself and the Lord Professor. The half-hour drive stretched to an hour, then to an hour and a half.

"What is he thinking?" he shouted again, and the car veered a little to the right. "How are we supposed to finish everything in just four weeks?"

"We'll just have to work a little harder," she managed through clenched teeth.

"Oh, we'll work harder, all right. We'll switch to a seven-day workweek," said Jay. "And I think what we're going to find up there on that hill will make him regret it."

Finally, they were back in the city center. Good thing that the winter vacation meant the streets were mostly empty, Samantha thought as their car clipped the edge of a sidewalk. Good thing for the people of Cambridge.

At last, Jay slowed at the entrance of a narrow alley—Rose Crescent, according to an old metal signpost at its mouth. The red and white circle below the name meant "No Entry" in any language. But apparently, not in one that Jay understood.

It was a tight fit even for the tiny rental car, and a pair of pedestrians rushed to get out of his way. And then, at last, he came to a stop in a front of a building of whitewash and timber, its lines bowed and bent from centuries of use.

Samantha noticed a hand-painted sign above the doorway, identifying the building as the "Ridge & Furrow." Above the name was a colorful scene of a medieval farmer and his ox plowing grooves across a field. She slammed the car door shut and raced to keep up with her uncle's strides. And when Jay pushed open the heavy oak door, he revealed a different world.

It was a pub, she saw at once, and wondered if she was allowed inside. But it was warm and cozy, more like a living room than any bar Samantha had seen at home. Sure, the Ridge & Furrow *had* a bar where adult drinks were served, and the whole place carried the sticky smell of spilled beer, but the warped wooden floors, crackling hearth, and sturdy beams told of comfort and custom. The aroma of frying fish wafted in from the kitchen, cut with the sharp smell of vinegar, and the leather chairs and mismatched oak tables cheerfully beckoned around the room. Following her uncle's example, she hung her coat on a hook near the door.

"I'm going to get us some lunch," he said. "In the meantime, why don't you introduce yourself around?"

She scanned the room. The others had beaten them by an hour or more and had settled in with drinks and food, or busied themselves with games. Despite Catesby's announcement, the mood seemed friendly and relaxed. But still, she felt strange about approaching anyone to say hello.

Now Stuart came to her rescue again, abandoning his game of darts.

"Welcome to the R&F, Samantha! What took you so long?"

His cheeks were still afire, but no longer from the outside cold. He held a sloshing pint glass in his hand. She smiled.

"My uncle took the scenic route."

"Oh, did he?" Stuart laughed. "I know what that's like. Glad to see you're still in one piece."

He leaned in conspiratorially, but his whisper was loud enough to rattle her eardrums.

"Did Jay explain what happened? Did he say why Professor Catesby's cut us short?"

"No." she said. "But he's definitely not happy about it."

"That old bampot's got something up his sleeve," Stuart began, but he was distracted by a bellow from the dartboard.

"Forsythe! It's your go."

Stuart's impatient opponent seemed much younger than the others in the pub, and his darker complexion stood out among his peers. He must have gone home to change, because he now wore a coat and a dress shirt, and his loosened scarf was striped with the pink and navy blue of Emmanuel College. His hair was an artfully teased collection of coal-black curls.

Evan was with him, and Samantha recognized him as his partner from the morning at the site. "Don't get your knickers in a twist, Kasim. We're coming," Stuart answered, then turned back to Samantha. "I need to teach our young friend here a thing or two about darts. Evan as well...though he claims he's already an expert."

This was true, Samantha thought. On the video-game version of the sport.

Stuart left her then, and Samantha pulled her notebook from her backpack to review her research, feeling a little left out. But she wasn't the only one outside the group of boisterous young men. In the pub's darkest corner sat Oona Jessel, half bowed over a table, her head in her hands in an attitude of woe. Her lips seemed to be moving, as if in silent communication with the long-dead college fellows in the portraits hung around her.

Just then Oona looked up, fixing Samantha with a penetrating stare as her mouth continued to move. Samantha could read her lips across the room, and the unvoiced words unnerved her.

"Despair and die," Oona was uttering, over and over again. "Despair and die. Despair and die. Despair and die."

Great, thought Samantha, trying to squelch her nervousness. Another one. Every excavation seemed to have its loner—a sinister shadow cast across the rest of the team. But surely Oona couldn't be as bad as Adam Quint.

Could she?

On an impulse, Samantha scanned the room, assuring herself that her uncle's old student wasn't among them here in Cambridge. Samantha remembered the chill of his fearsome gaze during his presentation at Jay's university and the guilt she felt on seeing his ghoulish scars. He would never forgive them—either her or her uncle. Never.

"Samantha! Join me."

The interruption could not have been more welcome. She looked to the pub's brightest nook, where Clare was waving her over. There, trophy rowing oars lined the walls amid the fading photographs of the teams who had won them.

"Off-putting, isn't it?" Clare asked, as Oona's mouth continued to move.

"She's learning lines for a play," the professor explained. "She's a very serious thespian. Talented too. I've seen her perform. But archaeological fieldwork doesn't seem to be to her taste."

Clare had a stack of volumes open in front of her, thick and old, and a notebook filled with thoughts and sketches.

"Your uncle has been away from British archaeology for some time," she said. "I'm trying to get him back in the swing of things, but he can be a difficult man to pin down."

Just then, Jay's laugh roared from the bar, where he was trading jokes with two undergraduates.

"It'll be good for him," said Samantha. "I think he's been a little depressed."

Clare smiled sadly.

"It'll only help if I can get him to focus! There's so much to review—torcs, brooches, loom weights, stone celts—he hasn't dealt with this sort of material since he was a student here."

There was a rush of outside air, and Samantha turned to see Cairn Catesby shuffle inside. With a dramatic swirl, he removed his coat, spraying snow on the students unfortunate enough to be sitting near the entrance. He was bound up in the striped blue scarf of Pembroke College and wore a pair of ridiculously oversized earmuffs lined with electric blue fur.

The room grew silent, but Catesby was oblivious to his effect on the atmosphere. He was a clumsy man, running into things as he ambled across the room. The change in temperature had fogged his round wire spectacles so that he failed in his first effort to find the coatrack. The second time, he only managed to hook an arm of the coat so it fell to the muddy floor as soon as he walked away.

He headed straight for Stuart.

"Forsythe!"

"Yes, Professor?"

"Lord Professor," Catesby corrected him. "I wanted to make clear that the tightening of the work schedule should not affect my regatta. How is the planning going?"

"Fine," Stuart stammered. "I mean, okay. I mean, I've made some preliminary enquiries."

"I understand, my dear boy. At least I think I do. You've plans to make plans, is that right?"

His small piggish eyes found Jay.

"This is your influence, Sutton. Your disease is catching!"

As Catesby's wet, hooting laugh filled every corner of the pub, Samantha could tell that the insult had hit its mark. She saw her uncle leave his conversation at the bar, readying some verbal assault. But Clare moved quickly, placing a firm hand on Jay's shoulder and leading him away.

Catesby turned back to Stuart.

"We're only three weeks out, and I'd like to see some progress. A boat race is a fitting honor for a peerage. For the title itself, if not for me."

The group dropped their gaze as Catesby lurched away from the table and back across the room. But there were a few hushed jeers as he wrapped himself once more in his scarf and collected his trodden coat from the floor.

"*Ave atque vale, barbaris,*" he said, swinging up one hand in a sort of salute. "*Ave atque vale.*"

But his grand exit was interrupted when he noticed his earmuffs were missing. His beady eyes flashed around the room, and the students seemed to shrink away. But, deciding that a dramatic departure was more important than the comfort of his ears, he abandoned his search, flung open the door, and strode out into the swirling snow.

a part of the government that's called Heritage They're in charge of a list of called "scheduled monuments," which basically archaeological sites that can't be destroyed. Stuart says that it's hard to get a site on this list, but I want to check.

Boodicca?
BOODAKA?
BOOTIKA? Bootica Boodicca?
Bootica
BOUDICA

Anyway, I thought it was a funny idea, at first, but I don't think any of us thought he would get so mad. It was like a switch went off in his head from normal to crazy.

It's such a stupid tradition that they don't let girls join. There's a woman on their emblem, for crying out loud!

MISCHIEF
MADCAPPERY
MAYHEM
ICENI

Vivant Romani = Latin for "Long Live the Romans!" But what is it?

I don't know if I'm imagining things, but I'm pretty sure that someone was following me. I haven't been this scared since the summer. At least Evan got me {contd}

# CHAPTER 5

"**V**ivant Romani is a terrible idea," said Stuart, his lovely accent escaping into the outdoor chill in cider-scented puffs.

They had been the last to leave the Ridge & Furrow. Awkward though it was, Catesby's display of power had cast a pall on the group, sending most of the team off to their colleges for early dinners. And now Samantha and her brother walked alongside Stuart and Kasim, out of Rose Crescent and into the vast Market Square. The two students had snuck their pints out with them, and Evan followed suit with his glass of currant-flavored barley water.

"What is it, though?" asked Evan. "Vivant Romani, I mean."

"The Emperor's bloomin' construction project," Stuart said, taking a sip from his glass and kicking a loose cobble to skitter across the snowy pavement. "It's why we're digging bloomin' holes in the middle of the bloomin' winter. He's in a hurry to get things moving. I've heard his finances are in shambles. He needs something to make him the kind of money he thinks a lord should have."

This only confused Evan further.

"But he's an archaeologist. Why would he want to destroy a site?"

"He wouldn't," Kasim explained, "if it were Roman. Lord Catesby doesn't give a fig for anything else."

"But there's a law, right?" asked Samantha. "You can't build something if it destroys a site."

Stuart shook his head, sitting down hard on the lip of the square's stone fountain as the light snow swirled around them.

"In America, maybe, but no, not here. And to be fair it would be impossible to build anything at all, if that were the case. They say that all of Britain is manmade, or modified by human hands. Archaeologists learn what they can before it's gone forever, and only in the rarest of cases would a discovery stop construction."

Samantha twisted a braided pigtail between her fingers. "How rare?"

Stuart let out a low whistle.

"Very rare indeed. It's a long, difficult process to get a site on the government's list of scheduled monuments. The Heritage Office has forms to fill out, applications, assessments. We don't have time. Four more weeks of excavation, and then it's the bulldozer for Wardy Hill, sure as sunrise."

She frowned. First, the metal detectorists and now this. England's present seemed to have a strained relationship with England's past.

"But if we do find out that Wardy's worth saving—something that we can get on that list—Catesby can't go on with his project?"

Stuart took another long sip.

"It's more complicated than that, Sam. Dr. Barrows works for Catesby, remember? That's why he picked her and not some outside archaeology service. It's not going to be easy on her if she says he can't go through with it."

"So that's why she invited us," said Evan.

"That's why she invited your uncle, anyway," said Kasim, pausing to drain his glass. "He doesn't work for Catesby, so he's free to say whatever he wants about the site and its importance."

Stuart nodded.

"And Catesby knows it. I was there when she told him that Jay would be coming. The Emperor looked ready to kill someone."

They sat quietly for a moment, marveling at the grandiosity of Catesby's self-love. Evan broke the silence.

"Well," he said, with a mischievousness that matched his uncle's, "the Emperor will be missing these."

From under his coat he pulled Catesby's bright blue earmuffs. Stuart and Kasim exchanged impressed looks.

"You stole those?" Samantha asked.

"He dropped them," said Evan, "and I picked them up. He just left before I could return them. What was I supposed to do?"

Kasim had an answer for that.

"Mischief," he said.

"Monkey business," said Stuart.

"Madcappery," Kasim replied, and Samantha noted that the three terms together sounded like some sort of motto.

"Duty calls," said Stuart, rising to his feet and hurling his pint glass to shatter in the shadows of the square. "Come on, then! For Boudica!"

"For Boudica!" Kasim replied, flinging his pint across the cobbles as well.

Caught up in the merrymaking, Evan heaved his own glass into the night.

"Evan!" Samantha cried. "Someone's going to have to clean that up!"

But her brother was too excited by the students' mysterious fervor to pay her any attention.

"For Boudica!" he shouted, loudest of all.

The half-remembered word ringing in her ear, Samantha bounded after the impish band and toward some kind of trouble.

———

Revenge would be theirs, they decided, in the form of sculpted snow.

They set up shop on the other side of the river—in the long section of open ground and imposing views known as the Backs. In summer, the footpath along the river must have been a splendid sight, Samantha thought, as they made their way down it. But the gardeners of the various colleges had let things get unruly during the winter holiday, and the scattered snowbanks and bare-limbed trees gave the whole area a look of wilderness barely held at bay.

If Stuart was right, Catesby's evening route would take him by this spot. The Lord Professor liked to take tea upriver at St. John's College. When he finished, he would cross the Cam at the covered Bridge of Sighs for a slow walk home along the Backs, enjoying the grand gardens and lawns of the older colleges that stretched out along the river.

And so they began their work on the pathway opposite King's College, the spires of its mighty chapel poking at the lowest of the dark and heavy clouds. It was to be the biggest snowman ever built, Stuart announced, and everyone wholeheartedly agreed. While Evan packed together a midsection, Samantha and Stuart focused on the legs, taking big armfuls of snow and heaping them into a lumpy pile. Kasim alone worked on the head, taking his time to get it right.

*Boudica.*

Samantha's thoughts wandered as she worked, settling on the odd word Stuart and Kasim had shouted some minutes before as a sort of rallying cry to mischief. And earlier, Jay had used it to describe Clare Barrows as she rallied the team around her.

"Who's Boudica?"

Kasim and Stuart looked up from their work, their eyes wild—with mischief, madcappery, and monkey business.

"Why, she's our lovely lady Queen!" said Stuart.

"Our stalwart, steadfast sovereign!" said Kasim.

"What?" asked Evan, trying to get in on the action. "Booty who?"

"Oh!" cried Kasim, in mock outrage. "He insults our queen! Fine him, fine him!"

"What are you guys talking about?" asked Samantha, as amused as she was bewildered. "Can someone please explain?"

"A fair request," said the red-cheeked Scot. "But one I can only partially grant, given the secrets I am sworn to protect."

"Secrets most solemn," said Kasim, approving.

"We are the Iceni," Stuart said. "Among the last of our kind. Sworn to protect her majesty's name against interlopers, scoundrels, and spoilsports—be they Roman or otherwise."

"And to bring charm and courtesy to the people of Cambridge."

"And to quaff carouses to its beautiful women, in the company of our peers."

Evan was intrigued. "So it's a club?"

"A society," said Stuart, "for gentlemen."

Over the next several minutes, and as the snowman began to take shape, the Iceni Society's great veil of secrecy was partly lifted—if great it ever was. It was a type of fraternity made up of some of the university's archaeology students. But Catesby's students were specifically excluded on account of their Roman focus. And so were women—all of them—no matter what they studied.

"They have their own societies," Kasim said, catching Samantha's disapproving scowl.

"Which we're not allowed to join," Stuart added. "Much as we'd like to."

Their frozen colossus was almost complete. Just as Stuart had hoped, it was the biggest snowman Samantha had ever seen. Its lowest part was shaped into a thick pair of legs while the midsection sagged above it, a hanging massive gut. And when Kasim heaved the head into place and stepped aside, everyone howled with laughter.

The sheer size of thing was funny on its own, but the stern features were what made it so hilarious. Kasim had used a crooked twig for a mouth, twisted into a testy little scowl. The nose was a stunted pinecone and the hair an ungainly wig of pine needles and leaves. Ears of snow stood out, ridiculously large. For eyes, Kasim had embedded a pair of shiny 50p coins, placed close together on the wide, white face.

The overall effect was uncanny, the likeness perfect. They were now face-to-face with Lord Professor Cairn Colin Catesby's massive snowman twin.

"A piece of art, my friends." Stuart managed, and slapped Kasim hard on the back. "Poetry in snow."

But they all knew that the snowman wasn't finished. Fishing the professor's earmuffs from his pocket, Evan stretched them as wide as they could go and squeezed them over the monstrous head, crushing the ears of snow. At last, they took a step back to admire their creation.

"And so we wait," said Kasim.

"And so we watch," said Stuart.

The four of them scattered to find cover in the shadows of the nearby willows. And just in time. Because as they took their places behind the tree trunks, the Lord Professor himself appeared upriver, shuffling toward them down the path.

He looked funnier than the snowman, with his blue-striped Pembroke scarf wrapped high around his head to protect his ears, and his hat pulled down to hold it in place. He walked a little like a penguin, his bundled head bobbing side to side. But no penguin bobbed with such fierce determination. Samantha almost pitied him—until she remembered his haughty bearing at Wardy Hill and again later at the pub.

Catesby walked with his eyes on his feet, so he didn't see the snowman until he was right in front of it. When the electric blue of the earmuffs entered his field of vision, he came to a sudden stop. For a moment, he just stood there, staring—two Catesbys, flesh and snow, standing face-to-face. And then one of those faces turned scarlet red.

Samantha heard her brother snicker. But Stuart and Kasim were unsmiling, their eyes gleaming with revenge. Catesby's own eyes had grown to twice their size. He shuffled around the snowman, his sideways motions driving the penguin comparison home. He seemed confused more than angry, unable to fathom how his earmuffs had arrived here, and on such a perfect caricature.

And then he lost his mind.

His hands shot out in front of him, shoving at the torso

of the snowman, trying to topple it over. But when only the head rolled off backward, Catesby's attack grew wild. He flailed at what remained, pummeling the mound of snow with punches and kicks, and emitting the wounded noises of his injured pride.

"My god," Kasim whispered in goofy horror. "This is fantastic."

"He's gone mental," said Stuart, and he and Evan laughed aloud.

But Samantha felt otherwise. It wasn't funny; it was scary. Catesby was completely unhinged. Twice he lost his footing, falling the first time into the remnants of the snowman and the second time backward, painfully on his rear. And when he noticed his earmuffs where they had fallen, on the very edge of the riverbank, he dove for them—sliding face-first down the slope, inches away from a fall into the icy River Cam.

They took this as their opportunity to run away. But there was no escaping this, Samantha thought as she sprinted and slipped along the riverside. Not really. Catesby's list of suspects would be a small one, and after his exchange with Jay at the pub, the Sutton kids would be at the top of his list. And then Evan sealed that fate for certain.

"For Boudica!" he shouted with unbridled glee.

His voice—distinctly American—could be heard up and down the Cam.

———

They ran and ran, fleeing the scene of their crime as fast as they were able. But even at a sprint, Samantha's much shorter legs could barely keep up. Her lungs burned as they ran south along the Cam's western bank, passing the colleges of Queens and Darwin, then back across the river at the Silver Street Bridge. With every turn, she expected to see Catesby waiting, ready to identify them. She would not want to be left out here, not by herself. But by the time they were in the narrow lanes of the town's medieval center, Samantha was falling far behind.

"Wait!" she cried out, as they darted through the alleyways. "Please, guys!"

But they didn't hear, or did but didn't listen. And then she was alone, the echoes of their footsteps growing faint in the afternoon gloom.

A turn down a side street spat her out near the wide parkland of Parker's Piece. Stuart, Kasim, and her brother were nowhere in sight. She stopped, panting, her hands on her knees. And then she turned to walk back to Trinity Hall alone, taking as looping a route as possible to avoid a run-in with their victim.

Cambridge's core was a nest of streets and alleyways, built over hundreds of years with little regard to order or purpose. It would have been a fun place to explore under different circumstances—when there wasn't an outraged English lord on the loose. Now, as she lost herself in the unfamiliar warren, all she felt was unease. The sky above had grown dark with winter clouds. The narrow, twisting lanes were empty—silent where snow dampened the echoes and loud where the softest sounds could bounce off walls and cobbles. She had no love for labyrinths and their strange acoustics—not after Chavín.

It was on bleak Petty Cury Lane where she heard the hurried footsteps of someone behind her. Was it just an echo? she wondered at first. She tested the theory by standing still for a moment. But the footsteps continued on their own for two steps, then stopped with a scrape.

She strained her ears as she pressed on through the lightly falling snow. And when it happened again outside the Guildhall, she was ready, spinning in time to see a shadow duck inside an alley—a thick muddy jacket and swirl of ragged scarves.

"Hello?" she said. No one responded. But someone was there. She could hear raspy breathing and see light puffs of condensed breath.

She was being followed.

And so she began to run again—back across the glass-strewn Market Square, then south and west and north again to shake her mysterious pursuer. She did not slow until she was safely through the Porters' Lodge, courtyard, and stairwell and behind the thick oak door of her room. Her pulse pounding, she crept to her window on her knees, peering beneath the curtain and into the shadowy alley below. Someone was there, walking alone in the empty lane. Whoever it was clung to the shadows, and she could not see the person's face until he passed beneath the lone streetlight.

The lamp turned the man's face a nasty orange. But still she recognized him. It was Ned Aubrey, the tall man from the night before. And he was in a hurry.

Aubrey wasn't wearing a scarf, though, and his jacket seemed thin and free of mud. Had he been following her? Not Catesby or someone else?

She let the curtain drop, sank to the floor, and held her knees tightly to her chest.

*Cálmate*, she told herself. Relax.

But she couldn't. All she could do was cower out of sight and wait for her brother's return.

———

But Evan did not come back to their room in the next hour. As the evening wore on and the sky outside grew blacker still, Samantha could not find the courage to stand, cross the room, and turn on the lights.

When her brother did return, he was soaking wet, shivering, and almost blue, but smiling all the same.

"Where have you been?"

"Iceni business," said Evan, disappearing into his room to change. "Can't say."

Her heart sank. So Stuart and Kasim had let him join their stupid club. Society, she corrected herself, meticulous even in the confines of her mind.

"You guys just left me."

When he came back into the sitting room, Evan did look a little sorry. But then his face lit up.

"I did bring you a present, though. It's outside. Follow me."

She was still rattled and stayed only a couple of steps behind her brother as they descended to the forecourt. Two bicycles were there in the lamplight, leaning against the wall, newly formed icicles hanging from the handlebars.

"Yours is the one with the bell," Evan said, pointing to the smaller of the two. Its paint was gone and the frame was rusted, but the chain was intact and the wheels seemed fine. It might come in handy, she thought.

"Stuart says everyone needs one at Cambridge. We even blew up the tires for you."

She didn't say anything as they walked back up the stairs. But when they entered the room, Evan could stand the silence no longer.

"Do you like it? Yes or no."

Still, she didn't answer.

"You better," Evan went on, his tone changed. "Tom almost killed me for bringing it through the Porters' Lodge."

She sighed aloud.

"Fine. I like it. But where did it come from? You didn't steal it, did you?"

Evan grinned again, his sly smile a replica of their uncle's.

"Can't say, Archaeo Kid. Iceni business."

She slammed her ancient door on its ancient hinges, rattling the ancient windows of her room.

## BRITISH SLANG THAT EVAN USES
## AND DRIVES ME CRAZY

- SOD OFF = get out of here, leave me alone
- PANTS = Underwear. (He thinks this is especially hilarious)
- BRILLIANT: Good or cool. I don't think he really understands this one.

The backhoe makes things go so fast. Maybe too fast! I'm worried that we're missing stuff.

**Oona** is just getting weirder and weirder. She's in Shakespeare's <u>Richard III</u> next term, but it's still weird. I'm going to try to avoid her.

Uncle Jay started telling me about Boudica, the Warrior Queen. I think he promised Clare he wouldn't, for some reason. Anyway, here's what I know so far:

If I had the wings of a sparrow
If I had the ass of a cow
I'd fly over Pembroke tomorrow
    the bastards below.

SPQR

When the Roman Emperor Claudius invaded England in 43 AD (CE) he made deals with some of the rulers of the Celtic tribes that were there already. For the Iceni, it was decided that the King didn't have to give up his land, and even when he died, only half would go to the Romans. The rest would go to wife, Queen Boudica, and their two ki... But when the King died, the Romans didn't keep their promise. Boudica objected,
    he Romans took her kids

# CHAPTER 6

The sun was out the next morning, but the temperature seemed not to know it. Ice caked the windows of Jay's car, and frost covered the Fens that streaked by outside in an indefinite blanket of white.

She considered telling her uncle about the previous night's events. Not the incident with Catesby and the snowman, though he would probably enjoy it, but about Ned Aubrey and his pursuit of her through town. She quickly dismissed the urge. Even if it had been Aubrey beneath her window, he might not have been following her. Perhaps it had just been her imagination. Now, in the light of day, she wasn't sure that she could trust herself. Not after Peru.

Besides, she did not want to upset her uncle. Jay was calm today. When the vans caught up at Coveney, the final village, he did not join them in their reckless race. And by the time he switched off the ignition, the students were already spilling out into the freezing morning, laughing and racing for the cover of the pillbox. Samantha pushed her own door open, and the cold seeped through her clothes as she trudged across the field and followed the rest of the group inside.

It made for an excellent lab. The former military fixture was in good condition—solid and sturdy with a door that locked. Most of the small space was filled with mismatched folding chairs. A small generator thrummed just inside the entrance, powering a space heater. Its coils glowed orange for the first few minutes of the team's arrival, then faded as the plug was freed for the electric kettle, in order to make tea.

Shelving had been brought in to house whatever arti-facts were to be uncovered, along with binders of various forms. The team's first couple days of field-walking and test pits had recovered enough animal bones and tiny bits of pottery to fill a dozen bags, and they sat all together on a shelf. Samantha smiled, recognizing the handwriting that labeled each bag. The finds were in Clare's capable hands here, and so was she. They would be safe this time.

As the group settled in and more water was put on for tea, Samantha gave a long glance through the small win-dows, out toward a hovering clump of hot-air balloons: green, purple, and one—like her backpack—striped in Union Jack red, white, and blue. It was easy to imagine the British soldiers who had been stationed here, their eyes trained through these narrow slits for any sign of a German invasion.

But the Second World War was so recent, as far as this place went. What about the lookouts posted here fifty generations ago? Or seventy? What threat did they fear? And what—or who—were they protecting?

These were the questions they were in a rush to answer before Catesby's development began its construction and their excavation came to its hurried end. But the others didn't seem to share her sense of urgency. As Jay and Clare finalized the plans for the day outside, Kasim regaled the team with stories of the night before—not the incident with Catesby, which he kept secret, but what happened after Samantha had fallen behind.

Only Samantha didn't find it funny. The team's convivial laughter interrupted the telling again and again. Kasim and his audience were agreeing about how the Cam was an excellent source of bicycles, as so many of them found their way into it over the course of year.

"And retrieving them makes for a suitable initiation exercise," said Stuart. "A winter's swim can test the mettle of a man."

From the sound of it, Evan's mettle had been tested. While Samantha fled an unknown pursuer, they had circled back to the Cam above Jesus Green. Still intoxicated by their daring prank, it had taken little convincing to get Evan out of his coat and jeans, and into the river in his T-shirt and underwear. Ten minutes later, two bicycles lay along the icy bank and he was close to hypothermia. Only a donated gym towel from a concerned passerby had saved him, and his new Iceni brothers had helped him wheel the bicycles back home.

"I did it for Boudica!" said Evan, and Samantha frowned, embarrassed for him. The comment seemed so forced. What could Evan possibly know of this age-old Cambridge club, all after a single night? He was humiliating himself. He was humiliating her. But then, to Samantha's displeasure, the male students answered her brother in unison.

"For our stalwart, steadfast sovereign," they chanted. "For our lovely lady Queen."

———————

As the team streamed reluctantly from the lab at last, Samantha found herself shivering in her jacket.

"Sorry, Samantha," said Kasim as they trudged across the field, scattering rabbits left and right. "About last night, I mean. I thought you were right there with us."

His arm around her shoulder warmed her somewhat, but his words felt hollow. After his story in the lab, she was certain that she had been abandoned on purpose. The Iceni Society was for "gentlemen," as Stuart had said, and they couldn't have initiated Evan with her there. She was about to tell Kasim so and register her hurt feelings, but he was off and away, bounding ahead to talk to Stuart and Evan and leaving her alone again.

"That hated wretch!"

The icy voice belonged to Oona Jessel, the beautiful, brooding student from the Ridge & Furrow—the actress who'd been rehearsing her part in a play.

"Foul devil, for God's sake, hence, and trouble us not!"

These were lines too, Samantha knew at once. But there was some real bitterness behind them. Oona could never be a member of the Iceni Society either, Samantha realized. She was excluded on two counts—both as a female and as Catesby's student—a scholar of the Roman Empire. But her voice was biting, full of spite, and maybe that was why Samantha found herself defending them.

"It's not like they invented it. Stuart says that the Iceni Society has been around for more than a hundred and fifty years."

Oona snorted, breaking character at last.

"And for a hundred and fifty years, it has given boys like these an excuse to act like barbarians. How stupid. How embarrassing for Cambridge, don't you think?"

Samantha studied Oona for a moment, taking in her fine clothes and carefully arranged hair. And then she looked over to where Kasim and Evan were trying to stuff handfuls of ice down each other's jackets. Maybe Oona was right.

But then another realization crossed her mind. The actress' words had been in perfect Californian English—an exact copy of Samantha's own.

"Are you…American?" she asked.

Oona gave a lofty laugh.

"Oh heavens no," she said, her voice British once again. "I've become a bit of a mimic, I'm afraid. Nasty habit. It began as a way to prepare for roles, but it's become automatic."

There was something unsettling about this trait too. Add it to the list, Samantha thought.

"All right, everyone." Clare began, as the group formed a circle around her. "There have been some changes to our schedule, as you are all aware. And our work will need to adapt accordingly."

A low rumble, and the ground seemed to shake. And when Samantha saw the monstrous object coughing up the slope, it was clear that she would not be needing her trowel today. She slid it into her back pocket, blade down. Clearly, Catesby's time limit called for a less gentle approach.

There was nothing gentle whatsoever about the backhoe. Jay had gone into the nearby village to retrieve it, and now Samantha watched as it appeared in a puff of exhaust over the crest of the hill, her beaming uncle at its controls.

It was a loud, nasty machine—its windshield cracked, its yellow paint peeling—and the noise it kicked out was as noxious as its fumes. When Jay brought the machine to a stop at the edge of the site, the small team's loud applause matched the volume of the engine.

"Power archaeology," he announced.

"This will save us loads of time," Clare said. She explained how centuries of farming had churned the surface of the field so that any artifacts it contained would be jumbled and unable to reveal any more information than the general pattern the test pits had already revealed. But beneath the farmed surface, pure archaeology awaited. It was there that the team could begin their units, and where excavation would provide a clear look at how this place had once been used.

Jay proved competent with the backhoe in his first few passes, skimming the topmost inches from the field in a series of jerky moves. But when he relinquished the controls to Clare midmorning, it was clear who the expert was. Samantha watched as the young professor steered the machine around the field, lowering its hefty shovel just enough to carve away the top of the plough soil in swathes only a few centimeters deep.

Samantha did more than observe. As some students returned to the pillbox to weigh and sort the completed bags, and as others prepared the sheaves of paperwork, she and her brother monitored each pass of the bucket, making sure it didn't turn up any hidden bits of buildings or burials, or break into the unploughed strata of the field below.

Only once did she have to raise her hand and signal—when her uncle was at the controls again, and when he dropped the shovel a little too deep. But during Clare's turn, Samantha could stand with her hands in her pockets, marveling at the precision of each graceful stroke.

It took most of the winter-cinched day, and by the time Clare clambered down from the cab, the sun was nearing the western horizon. The long shadows did something to the field. Marks could be seen on the machine-smoothed surface: traces of something that had once commanded the hilltop. But as Samantha felt the welcome thrill of discovery, it was clear that Evan did not share the sentiment.

"That's it? That's all there is?"

"Calm down, Evan," Samantha said, and her brother fixed her with a nasty glare.

"Hey, Archaeo Kid. Why don't you sod off?"

She groaned. Mention of her hated nickname was expected, but the use of British slang was something new. Some of the Iceni language was rubbing off on him or— more likely—he just wished it was.

Still, the field's mysterious markings beckoned. She took a long look before trudging back to the pillbox to collect her belongings, and stopped halfway to turn and look again. Jay and Clare were still at the edge of the machine-scraped field, gazing out at the results of their hard day's work.

Samantha smiled. Maybe it was the way they were standing—shoulders touching, leaning close—but Samantha could sense magic at work. She knew love when she saw it.

But then her uncle did something to break the spell.

"She was here," Samantha heard him murmur. "I just know it."

Disappointment creased Clare's pretty face. Jay had ruined the moment. The British professor shook herself free without a word and strode off, leaving him stammering and alone.

And ashamed, Samantha realized, as he caught his niece's worried stare.

———

"Your brother and I have some catching up to do, Sam. I'm sure you understand."

And Samantha did understand, even if it hurt her feelings. Jay and Evan shared a different sort of bond—one that sometimes made her jealous. Only her uncle could talk her brother out of his archaeological funk, and only Evan could distract Jay from troubles of his own.

So she piled into one of the excavation vans with the boisterous team, caught up in the current of their mischief, madcappery, and monkey business despite herself. She squeezed into the rear seat just as the others broke out into a raucous song about Catesby's college, with lyrics more filthy than any she'd heard before.

But the student beside her wasn't singing, just mumbling something horrible into her scarf.

"Despair and die. Fill thy sleep with perturbations."

Samantha looked up with a start. Oona was practicing her unnerving lines again. Her pale eyes were burning straight ahead, as if in a trance.

"Tomorrow in the battle, think on me. Despair and die."

Samantha sank in her seat, Shakespeare's curses wending their way into her subconscious. And as the van raced its twin across the darkening countryside, she urged it faster on.

———

She found Jay at a picnic table in Trinity Hall's Back Court, bent over a book by the soft glow of an outdoor lamp. It was a freezing out, especially now that the sun had gone down, but she knew that Jay's trick for concentration was to study in the cold. Even in California he would turn the air conditioner on full blast whenever there was some new lecture to commit to memory or some complicated article he had to write.

She shivered as she sat down opposite her uncle, the cold of the bench searing through the back of her jeans.

"Doing my homework," he said, gesturing at his copy of *Marshland Communities and Cultural Landscape.* "I want to stay on Clare's good side."

Or earn your way back to it, Samantha thought, remembering the mysterious disagreement she'd witnessed at the workday's end.

They sat a moment in silence. Samantha wanted desperately to talk to him about his relationship with Clare, about Adam Quint, about what was going on with his own career. But being alone with her uncle felt strange somehow. They hadn't spent much time together since Peru, and the specter of that misadventure hung over them still.

"Hungry?" he asked her.

He pointed to where an open bag of potato chips sat on the table—or crisps, as she knew they were called here. She took one out and sniffed it, recoiling at the unexpected odor. Lamb and Mint, the bag said.

"I've also got Prawn Cocktail," Jay offered, but she made a face and shook her head no.

She looked out over the college's vast lawn. The towering, leafless willow at its center cast a weird silhouette on the darkening sky. Beyond was the Cam itself, swollen in its banks. To the right was a squat brick building, two stories high.

"That's the Old Library," Jay said, as eager as she was to break the silence.

At this Samantha brightened.

"How old?"

"Five hundred years, at least, and full of secrets. It's supposedly built from the wrecks of the Spanish Armada."

A flame kindled up inside her. She loved libraries, whether she was conducting some focused research of her own, or just wandering through the reference section and opening books at random. There was something so satisfying about holding a book in her hand. The words inside seemed much more considered, so much more permanent than anything she could read on a computer. And she loved the idea of being surrounded by hundreds of them in a single building, encircled by rows and rows of human knowledge. She would have to explore this one too, as soon as she had the chance.

But Trinity Hall's Old Library was peculiar. A door was built into the side, high above the ground, opening out into nothingness. Whatever this door had once led to—a bridge, a battlement, some secret annex—was long, long gone.

"Fun, isn't it?" Jay said, following her line of sight. "In the Tudor period, there was a bridge connecting the library to the Master's residence across the way."

Catesby would enjoy something like that, she thought.

Crossing high over the heads of the students so he wouldn't have to mingle or muddy his boots.

They shared a smile, and just like that their old closeness returned. They were bound together once more by their love of the past. Maybe now was the time to ask the question that had bothered her all day.

"Who's Boudica?"

Jay looked up with a start.

"Where did *that* come from?"

"From you, partly. Remember? You said Clare was like Boudica, the other day. And Evan keeps saying it too—shouting it, actually. I think it has something to do with Stuart's club."

"Oh right!" Jay grinned, his pride unmistakable. "I hear your brother's in the Iceni Society! The Sutton tradition continues."

Great, Samantha thought, so Jay was a member as well. She tried to refocus.

"Boudica, though. Who was she?"

Jay shifted on the bench.

"A very powerful ruler, Samantha. A warrior and a queen."

He seemed reluctant to elaborate.

"Queen of England?" she prompted.

"Part of it. She was the ruler of the Iceni—one of the Celtic tribes that lived in Britain, until around two thousand years ago. She's famous for fighting back against the Roman invasion."

Samantha nodded. She had read this somewhere in her

hurried research to prepare. And as Jay went on, the story came back to her—the queen who'd taken on the most powerful empire the world had ever known.

"At its height, Rome controlled a huge part of the world—from Spain to Armenia, Egypt to France."

"But not England," said Samantha.

"Right. At least not at first. Britain was a cold, wet place back then—pretty much like it is now. For a long time, the Romans were content with trading with the Iron Age Celtic tribes—importing their tin and wool. They didn't want the whole place for themselves."

"Until?"

"Until a particular emperor came to power. A guy with something to prove. He was old, in bad health, and with a stammer that made him hard to understand. He needed a way to make a strong impression. He needed someplace to invade."

Jay ran his fingers through his dark brown hair, as he always did when he was telling a story. The Roman army could have brought all the tribes of Britain to their knees, he explained, if it had felt the need. But war was expensive and hard to manage so far from the homeland. So the Romans developed a system. The native British kings could live out their lives in peace if they agreed to will their land to the Empire when they died and their people to Rome as subjects.

"But there were exceptions," Jay went on. "Things were different for the richest Celtic rulers—like Prasutagus,

King of the Iceni and husband to the great Queen Boudica. With lots of their own wealth and strong connections with Rome already, the Iceni were no ordinary tribe. So, it was agreed that only half of the kingdom would go to Rome when Prasutagus died, while the rest would go his kids."

Jay paused to make sure that Samantha was following. She was—intensely so.

"Anyway, they had a deal. But it wasn't one the Romans intended to keep. When Prasutagus did pass away, the emperor went back on his agreement with the Iceni. And this was what caused Boudica to take action."

An ancient queen? A warrior? That was an image Samantha could live with—the true Iceni, led by their fearsome queen.

She blurted out her biggest question.

"Does Boudica have anything to do with Wardy Hill?"

An eager smile broke across Jay's face.

"Maybe, Sam. Just maybe. In fact, some people say…"

But then he caught himself, as if remembering some promise of his own. He gave a sheepish sigh.

"Sorry, kiddo. I don't want to spread rumors about what might be up at Wardy. Catesby would have my head, and even Clare got mad at me this afternoon for mentioning the possibility."

He cleared his throat.

"And they do have a point, Sam. We're archaeologists, after all, not historians. We don't go looking for evidence of specific people or events. For us, it's the other way around.

We let the evidence do the talking and construct the story from what we find."

Samantha nodded, her mind still swarming with images of Roman soldiers and ferocious Iceni Celts locked in combat. She could see the fearsome warrior queen, steering her chariot through the battle.

"So, no more Boudica talk, okay?" Jay asked. "You'll let it go?"

She promised him that she would, and Jay was content. They had a deal. But it was not one Samantha intended to keep. She wasn't done with Boudica. Not even close.

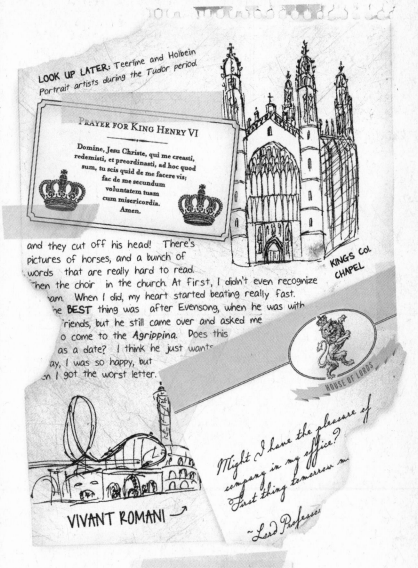

**LOOK UP LATER:** Teerline and Holbein Portrait artists during the Tudor period.

PRAYER FOR KING HENRY VI

Domine, Jesu Christe, qui me creasti,
redemisti, et preordinasti, ad hoc quod
sum, tu scis quid de me facere vis;
fac de me secundum
voluntatem tuam
cum misericordia.
Amen.

KINGS Col. CHAPEL

and they cut off his head! There's
pictures of horses, and a bunch of
words that are really hard to read.
hen the choir in the church. At first, I didn't even recognize
am. When I did, my heart started beating really fast.
e BEST thing was after Evensong, when he was with
riends, but he still came over and asked me
o come to the Agrippina. Does this
as a date? I think he just want
ay, I was so happy, but
n I got the worst letter.

HOUSE OF LORDS

VIVANT ROMANI →

Might I have the pleasure of
company in my office?
First thing tomorrow m

~ Lord Professor

SSFNb2-WH: 7

# CHAPTER 7

**K**ing's College Chapel. Samantha had decided that there couldn't be a more magnificent building—not in Cambridge, not in England, not in all the world. And each time she passed it, she fell once more under its lyrical spell.

It looked just like a song would look, if music could be built with stone. The chapel rose from the snowy ground with the growing thunder of percussion, up to where its graceful steeples formed a marble melody against the sky.

And that was just the outside. Tonight, as she followed her uncle and brother from the King's College forecourt and into the softly lit space, she was struck dumb once more by the haunting, heavenly music of its construction. On this she and her uncle seemed to agree.

"My favorite place in Cambridge, guys," said Jay, as he held open the heavy door. "If not the entire world."

She was immediately struck by the height of the walls. They seemed to be made up more of windows than of masonry. Narrow stalks of marble separated the giant panels of stained glass, rising like the slender trunks of tall white trees. And the ceiling—the ceiling!—interlocking webs of pure white stone, carved into arcs and points and spokes and the stark white coats of arms of English royals.

"Wow," Evan muttered, forgetting his frustrations with distant Annie Cartano and nearby Wardy Hill.

Samantha gazed and gazed until she felt dizzy. She took a moment to rest her neck, then looked up to gaze again. A great wooden screen split the long central nave, and they followed their uncle through its grand opening to take their seats among the high-backed stalls. The air smelled of incense and wood, a memory of some long-gone forest. Samantha cast her eyes upward once again. Through the windows, the sky was almost completely dark. But such was the stillness and purity of the light within the chapel that all the clamor of the outside world—looting and madmen and warring professors—seemed impossibilities. All was still in this great space. All was at peace.

The spell was broken when she saw faint graffiti scrawled in ugly red on the wall beside the altar. Samantha could just make out a large drawing of an animal, maybe a horse, and some illegible traces of words. Who could do such a thing? Who would desecrate the beauty of this place?

"Don't worry," Jay whispered, following her angry gaze. "They caught the guy who did it."

"Good!" she said, her voice echoing more than she would have liked. "I hope he got in trouble!"

"You could say that," said Jay. "They cut off his head."

Samantha turned to stare at him. But Jay was smiling, enjoying her confusion. There was clearly more to the tale.

"This was in the seventeenth century, Sam. And actually, he was already dead. But it was for treason, not for vandalism or for the fact that he used this church as a stable."

Another story, Samantha thought as the rest of the seats were taken and the candles lit. Another knot of complexity in England's tangled past.

The sudden sound of the organ filled the space. So deep and resonant were the first few chords that Samantha could feel the vibrations to her core. Then, as the music continued, a line of boys shuffled in, filling the choir stalls across from them. Some were Samantha's age or slightly older, while some—especially the little ones in the front— couldn't have been more than eight or nine. In their long white shirts over longer red robes, they looked like they were from another time. She sat awestruck and ignored Evan's mocking chuckle.

"Wow," he said. "You couldn't pay me to wear something like that."

But even he fell silent when the boys began to sing. The music was soft and pure but wielded a hammer's force. It filled the space, rebounding from the intricate ceiling and misting back down like gentle rain. Beside Samantha, her uncle closed his eyes and let the harmonies take him.

When the last echoes gave way, there was no applause from the congregation. There was no sound at all. And when the deacon took the podium and gave a short welcome to the small assembly, it seemed a rude incursion. But soon, he surrendered the chapel again to the boys, and once more they filled the nave with glory.

This song—said the printed program that lay across Samantha's knees—was the prayer of King Henry VI, set to music. The words were simple and spoke of peace—strange, when Samantha thought about the man who wrote them, and his brutal wars across England and parts of northern France. But it was he who had had this chapel built. And for that, Samantha could almost forgive his bloody legacy. This was England, after all. Its entire history was bathed in blood.

Again the deacon interrupted, reading aloud a story of another Iron Age people—a desert civilization, half a world away. Samantha knew these tales—and even loved them when her mood was right. But how foreign they seemed here. How out of place. It seemed so odd to speak of dry and distant Bethlehem on the edge of the watery Fens.

The next song fit the setting, though, and brought the service back to England:

*In the bleak midwinter, frosty wind made moan.*
*Earth stood hard as iron, water like a stone.*

As the candles flickered, and as the congregation grew quieter still, one voice raised above the others—rich and pure and strong. All eyes turned toward the soloist.

*Snow had fallen, snow on snow, snow on snow.*
*In the bleak midwinter, long ago.*

Samantha felt a faint hint of recognition as the boy concluded his solo. But Evan knew at once and nudged his sister hard. The singer was Graham Aubrey—the boy with the metal detector. He looked so different in his cassock, his hair combed flat, scrubbed of dirt and mud. The candlelight made his big blue eyes look soft, and the arch of his eyebrows showed his deep concentration.

"He sings like a girl," her brother said, harsh in her ear.

"No, he doesn't," she spat back.

And he didn't. Not at all. Graham's voice was clear and high, but there was nothing girl-like about him. She loved how deliberate his singing was—how his lips formed each word precisely, and how attentive he was to the conductor's movements. He looked so focused. So handsome. She couldn't pull her eyes away.

The solo ended, far too soon, and Graham's voice fell back among the others. For a nervous moment she wondered if he had seen her, as close as she was to him across the nave. But his concentration was too strong for that, lost as he was in another world.

When the song came to an end, though, Graham did seem to glance her way—probably drawn to the intensity of her staring. She looked down, embarrassed, and was pretending to study the program in her lap when the deacon again took his place behind the lectern and broke the ancient spell.

———

After the service came to a close, the Suttons lingered for several moments in their pew. Only when the last echoes faded did they wind back through the nave and out the door onto the rain-slick cobbles outside. The freezing rain roused them from their daze, and they hurried to gather under Jay's umbrella.

"Samantha?"

It was Graham, separating himself from where the other choirboys were milling beneath an overhang. They had all changed clothes, and they were no longer angels—just boys again, like boys anywhere. And there was nothing angelic about their crude chatter.

"Go on, Aubrey!" shouted one, behind his hand.

"She's *fit*!" added another.

Graham waved them all away.

"Your name *is* Samantha, isn't it?"

Samantha nodded, a little too startled to speak.

"I thought I saw you in there," he said. "Did you enjoy the service?"

She nodded again. But Graham was expecting an answer.

"Your solo was really nice," she managed. "I had no idea you could sing like that."

She wished immediately she could take it back. She had met the boy once, and under very strange circumstances. How could she know anything about him?

But her brother had no such reservations.

"Wow," said Evan, "He can loot archaeological sites *and* he can sing like a girl. What a lot of talent."

To her great relief, Graham ignored the insult and answered her awkward statement instead.

"Hope so. We have the Christmas Eve service in a few days' time. International radio broadcast."

"Wow," she said, realizing that she'd heard the program herself on Christmases past, tuning in with her uncle when he visited their home in Davis, California, for the holidays.

Suddenly, Ned Aubrey was there among the dispersing crowd. He glared in their direction, and Jay seemed suddenly eager to leave.

"Sam?" he called. "You ready to get going?"

But Graham spoke up before she could depart.

"Do you want to pop 'round sometime and look at the collection my dad and I have made over the years?"

She nodded, a little too enthusiastically.

"Here's my address," he said. "Come by any time."

She took the piece of paper and squeezed again under Jay's umbrella, flinching a little from Ned Aubrey's stare.

"Cheers then, Samantha," said Graham.

"Bye."

Her heart was singing—the sound of Graham's glorious solo. The teasing started immediately.

"Aww. The Archaeo Kid's got herself a boyfriend!" said Evan.

"Atta girl," said Jay.

But neither bothered her at all. A good-looking boy had invited her to do something. Did this count as a date? She wasn't sure. But it was a first, whatever it was.

She looked back for a last glimpse of Graham, and her eyes fell on his father instead. But for now, even Ned Aubrey's cruel stare couldn't dampen the moment.

———

Tom looked up from his newspaper as they entered the Porters' Lodge, setting down his cup of tea.

"There's a message," he said, sliding a folded piece of paper across the desk.

"Who from?" asked Jay, reaching for it. But the porter held it tight.

"Not for you, sir. For the young lady and gentleman."

Samantha exchanged a startled look with her brother, then took the paper and smoothed it flat. The page was embossed with the Lion and Unicorn of the British House of Lords. Below, a short message appeared in massive looping script:

> *Might I have the pleasure of your company in my office? First thing tomorrow, if you please.*
> *—Lord Professor Sir Cairn Colin Catesby,*
> *Baron Catesby of Coveney*

The summons alone was enough to make her anxious, but what was sketched out beneath it made her tremble so much that Evan snatched the paper from her hand.

Drawn at the bottom of the page was a crude and ugly snowman, an enormous pair of earmuffs stretched over its bulbous head.

"Uh-oh," said her brother, and shoved the paper into his sister's pocket before their uncle could see.

Evan could keep it, for all Samantha cared. It was her second invitation of the evening, but the first to send her pale and shaking to her room.

————

Samantha had suffered nightmares since returning from Peru. But that night's dream was something different. That night she dreamed of Boudica.

The story Jay had told her came alive in her mind's eye, filling her sleep with perturbations—Oona's muttered curse come true. An image of a man took shape in her imagination, middle-aged and awkward, wrapped though he was in the fine robes of an emperor of Rome. But the man's imperious face with the prominent nose and ears looked like someone she knew.

Cairn Catesby. There was no mistaking him.

Her dream view shifted, and now she was high above the earth, with Britain spread out below her like a map. Across it coursed the red ribbons of Rome's powerful legions, spreading north and west from the southeastern coast. When her view swept downward, fast and close, she could see the man who led them. This, she knew, was the emperor's governor general. But her mind had assigned him the cruel face of Ned Aubrey, Graham's menacing father.

She watched as the governor general made pacts with

one British king and then another, and then the special promise that the Empire never intended to keep. And as the trusting Iceni king clasped the Roman general's hand, it was Jay's face that smiled in open friendship, and Clare's—as Queen Boudica—that stared warily on.

The dream jumped in time. To her horror, Samantha watched the death of the king with the face of her uncle, and Boudica mourning beside his deathbed, holding her children close. Samantha saw her brother there, scared and threatened, and beside him her troubled self.

Then, a cold wave of terror. Samantha saw herself running through the watery Fens, fleeing Aubrey on his slathering horse. He was gaining, his armor clanking, his smile thin and cruel.

And suddenly she was in modern Cambridge, scrambling through its narrow, twisting lanes, the sound of the pursuit muted by the piled snow. She tripped and could not find her footing. But then, just as Aubrey's gauntlet closed on one of her braids, threatening to yank her off her feet, Samantha awoke, pulling herself upright and flinging her heavy blanket to the floor.

She could still smell the cold, wet earth. She could still feel the panic. But it was morning now, and she needed to be ready for the day.

She had an appointment, Samantha remembered, with the Emperor himself.

---

Samantha expected no game of "Sutton Who" this time as she and her brother arrived at Catesby's office. The Lord Professor had to know who built the snowman. Only someone on the team could have taken his earmuffs, and only two among them would have cried out in an American accent as they fled the scene of the crime.

What would he do to them? Would he yell at them? Send them home?

Then she noticed some new lettering by Catesby's name on the door, where someone had scribbled "Emperor" next to his name and titles. The act of defiance cheered her on, but it took a few moments before she'd gathered the courage to knock.

She raised her knuckles to the wood but stopped. She was sure she heard voices inside—very faint—and she dared not interrupt.

"Enter!"

Catesby's bellow startled them both, and Evan pushed open the door.

Inside, the office was snug and inviting. A morning fire roared in a hearth on one side of the room, casting a flickering glow across the spines of the bookshelf opposite. The warmth of the fireplace drew out the pleasant aroma of the leather furniture and the peaty smell of the artifacts arrayed in trays below the window.

Samantha scanned the room, looking for the other half of the faint conversation she had heard from the hallway. But the Lord Professor was alone, seated as his desk, a typed manuscript of some kind spread across his desk. Samantha gave him a wary look, readying for his anger to unleash. But it did not come. Instead, his tiny eyes looked cheerful behind his wire-rimmed glasses, and his smile showed both rows of his crooked teeth.

"Ah, my portraitists!" he cried out in greeting, "My Teerline and Holbein of the snow!"

Samantha felt her brother fall back.

"Don't try to deny it," Catesby went on, motioning them into the room. "Your modesty won't do. A young American voice is not something one hears often on the banks of the Cam."

"It was just a joke," said Evan, his eyes on his shoes.

"And I applaud you for it! Cambridge has always enjoyed a rather shocking tradition of pranks and mischief. I'm sure it was all in fun." Catesby's sleepy voice grew menacing behind his smile. "Just as my reprisal will be."

There was a long silence. Samantha shifted on her feet.

"But that will wait," Catesby said at last. "Come, come. I'd like to show you something."

He led them to his examination table, past the trays of Roman nails, colorful Roman glass, and bits of corroded Roman arms and armor. Something lay on the table's far end, covered by a red silk cloth.

"And so, my young friends. I ask you: what has brought you to our sceptered isle?"

Samantha could tell that there was a particular answer he was looking for.

"Working for our uncle, I guess?" Evan ventured. "Er…I mean…for Dr. Barrows?"

Catesby's eyes narrowed.

"Dead wrong on both counts."

His turned to Samantha, awaiting her response.

"Working for you?" she offered, figuring that flattery might be what he was looking for. Catesby chortled at her efforts to please.

"Closer, ever closer. But wrong again."

He took hold of the shiny red sheet.

"You are here to serve the glory of Rome."

With a flourish he pulled the cover from the table, revealing the marvel beneath. And while Evan let out a thrilled gasp, Samantha could only stare.

Before them was a massive architectural model, constructed of balsa wood and foam. At first, Samantha took it for a 3D depiction of some major archaeological site—complete with grand colonnades, temples, amphitheaters, and villas. But its parking lot, ticket booths, and concession stands indicated that it was not a thing of England's past, but something of England yet to come.

"Vivant Romani," Catesby pronounced, "or 'Roman Adventure Pleasure Park,' if my somewhat timid developers get their way."

Only now did Samantha see that she was looking at a theme park—one where the theme was very well-defined.

"Haven't you dreamed of competing in gladiatorial combat?" asked Catesby. "Witnessing the Battle of Actium from the deck of Augustus' *triremis*? Cheering the execution of savage Gauls? Have you not craved the chance to mount a chariot and race for the honor of Jupiter?"

Samantha saw that tiny plastic visitors were doing just that on the model before her—frozen in motion as their tiny robot horses circled a reconstructed Roman circus. But there were normal rides as well: ornate bumper cars, a carousel decked out with Roman war elephants, and a flume ride designed like a three-tiered aqueduct. The enormous pillar she had taken for some ancient monument was in fact Trajan's Column Drop—the kind of freefall ride that Evan liked best.

Her attention then turned to the gentle hill at the middle of the model, where a nest of looping track was perched. Catesby followed her gaze.

"A technological marvel," he said. "My engineers assure me that nothing so dashing and daring has ever been attempted before."

But Samantha's focus was not on the roller coaster but on the rise on which it sat.

"That's Wardy Hill," she said, recognizing it by its contours.

"Indeed," said the Lord Professor. "My Wardy. The one bit of higher ground in the entire region. People will see the park from miles away."

"But the archaeological site," said Samantha. "This will completely destroy it."

Catesby's proud smile did not fade.

"I'm taking the necessary steps, as you are no doubt

aware. With your help, Dr. Barrows and your uncle will retrieve whatever paltry evidence they can, and then we will proceed."

This matched Stuart's explanation from the day before. But Samantha still wasn't satisfied.

"But you can't, right? Not if there's something there. Something important, I mean."

This time Catesby laughed aloud.

"My dear girl," he said, "This is not America. We don't preserve every savage hearth and rubbish tip we find. We simply haven't the luxury. Progress should not come at the cost of England's true past, of course, but that past began with the arrival of Rome."

"What's it called?" Evan asked, pointing at the roller coaster at the center of the park.

"The *Imperator*!" Catesby proclaimed. "The Emperor! But I feel inspired by your spirited sister, here. Shall I change it to *Imperatrix*, the female form?"

Samantha frowned, not swayed by the flattery. Still, she regretted her next words as soon as she'd uttered them.

"Maybe you should call it '*Boudica's Revenge*.'"

There was another long silence, and a cold fury came over the Lord Professor's face.

"What?" he said through his clenched, tiny teeth.

Evan was happy to enlighten him.

"Boudica," he said. "You know? Our stalwart, steadfast sovereign? Our lovely lady Queen?"

The Lord Professor took a couple steps toward him.

"That name," he spat. "Shall not be uttered in my presence."

"Which name?" said Evan, enjoying the display. "Boudica? How come?"

Catesby's face darkened from red to purple.

"Out," he whispered. Then his voice rose to a wet bark. "Out!"

He swept the air before him with his hand, knocking the balsa Imperator across the model, toppling the roof of the Diocletian Dodg'ems, and upsetting the queue of tiny figures by the Vestal Virgin gift shop.

"OUT!"

Samantha needed no convincing. But Evan was still working on some witty comeback, and she had to grab his arm to force him from the office.

There was a crashing noise behind them when they reached the hallway, and an angry cry in Latin. The Lord Professor's rage continued, chasing them from the Department and into the early morning chill.

"Well, that was fun," said Evan, as he zipped his jacket tight.

But Samantha wasn't ready to joke about it. Only one thing was clear from Catesby's eruption: while Boudica herself might be long gone, her adversaries were more alive than ever.

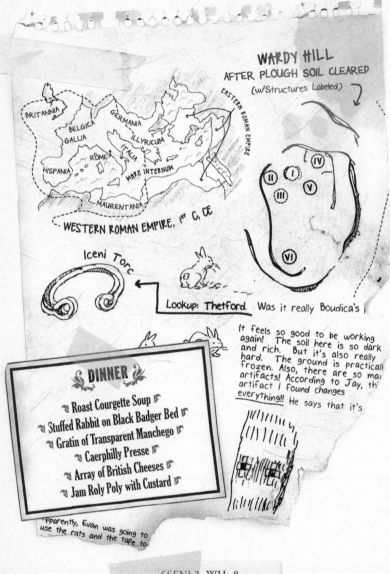

WARDY HILL
AFTER PLOUGH SOIL CLEARED
(w/Structures Labeled)

BRITANNIA
GERMANIA
BELGICA
GALLIA
ILLYRICUM
ITALIA
EASTERN ROMAN EMPIRE
ROME
HISPANIA
MARE INTERNUM
MAURENTANIA

WESTERN ROMAN EMPIRE, 1st C, CE

Iceni Torc

Lookup: Thetford. Was it really Boudica's

It feels so good to be working again! The soil here is so dark and rich. But it's also really hard. The ground is practicall frozen. Also, there are so ma artifacts! According to Jay, th artifact I found changes everything!! He says that it's

**DINNER**

Roast Courgette Soup
Stuffed Rabbit on Black Badger Bed
Gratin of Transparent Manchego
Caerphilly Presse
Array of British Cheeses
Jam Roly Poly with Custard

pparently, Evan was going to use the rats and the tape to

SSFNb2–WH: 8

118

# CHAPTER 8

It's true," Jay said some thirty minutes later, as they whipped north and east through the dawn-lit country-side. "Cairn's worst enemy has been dead for more than two thousand years."

He turned to look at his nephew, and they veered a little into the oncoming lane.

"Who, Boudica?" Evan asked, as the car jerked back straight. "What's his problem?

Jay laughed.

"Where to begin? He's always had a thing against the Celts, for one thing. They were just savages, in his mind—to be forgotten, not celebrated or admired."

And then his voice took on Catesby's resolute tone, and a bad approximation of his accent.

"The study of the past should edify the present! And there was nothing edifying in Britain before the coming of Rome!"

Jay slipped back into his own voice.

"Of course, the idea that one of their sites might upset his grand ambitions has pushed him over the edge."

Samantha's imagination whirred. So that was it, wasn't it? Catesby was worried about what they might uncover. Was there some trace of the Warrior Queen on Wardy Hill, ready to be found? Did Boudica herself await them?

But only Clare stood waiting as Jay's rental car rolled to a stop in the Fenland gloom. She greeted her colleague with a forgiving smile, and Samantha with a long, warm hug.

"Today the real archaeology begins," she said. "Now that we know what we're working with."

Samantha gazed out across the field. Rendered perfectly flat by the backhoe, it looked exposed and vulnerable, spread out before them like a patient on a table.

Maybe Catesby had reason to worry. What was clearer now was that there had once been something here—something huge and formidable. Samantha could see how the site was ringed by a pair of shallow troughs—the remnants, she guessed, of ancient defenses. There were smaller marks within—individual buildings, now long gone. She couldn't wait to carve into the soil and to discover the secrets it might contain.

"Beautiful," said Jay, and from the direction of his gaze, it wasn't clear if he was speaking about the site or his beaming British colleague.

"Magnificent," said Clare. "A classic Iron Age ringwork."

And maybe Boudica's fortress, Samantha thought, but forced the presumption from her mind.

"Are those building foundations?" she guessed, pointing at one of the six circular scars enclosed within the long-gone walls.

"No, not foundations," Jay said. "A good guess, though. Try again."

Thinking hard, she cast her gaze up across the Fens and to the clouded sky. She felt the chilled fleck of raindrops on her face—just two of them, one on each cheek. Such weather seemed normal here. It fit the landscape. And it answered her uncle's challenge too.

"It's from rain coming off roofs of buildings," she said, surprised at how sure she was of her answer. "The dripping water carved ditches over time."

Jay looked genuinely impressed.

"You're right, kiddo. Exactly right. They're like shadows, in a way. But these channels—'eaves gullies' they call them—contain a lot of information. They're great sources of data on what sorts of buildings they once surrounded."

"We'll be digging them out?"

"Them, and all along the other field marks as well. We have a lot of work ahead of us, Sam, and not an awful lot of time. It's not going to be easy."

But Samantha was ready. As soon as the vans arrived and the team dispersed, she pulled her trowel from her pocket, eager for the workday to begin.

---

"I've got it, lassie," said Stuart, waving off her offer of help. "Just you take it easy."

From the pillbox, he'd lugged a screen, a bucket, a shovel, and a pick, and now he let the whole assemblage crash into a pile at Samantha's feet. Which of Britain's secrets had these tools uncovered? she thought. Had they located the floors of ancient monasteries? The walls of castles? Had they unearthed the graves of knights? And in the coming days, would they find a warrior queen as well?

But there was work to do, getting started, and she hurried to help Stuart in the task. Their first assignment was on the ringwork's outer wall, close to the road, and with a level, tape measure, and a string they set up the unit—one of the careful, perfect holes on which all excavation was based.

"You've still got it, Archaeo Kid!" said Stuart, setting the empty bucket down for her to fill again. "Like a duck to water."

And Samantha did still have it—her summer's skills came back at once, and she moved with confidence and speed. She had missed this feeling: the sensation of the earth against her trowel blade, the satisfaction of brushing clean the unit's even floor.

But Wardy Hill was different in its digging. Here, ice ran through the soil in long clear veins and bound the mud into stubborn clumps. The density of artifacts was staggering. The plough soil was so thick with tiny potsherds that each frozen clod bristled, hedgehog-like, holding its secrets close. Each clump needed to be forced through the lattice of the screen, and Stuart's face was already red from the effort.

As the day went on, and as pottery began to emerge in

massive quantities from all the units, Jay and Clare brought the more interesting sherds around to show the students, both to educate them and as a way to spur them on. Clare recognized all of the sherds by their color, texture, and thickness, and could pick out their age and style. Some dated back to the Late Bronze Age, she said, around three thousand years ago. Somewhat more exciting were the slightly newer fragments, dating back to Roman times. These included a salmon-colored piece of Samian ware, brought all the way from Gaul—what France was called back then. Samantha marveled at the image it evoked of stacks of crated pottery in the holds of Roman galleys, clanking across the English Channel as toga-clad sailors worked the oars above.

That didn't mean the site was Roman, though, as Jay was quick to point out. In fact, it likely meant the opposite.

"If the Romans used this place in any meaningful way, we'd be finding more Roman material. Lots more. Sure, some seems to have come here through trade. But if anything, these people seem to have purposefully rejected what the Empire had to offer."

Rejection. Rebellion. The Warrior Queen came rushing back to mind.

"People like the Iceni," Samantha whispered, when Clare had moved away and out of earshot.

Jay's eyes narrowed.

"Sam! Clare will kill me if she hears you even mention Boudica. No more of that, remember? I thought we had a deal!"

This was the closest her uncle could come to being stern, and Samantha felt a sting from his rebuke.

"Sorry."

But when she looked up again to meet his gaze, she saw no anger there. The answer to her question glinted back at her instead: a silent, ardent "yes."

————————

"Just you tonight, miss?"

Tom was stationed in his usual spot at the Porters' Lodge's vast desk, a colorful tabloid spread out before him and a mug and teapot stationed close by. He glanced up at her as she came in, then folded the paper away.

"My uncle is with Dr. Barrows," Samantha said, "and my brother's off with his friends."

Tom grunted. He clearly was aware of how Evan was spending his time these days, crashing his way through the ancient town with his rowdy band of brothers. It was just as Jay had said: porters know all.

This gave her an idea.

"Tom? Do you know anything about the Iceni?"

The porter crossed his massive arms.

"Well," he said. "I can tell you that they're not allowed in Trinity Hall. Not as a group, anyway. Not after last May Week. The front court lawn's still not fully regrown, and they haven't reimbursed the college for what they did to the cupola."

Samantha shook her head.

"No, not those Iceni. I meant the real ones. The Iceni from the Iron Age."

"Ah, I beg your pardon. The destroyers of Colchester, you mean, and not of flower beds. What is it that you want to know?"

"Was Boudica from here?"

Tom's stern face widened to a smile.

"Oh, no, miss. Thetford was her capital, or so they said in school. All the way on the other side of the Fens. They've found her whole palace there and her royal treasury. It was in all the papers."

Samantha's heart sank. The site of Boudica's capital seemed to be a settled question.

"No," Tom continued. "Cambridgeshire wasn't where the Queen *ruled* from. It was where she…"

But at that moment, Evan burst into the Porters' Lodge. His cheeks were flushed with whatever latest mischief, madcappery, and mayhem the modern Iceni were now unleashing on the good citizens of Cambridge.

"Tom! Just the man I was looking for. I need a hammer, a block of ice, two yards of sticky tape, and some live rats. Mice would work, though, in a pinch."

"Evan," Samantha snapped. "You're interrupting."

But her brother's demands had put Tom out of his obliging mood.

"I can't help you, miss. Your uncle and Dr. Barrows are the experts. You should ask them."

He spread out the newspaper once more.

"What about me?" asked Evan.

"What about you, sir."

The words were flat. Not a question.

"Uh, hello? The ice? The rats? What about me?"

Tom did not look up.

"You, sir, are a puffed-up little prat. I'm not here for your amusement, and neither is Cambridge. This isn't a fancy dress party. It's the best university in the whole world. Show some bloody respect."

With that he returned to his reading and, for the first time Samantha could remember, Evan had nothing to say.

———————

Her thoughts were on Graham the next morning as she set to work, his singing voice as clear in her mind as in real life. She pulled her trowel across the unit floor to the remembered rhythms of his solo:

*Earth stood hard as iron, water like a stone.*
*In the bleak midwinter, long ago.*

Another pass and an artifact popped from its mud casing like a piece of shrapnel. She yanked off one glove and plucked the object from the unit floor to examine it.

The thing in the palm of her hand was a modest piece of wood, slightly curved and banded through its center with a design of squares and crosses. These decorations were in metal and had almost rusted away after centuries of Fenland damp. But it was clear that this had been something special, whatever it was. After days of finding little more than the stuff of bare survival, there was something personal about this latest find. The people of ancient Wardy had wanted nice things too. They had wanted things that were pretty.

Samantha rocked back on her heels, squinting in the force of the wind. Stuart had gone into the pillbox for a midmorning cup of tea.

"Uncle Jay!" she called, sending a nearby cluster of rabbits scattering across the field.

Because of the way his face went flat when she handed him the object, at first she thought she'd made him angry. Had the find somehow hurt the project? Was it modern, maybe, showing that the site had been damaged beyond repair?

But his words told a different story.

"Oh, Sam," he said, "Catesby's going to hate you for this."

———

"Let's be cautious," Clare said, as they huddled around Samantha in the lab, pushing and shoving for a better look. "Level heads, please. All of us."

She seemed to be looking at Jay.

"But what is it? What did I find?"

"A piece of a bucket, Sam," said her uncle. "Or some sort of tankard. From the roundness of the curve, you can see how big the complete vessel would have been. Maybe 15 centimeters or so in circumference."

He showed her, holding the object up and completing an imaginary circle in the air.

"A bucket?"

Evan's furrowed brow showed that he wasn't impressed.

"More interesting than it sounds, kiddo," said Jay, "I promise. It's a drinking vessel used for feasting. It's also the kind of thing we find in high-status Iron Age sites—usually linked to someone of royal status."

"Someone like Boudica?" Evan asked.

"All hail our noble Queen!" said Kasim.

"All hail our stalwart, steadfast sovereign!" Stuart began.

As Jay smiled, Samantha remembered Tom's unfinished explanation: it's Cambridgeshire where the Queen…what?

Clare interrupted her thoughts.

"Listen, everyone, and listen well. We are not historians. We don't construct a version of events, then decorate it with the artifacts that we find. We're archaeologists. We let the artifacts tell the story. We let them speak for themselves."

But Jay's enthusiasm overwhelmed his good sense.

"But don't you hear it, Clare?" he joked, cupping a hand behind his ear and leaning in toward Samantha's open hand. "This one *is* speaking. It's saying 'Boudica!' Boudica!' I hear it, loud and clear."

Most of the group laughed in their exhilaration, Jay's enthusiasm pulling them in. But not Oona, whose pale eyes burned coldly in Samantha's direction. And definitely not Clare, who set down her tea, bundled herself in her jacket, and headed out alone into the cold.

"Preposterous. And worse, uninformed."

Samantha saw Clare flinch at Catesby's pronouncement. The slam of his fork brought stares from the kitchen staff as they ate their own dinners at the long tables of the dining hall. But the Emperor's cries brought only a defiant chuckle from Jay Sutton, and Samantha regretted sitting between the two professors, caught in the bitter crossfire.

"Gee, Cairn. Tell me how you really feel."

Jay was playing host, inviting his British colleagues to attend Trinity Hall for dinner. And while Clare had remained silent and withdrawn, Jay and Catesby's rivalry had begun to shoot out sparks.

They sat at the high table, reserved for professors and visiting guests. The lofty ceiling arched high above them, the walls supporting it painted white and light blue. But this was only a facade. Samantha knew that just beneath the fresh, eighteenth-century veneer were the original oak beams and grim, smoke-soaked stones, thrown up at a time when plague devastated England's cities and lines of kings poured their armies into endless bloody wars. The conversation at the dining table seemed similarly layered: a coating of civility spread thin over a history of strife. And Lord Catesby's outburst had knocked some of the paint loose from this construction.

The Lord Professor's next words were directed at Samantha.

"Your uncle's expertise seems to extend far beyond his

experience," he said, rocking back in his seat and folding his arms. "His American confidence is undiminished, I see."

Samantha shrank in her seat. Evan would have voiced his displeasure with Catesby's emphasis on the word "American." But he was out with Stuart, Kasim, and the other Iceni Society members at an Indian restaurant in town, celebrating the find that she had made. That Samantha herself was excluded wasn't fair, of course, but it didn't seem unusual to anyone else.

"All he said was that the excavation has been more interesting than he expected," she said, trying hard to meet the Lord Professor's tiny, twitching eyes.

"*Interesting* it may be, at least when compared to the vulgar rubble of his usual New World sites. But if you'd paid attention, you would note that he made claims about Wardy Hill's *archaeological importance*. Which is quite different, indeed, and wrong from beginning to end."

"Cairn's just nervous, Sam," Jay said. "All he wants is a little Anaheim magic way out in the Cambridgeshire Fens, and now the past will rise up to stop him. His beloved theme park will be ruined by ruins."

Samantha frowned. She had no desire to be the go-between in the escalating argument. But Catesby's mouth had twisted into a small, crooked smile.

"Ruined by ruins? Good God, Sutton. Terrible, but brilliant."

This broke the tension, and as Jay laughed heartily and

Catesby hooted his great wet guffaw, Clare and Samantha shared a nervous smile.

Until the Lord Professor spoke again.

"Remind me, Sutton. In what area of British archaeology do you specialize?"

"I don't, Cairn. I'm a generalist, as you know, just as I was when I was a student here. But I remember what I learned from you. I can still tell my tegulae from my imbrices."

"I can too," said Samantha, feeling a sudden need to stick up for her own presence. And she could, from her research, distinguish between the two types of roof tiles, common finds on almost any Roman site.

"Oh, that *is* a relief. Barrows, Jay Sutton has all the knowledge of a schoolgirl of ten."

"I'm twelve," Samantha said, her voice steely. "And I'll be thirteen soon."

"My apologies, my dear girl. I stand corrected. Sutton, you have the expertise of a twelve-year-old schoolgirl, going on thirteen."

Jay half stood, ready to defend her, but Clare intervened.

"All right, everyone. All right," she said. "Let's just enjoy the meal."

Samantha looked down at her plate, where her food was arranged in little gray piles around the college coat of arms. A printed menu had been laid across her place when she sat down, and now she used it as a sort of field guide. *That* must be the stuffed rabbit, drowning in a pool of greasy beans. And *this* could be a "gratin," glistening under a soup of "transparent Manchego." Only by a process of elimination could she finally guess the whereabouts of the "caerphilly presse"—its identity a mystery even after her first wary bite.

She stabbed a hunk of rabbit with her fork and bit into it, a small geyser of grease bursting in her mouth. She took a long, long sip of water before trying her luck with a different shimmery puddle.

A bang and the sound of running pulled her attention to the end of the hall. It was Evan, grinning wide, a scowling Tom right behind him on his heels, holding out a folded robe.

"You cannot be seated, sir. Not without a gown."

Evan only laughed. It was a game to him—and revenge for Tom's earlier string of insults.

"No way. I'm not wearing one of those. I don't care about the rules."

He should care, Samantha thought. The college calendar designated this meal as a Formal Dinner, which meant that in order to be seated, everyone needed to wear nice clothes, topped off by a flowing black robe.

The garment was used across the university and important enough that Clare had loaned Samantha an extra. Catesby's was well cared for but far too tight, a reminder of when he was a smaller man. Jay's had been fished from the depths of his closet in California and had the formality of a wrinkled garbage bag.

But this was tradition, and as her uncle had reminded her many times on this visit, tradition didn't have to make sense.

"Then I'll see to it that you won't be served," said Tom, his voice not betraying his red-faced rage.

"Fine with me, Tom old boy," said Evan, settling into a chair beside his sister. "I already ate."

Jay held out his hand.

"I'll make sure he puts it on."

Tom handed the robe over but did not leave the hall until Jay had draped it across his nephew's back.

Only now did Samantha see the state of her brother's clothes. His shirt and pants were covered in sprays of curry, with chunks of it stuck in his hair and orange streaks of sauce from his temple down his cheek. One eye burned red from its contact with the fiery food.

"What happened to you?" she asked.

"Food fight," said Evan. "Right in the middle of the restaurant! Oh, it was so much fun."

Samantha didn't know what to say. The Iceni had thrown food at each other? In a public space? What about the other diners? And what about the restaurant staff, who would have to clean it up? But Jay was laughing, and Catesby was too. Yet another Cambridge tradition—how things had always been done.

"Good, kiddo. I'm glad you guys were celebrating."

Jay realized his mistake too late.

"What was the occasion?" asked Catesby.

"Didn't they tell you?" said Evan, stabbing a wet piece of gratin from his sister's plate. "Boudica was at Wardy Hill. We can prove it."

"What?" asked Catesby, his sleepy voice hard once more.

"Boudica? You know, the lady who beat the Romans?" said Evan, his mouth full of food. "We found her bucket."

Samantha didn't bristle at the word "we." For the moment, it was not a discovery she wanted to take credit for, especially as Catesby's face grew red and his grip turned whiter and whiter around his dinner fork.

"Don't worry, Cairn," said Clare. "We've not found anything linking Wardy Hill to Boudica or any other historical figure. Samantha here did recover a beautiful wooden stave from some sort of vessel, but so far it seems to have been an isolated find."

"Does make you wonder, though," Jay said with a mischievous grin. "A high-status, late Iron Age item in the middle of a prominent East Anglian ringwork? I think a Boudica connection is well within reason."

Catesby flew to his feet, jabbing his fork in Jay's direction and far too close to Samantha's face. "Rubbish!" he cried, as his chair wobbled, then fell. He stormed from the table and off the raised platform, stumbling awkwardly between the tables of the dining hall.

"Rubbish!" he cried again.

Halfway across, his gown caught the corner of a bench and sent it tumbling to the floor as well.

"Rubbish!" he bellowed, pushing his way through the great oak door. When he slammed it shut behind him, the noise was like a crack of thunder.

For a moment, the rest of the table sat in stunned silence. Samantha was the first to speak.

"Why would Boudica have anything to do with Wardy? In theory, I mean."

Jay smiled.

"I guess I've said too much. But you should be the one to tell her, Clare. You know the history best."

His colleague frowned.

"I'd rather not."

Jay ran his hand through his dark brown hair.

"Okay then, Sam. I'll give it a shot. After the Romans stole Boudica's lands, they beat her up in front of her people. But it was after they attacked her two children that she swore her revenge."

"Jay," Clare said in a warning tone, but he only went on, his voice dropping to a whisper.

"Her first target was the Roman capital of Camulodunum—what we call Colchester, now. It was a sizeable city, even back then, and where Roman soldiers went to retire with their families. But they weren't eager to fight this terrifying warrior queen. Instead, they locked themselves into the temple built to honor the emperor and waited for someone to come to their rescue."

Jay paused for dramatic effect, and Samantha leaned forward in her chair.

"But no one came. Boudica and her forces swept into the town, burning and pillaging everything in their way. And when she reached the temple where the townspeople were taking refuge, she had it burnt to the ground and then tore apart the sacred statue of the emperor."

"Jay," Clare said again. "That's enough." The words carried more than professional annoyance. "Let's focus on the archaeology, all right?"

Jay nodded, smiling at the interest he'd caused. But it wasn't all right with Samantha. What did Boudica have to do with the site? She would have to find out. And if the Warrior Queen was still at Wardy, Samantha would be the one to discover her.

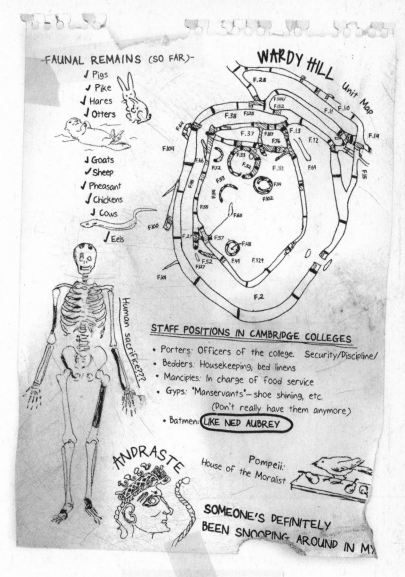

-FAUNAL REMAINS (SO FAR)-
- ✓ Pigs
- ✓ Pike
- ✓ Hares
- ✓ Otters

- ✓ Goats
- ✓ Sheep
- ✓ Pheasant
- ✓ Chickens
- ✓ Cows
- ✓ Eels

WARDY HILL Unit Map

Human sacrifice??

STAFF POSITIONS IN CAMBRIDGE COLLEGES
- Porters: Officers of the college. Security/Discipline/
- Bedders: Housekeeping, bed linens
- Manciples: In charge of food service
- Gyps: "Manservants"—shoe shining, etc.
    (Don't really have them anymore)
- Batmen: LIKE NED AUBREY

ANDRASTE

Pompeii:
House of the Moralist

SOMEONE'S DEFINITELY
BEEN SNOOPING AROUND IN MY

SSFNb2-WH: 9a

# CHAPTER 9

**S**amantha shivered, pulling her jacket tight.

It had been a struggle to get out of bed before even the first glimmer of dawn streaked the sky. And when she had, she was tempted to retreat back under the covers. It was freezing cold: the perfect time to comb through the few books she had brought from home, looking for mention of Camulodunum, the Iceni, or Boudica herself.

But she had made a promise. She unlocked her bike and wheeled its rusty hulk into the middle of Trinity Lane. It groaned with each turn of the pedals and screeched with every bump—crying out as if it had been dragged from the river against its will. Evan had gone on ahead. There was no one on the streets of Cambridge—no one at all—and Samantha was alone with the ghosts of her imagination.

The route opened up as she reached the river's edge, bathed in the faintest, bluish light of dawn. The path ahead was damp from snowmelt, and Samantha skirted its swollen, icy puddles as she made her way upriver in the dark.

This is where Catesby's regatta would be held in exactly two weeks' time. Or, as Stuart had taken to calling it: "Catesby's Bloomin' Regatta."

"It's the Winter Holiday," he had said the night before, as the archaeological team convened for darts and pints at the R&F. "How am I supposed to get enough rowers to fill a single boat, let alone enough for a proper race?"

"Why do it at all?" Kasim asked, pulling a dart from the board to throw again. "Let's just put his lordship in a scull, hand him a paddle, and give him a shove. He can be his own bloody regatta."

Stuart grinned darkly.

"I bloomin' well would, believe me. I'd give him a shove into the bloomin' river without a bloomin' boat, if he weren't the head of the whole bloomin' department. He holds my life in his hands, doesn't he? No. The Emperor wants his regatta, and I'll have to give it to him."

"I could row," said Evan. "I'm actually pretty good."

Pretty good, Samantha almost offered, at the video-game version of the sport.

"Brilliant," said Stuart. "But we need more. Pity that the Iceni Society's best rowers are all away on research. Galahad's in Belize, and the Cerne Giant's down in Dorset."

"Ring them up," said Kasim. "Galahad's away, it's true, but Gog and Magog are at the Fitzwilliam over the holiday, working on their replicas. I'm sure they'd both be keen. The Cerne Giant will come tonight if you ask him. And the Green Man's just in Norwich."

Stuart did a silent tally on his fingers.

"That's seven, counting us three," he said. "One more."

"What about me?" asked Samantha.

"Oh, that I'd love to see," said Evan. "You couldn't even reach the paddles."

"Blades," said Kasim. "not paddles. But I'm afraid that Evan's right. It wouldn't work."

"No, not to row," said Stuart, a twinkle in his eye. "But there is something you could help with, Samantha. In fact, I think it's something only you could do."

Samantha had heard such a pronouncement before, and she felt a buried, creeping dread. Those were the words that had put her in so much danger the summer before, squeezing through the Temple's haunted tunnels, chased by bats and madmen.

"We'll be able to fill the eighth seat, easy. The Viscount will do it, I reckon. Him or the Yeoman, if we can get him back from Wales. No, Sam, what we need is a coxswain. The person to steer us, to make sure we're all in unison."

Samantha's small size was ideal for the position, he went on to explain, since she'd fit in the tiny seat and wouldn't weigh the boat down as it glided across the water.

"You'll be magic at it, Archaeo Kid," he promised. "We'll show you how."

And so Samantha had agreed. It wasn't the Iceni Society, but it was the closest she could come.

Now, as she steered her bike around the icy puddles in the path, the expanse of Midsummer Common stretched out to her right, its wintery covering making a mockery of its sprightly name. To her left, the murky Cam flowed back toward town, the scattering of leaves on its surface betraying the swiftness of its current. Soon, she reached the first of the college boathouses and crossed the Cam at the Green Dragon footbridge. She was late—her watch said 6:05. She stood up on her pedals and sped up the riverside road.

Through Jay, Stuart had arranged for the group to use the equipment of the Trinity Hall Boat Club, as well as its boathouse. It was a two-story affair, black and white and sturdy, crammed among the others along the river. The upper level could be reached by an outdoor staircase. But while the windows above were dark, the garish light of bare bulbs streamed from the open garage doors beneath.

A group of students was waiting there, huddled among the racks of eights and fours. So deep were the early morning shadows that she could not make out anyone's face. But she recognized Stuart and Kasim by their familiar voices, and her brother from his mischievous laugh. She was in the right place.

"Cox is here!" Stuart called out.

"Sorry," she said, a little out of breath. "*Someone* didn't wake me up."

"You're late, coxswain," Kasim grinned. "Fine her!"

"Fine her!" cried Evan, and then it became a sort of chant. "Fine her! Fine her! Fine her!" ringing off the concrete and the brick.

But Stuart put an end to it.

"We'll let her off easy today, lads. But Archaeo Cox, you should know that the fine for tardiness—and all other offenses—is a morning dip in the Cam!"

Shivering, she eyed the ice along the concrete apron and the bobbing sheets of it on the river. She would have to try to avoid the punishment.

"Lads, this is Samantha Sutton. Samantha, this is your crew."

And then he introduced them one by one.

"This is the Cerne Giant, who's just driven in," he said, pointing at a short student at the end. "We call him that on account of his legendary stature. You know Kasim, of course, and your brother there. And this is the Green Man, who has a touch of seasickness."

"Not on rivers, though," said the student, whose face indeed seemed green. "At least, not typically."

Stuart continued down the line.

"Here are Gog and Magog. They're students here, but locals. They know the river well."

The twins, true giants, gave her a friendly nod.

"And this is the eighth member of the boat. Your bowman," said Stuart, pointing out a sleepy-looking fellow at the end. "The Viscount."

There was nothing regal about him, despite his lordly nickname. He was by far the most disheveled of the bunch.

"Why do you call him that?" asked Samantha.

"Well, because he's a viscount."

"It's true," said the Viscount, sleepily. "But they never seem to respect my title."

"Right!" said Stuart. "First thing, Archaeo Cox, is to get the boat in the river."

"That's my job?"

He smiled.

"It's your job to make us do it. But don't worry. I'll show you how."

They moved inside, falling into a line along the boathouse wall. Stuart had her repeat his whispered commands, goading her to shout them louder and louder. And to her great satisfaction, the team reacted in unison whenever she issued an order: lifting the boat from its rack when she shouted, "*Hands on*," swinging it down to waist height, and carrying it outside to the water's edge. Even her brother did as she instructed. She could get used to this.

Now Samantha saw that the Cam was swollen far beyond its banks, up and over the concrete apron of the shore. The rowers were all barefoot or in socks, and the thin layer of ice on the water's edge crackled as they stepped through it. It was too late for Samantha to remove her shoes, and she felt the frigid river seep between her laces and then—as she walked farther—soak through around her toes.

The boat was a long, beautiful, graceful craft—especially in the strawberry light of dawn. Eight spots for eight rowers filled the space inside—their seats capable of sliding backward and forward as the rowers took their strokes. Each member of the crew controlled a single, jet-black oar, either off to the right or off to the left, which latched to the boat with a metal rigger. What Samantha had not imagined, though, was that the rowers all sat backward. Only the cox could see where they were going. Her responsibility was huge.

Before she knew it, she was in the coxswain seat, with Stuart facing her in the stroke position, his bare feet strapped into the shoes on his footplate.

"Okay, Sam. Keep hold of that loop of rope there. It controls the rudder so you can steer."

"This is going to be ugly," said Evan, behind him in the seventh position.

"Do make sure we don't hit anything, Cox," shouted the Cerne Giant from the three seat. "It's never pleasant running into the bank."

"Broke my wrist when *he* tried coxing," said the Viscount in bow. "Can't say I appreciated that."

The comments did nothing for her confidence. But with Stuart's guidance, her job proved easy after the first few minutes—or at least not too hard. Shouting everything he told her into the headset she'd been given and following his careful instructions, she maneuvered the boat into the middle of the river. And soon, with a lurch, they were off and gliding across the surface in mighty, rhythmic bursts.

She felt as if they were flying. The boat moved like an eight-winged swan, skimming the surface of the Cam. Such transport must have been normal once, Samantha realized, when the entire region was rivers and fens. Boudica herself must have traveled this way. But now Samantha commanded her own Iceni crew, and her orders were followed without hesitation or complaint. And it was she who was the stalwart, steadfast sovereign this morning, the lovely lady Queen.

———————

An hour later, the boat was back in the boathouse and the rowers were en route to Wardy Hill, their clothes damp and stinking with the particular odor of the River Cam. Samantha was more eager than ever to get to Wardy and drummed her fingers impatiently on the window as they left the motorway behind them.

But as desperate as she was for the workday to begin, she longed for the Fens themselves. Cambridge was a clamor of ages, of rules and male tradition, of rigid buildings, tight alleys, cobbles, and stone. The Fens were free of all that. There were no doors here that were closed to her, no prescribed paths or *Patris, Filii, Spiritus Sancti* before the noonday meal. This felt like Boudica's world, even now, where a girl could become a warrior and a queen.

Boudica's world that morning was a freezing one. It had been cold out on the Cam, but it had been nothing like this. The day's special chill found her as soon as she stepped out of the van. The wind carried flecks of ice, stinging her face and neck. Even her hands grew numb, padded and awkward in their thick gloves. Samantha pulled her hat down over her ears and zipped the collar of her royal blue jacket up as far as it would go. Jay did the same. And when they caught sight of each other, she could hear him laughing through his scarf.

"You look like a *gladiatrix,* Sam. Look at all your armor!"

"I feel more like an astronaut."

Evan, for his part, still wouldn't set foot outside the van.

"Come on, Ev," said Jay. "It'll be much warmer in the lab. And we have heaters to set up by the units."

Sure enough, Stuart and Kasim were wrestling a pair of 44-gallon drums from the back of each excavation van, along with kindling and wood. The solution was rustic, Samantha thought, but it would help. As long as fires could be lit in this damp, and there were enough to go around.

The team had swelled in number. It had been Stuart's idea to take the whole boat to Wardy—not the boat itself, of course, but its rowdy Iceni crew.

"With the new deadline, we'll need more manpower," he said. "And this lot has nothing better to do."

It made sense to Samantha. They were all archaeology students, after all. It didn't matter that the Viscount did his fieldwork in Western China, or that the Cerne Giant studied geoglyphs across England's south. They all knew the same basic methods, and that was all that was needed for something like this.

Still, not everyone seemed happy with the new additions.

"Stuart," said Clare, as the vans emptied out. "You should have run this by me."

"I thought you'd be pleased, Professor."

A frown creased her pretty face.

"It's not me you need to worry about. It's Professor Catesby. He wants to approve every member of the team."

Stuart looked a little panicked.

"Should I ask them to leave?"

Jay interjected before Clare could respond.

"No, no, of course not. We need all the help we can get!"

It took two tries to get the workday started. The fires had been lit for half an hour when they made the first attempt, the team fanning across the site to their units, tools in hand. Samantha loved the sight of the fires piercing the gloom. The orange glow of each metal barrel looked like a beacon and was surely visible for miles around. But they had not been burning long enough to make a difference to the soil. Samantha could make no headway whatsoever with her trowel, no matter how much weight she put into each stroke. She threw it aside in frustration, upsetting a shuddering rabbit nearby.

"Fine her!"

It was her brother crying out across the field.

"Leave me alone, Evan."

"But you've assaulted a sacred, sanctified hare! The auspicious augur of the divine Andraste! Goddess savior of our Queen!"

He raised his voice.

"For Boudica!"

To Samantha's annoyance, the other Iceni Society members responded with gusto, and the Warrior Queen's name crackled through the cold morning air.

"That's a rabbit, Evan. Hares are much bigger."

It was all she could think of to say.

Nearby, Clare was attacking the frozen earth with a pickax. On her second stroke, the sound of the handle splitting in two turned heads all around the site.

"Sorry!" she said, holding up a gloved hand. "A little overeager. Shall we give the earth a little more time to thaw?"

The reprieve was welcome. The new, swollen crowd milled around the pillbox and filled every corner of the lab inside—or almost every corner, as no one seemed to want to be close to Oona. But the rest were a happy group, laughing as they fashioned snowballs from the surrounding patches of ice or wrestled each other kicking to the ground.

"Shut the bloody door!" said Kasim. "You're letting in the damp!"

Samantha felt a mug being pressed into her gloved hand.

"This'll help, Archaeo Cox," Stuart said, as she took a long draw of the hot tea. "Just like California out there, eh?"

She shook her head. The low temperature alone was striking, but there was a dampness to it that clung to the body and assaulted the senses in a way she had never experienced.

"Better than it must've been like in Iceni times," said Kasim. "We have it pretty good."

This was true, Samantha thought, and it brought new questions to her mind. What was so important that people had lived here on this hillside, exposed to the arctic blasts of damp and chill? What had they been protecting, exactly? Or who?

―――――――

But it wasn't just potsherds that popped from the mud an hour later, when work was able to begin. Bones were emerging from the open units and were being passed around. The local species attracted the most attention: eels, pike, hares, and otters. But most were goats and sheep, pheasants and chickens, cows and domesticated pigs—typical farmyard fare.

"These people weren't used to living off the land," said Clare. "They were accustomed to the good life, not the wilds of the Fens."

The good life? Samantha wondered. The royal life?

She had to write this down, she realized. She opened her backpack, now streaked with mud. But her notebook was not inside. Had she left it in the boathouse that morning? Was it back at the college in her room?

Samantha shook her head, annoyed with herself. This wasn't the first time she had let this happen. Even though she tried to be sure to leave it in her backpack—back at the boathouse during the morning's row, or at the pub after work—there were still times when she would find it missing, only to have it turn up again on her desk in her room. Maybe she should wear it from her neck again, Samantha thought. This had never been a problem before Peru.

But today Stuart saw her frustration and presented her with some loose paper and a pen.

"Nae danger, Archaeo Kid. Just copy your notes over later."

They opened their next unit in the heart of the site,

where the inner ditch abutted Structure I. The nearest heating drum was a few meters away, and only when the wind was blowing in the right direction could she feel its fragile warmth. She would have to work harder to warm herself and to keep from freezing.

"We can switch if you like," Stuart said, when she'd dug down to the level of her waist.

She shook her head. Aboveground, the wind shrieked bitterly. It was warmer below the unit's rim, the silence total but for the scraping of her trowel across the earth.

The work was still difficult, though. Every stroke crunched through ice crystals or caught on frozen mud, and popped them from the unit's floor in infuriating clods.

After pushing the loose chunks into her bucket, Samantha saw that one artifact stuck out from the profile. She didn't dare pry it free. It was another bone, but there was something different about it.

"It's not bovine," Stuart said, taking her place in the unit. "That's for sure."

He reached into his satchel and pulled out a pair of wooden chopsticks.

"These work better for something like this," he explained. "They won't scratch it up."

He used the chopsticks to clean the bone completely, digging slightly into the profile to slide it fully free. But other scrapes already extended all along the bone—cuts and gouges so deep that she knew she hadn't done it accidentally with her trowel.

"Bloomin' hell," said Stuart, tracing the markings with his finger.

"Are those from butchering?" she asked.

"Of a sort. But the kind done with a sword, and on a battlefield."

He turned to face her, a dark smile upon his lips.

"Samantha, this bone is human. And I've never seen anything like it."

————————

The professors bounded over as soon as Stuart called for them, arousing the interest of the entire team. And soon, everyone had gathered to watch the dead emerge from the unit's frozen floor.

The bone Samantha had first uncovered was a femur, but a few prods with a chopstick turned up slashed bits of an ulna, ilium, fifth proximal phalanx, and frontal bone—what any normal person would call an arm, a hip, a little toe, and a part of a skull. All were left in place until Stuart could photograph them and measure their location, and then handed up to the rest of the team to pass around.

Samantha didn't feel the least bit guilty about disturbing the grave. Maybe it was because this individual's death had been so gruesome and her own transgression so trivial in comparison. Her only reactions were a crackling, electric pride for her discovery and impatience to hear what it might mean.

The remains did have a story, and her uncle was eager to be the one to tell it. The individual had been a man, Jay stated, and the deep cuts on the arm bone showed where he had thrown up his hands in futile defense against a crashing blow from an axe or sword. And then, after he'd fallen, his body had been completely dismembered. There were saw marks on the ends of the arms and chopping blows on the legs, showing—Jay explained—how the unfortunate victim had been "taken apart."

"A sacrifice to Andraste, maybe," he concluded, and at the mention of Boudica's patron deity, a nervous rustle went through the team. Clare tried her best to head off the excitement.

"What I'm sure Dr. Sutton is saying is that this is a typical Celtic practice. Prisoners of war were often taken to water and sacrificed to the gods as tribute. I'm sure he is not suggesting that we speculate as to who this individual was, or who killed him."

"Right," Jay said, his eyes in a mischievous squint. "For example, I shouldn't tell Catesby that we've dug up a Roman soldier, brought to Wardy as a sacrifice to the Iceni goddess of war."

The male members of the team laughed aloud. And Samantha couldn't help but join them.

"Don't," Clare said, her voice as icy as the weather outside. "I beg of you."

The excitement of the day didn't fade that evening and continued to warm Samantha on her walk back to Trinity Hall and through the welcoming Porters' Lodge. She felt so stupid, leaving her notebook behind. She longed to transfer her day's observations to it and feel its familiar weight around her neck.

So eager was she that she barely registered Tom's visitor, wrapped in scarves and a scruffy wool jacket and engaged with him in some hushed conversation. She squeezed through into Trinity Hall's ancient forecourt and up the ancient stairs toward the ancient door of their ancient, cozy room. Samantha let out a relieved sigh when she found her notebook waiting for her on her desk, its cord coiled in a tidy spiral. But then she noticed something written across the open page.

III.4.2 7698C

SSFNb2-WH: 9b

She stared for a moment, the bold numbers and capital letters making it difficult to tell if the writing was her own. Was this something she had come across in her reading in the autumn when she was preparing to come? She didn't remember clearly. Her preparation had been so rushed. But this—this was wholly unfamiliar.

And then she turned to look around her room, and the last of her excitement left her.

Her belongings had been rearranged—her bed remade, her neatly folded sweaters refolded even neater. The books she'd brought for research were now placed in an orderly stack on the bookshelf—and not on the nightstand where she'd left them. She hurried to check the fireplace, where she and her brother hid their cash beneath a loosened slab. It was still there, all of it. But still she knew: someone had been in her room.

Just then she heard the groan of the door across the narrow landing: her uncle returning. She ran to meet him and to see if his room had been tampered with as well.

It had. That much was obvious. The whole place had been cleared of Jay's characteristic mess. His binders of notes and photographs lay across the low coffee table in new, neat stacks.

"This isn't good," he said, surveying the room.

"Mine is like this too."

"We've got to tell Tom," said her uncle. "Right away."

They hurried to the Porters' Lodge in silence, Jay leading the way.

"Tom!" cried Jay, throwing open the door so violently that the porter dropped his biscuit in his steaming cup of tea.

"Sir?"

"The condition of our rooms. This is unacceptable."

"Not cleaned to your liking, sir?"

Jay's eyes narrowed.

"You could say that."

"I'm sorry, sir. The bedder's just left. Must've…"

Jay finished the thought for him.

"…been traumatized, trying to clean up after me!"

Samantha stared at him, realizing he didn't share her suspicions.

"Uncle Jay, it's not just that."

He brushed her concern aside.

"There's really no need to send anyone in there, Tom. It's not fair to them. Actually, I like a certain amount of disorganization. It sort of helps me stay…organized."

Tom smiled.

"I remember."

"Of course you do. I'm still the same old mess. And the same gene seems to have passed to my nephew. Please tell the bedder that there's no need to bother with the Suttons. We're beyond all hope."

Samantha couldn't help but frown at the pronouncement. Were they beyond all hope, indeed?

---

It still didn't sit right that evening, when the team assembled at the Ridge & Furrow. *Relax*, she told herself—for the thousandth time since Peru. Her mind was just playing tricks again, finding danger where it wasn't and fear where there should only be fun. Still, the notebook's string was safely around her neck once more, tucked into the protection of her jacket. And there, she had decided, it would stay.

"Bedders," said Jay, his own research materials spread out across the sticky table. "That's one part of Cambridge I could never get used to—all the people here to wait on you. And I'm not talking about the porters. I mean the kitchen boys, the manciples, the gyps, the batmen…"

"*Batmen?*"

"Probably not what you're thinking, Evan. They're sort of like personal servants. It's not really a Cambridge thing, at least not anymore. But our pal Catesby had one, back in the day."

"Really?"

Jay nodded.

"And you've met him. Ned Aubrey—the guy with the metal detector. I thought he looked familiar, but it was Clare who reminded me who he was. Aubrey was Cairn's batman at Cambridge, once upon a time."

Samantha wondered about the connection between the two men and just what it might suggest. "Anyway," Jay went on, "I was never comfortable with all the staff, the whole upstairs-downstairs thing. It sounds so fun in theory, right? But it's a pretty weird tradition."

"Doesn't have to make sense," said Evan with a shrug.

Samantha saw her opportunity.

"Do you know what this means?"

She pointed to her open notebook. But when Jay saw the strange inscription upon its page, he laughed aloud.

"Why the sudden interest in Roman graffiti, Sam? Have you gone over to Catesby's side?"

"What does it mean?"

Jay rummaged through the stack before him. Most of his books were on the British Iron Age, but there were volumes on the Roman Empire as well—showing that Jay was readying himself for whatever test Catesby might throw his way. Now he opened a fat, old book about Pompeii and flipped open to a certain page.

"Here you go, kiddo. The inscription from Structure III.4.2, the House of the Moralists. I bet I know why you wrote it down. This one's particularly creepy."

Inscription 7698c was incomplete, but from the open volume before her, it seemed as if the decipherable section had been translated long ago:

ABANDON YOUR TIRESOME MEDDLING NOW, OR RUN FROM HERE AND HIDE YOURSELF AT HOME.

She stared at the volume's open page and then at the entry in her notebook. Whatever their original meaning, the ancient words were now just meant for her. It was a threat—a warning to flee Wardy, flee Cambridge, or flee from all of England, and to leave Lord Catesby's plans alone.

Unless, of course, she had written the note herself, and her summer's fear was still inside her and poisoning her reason.

*Cálmate*, she told herself. *Relax*.

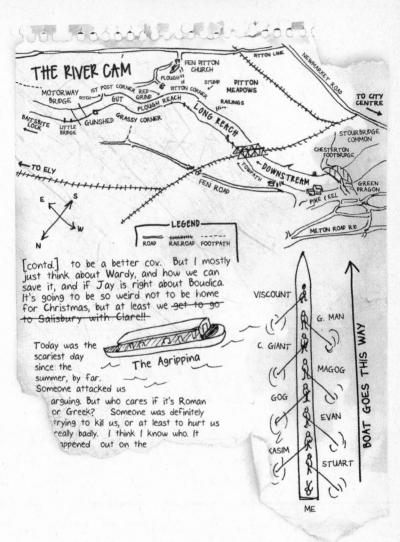

[contd.] to be a better cox. But I mostly just think about Wardy, and how we can save it, and if Jay is right about Boudica. It's going to be so weird not to be home for Christmas, but at least we ~~get to go to Salisbury with Clare!!~~

Today was the scariest day since the summer, by far. Someone attacked us

arguing. But who cares if it's Roman or Greek? Someone was definitely trying to kill us, or at least to hurt us really badly. I think I know who. It happened out on the

# CHAPTER 10

Samantha's new unease was no match for the driving Cambridge rhythm.

Her days began in predawn blackness, when the greatest of fortitude was required to leave the warmth of her heavy blankets. She would slide from her bed, twist her hair into matching braids, and stumble to the outer room for a sleepy bowl of cereal. Evan wouldn't emerge until she had already left the staircase, catching up with her in the Porters' Lodge with his mouth still full of breakfast.

On their rusty, rustic bicycles, they would creak through the blue-black darkness—around the bend of Trinity Lane, past old St. John's College and regal Sidney Sussex, around the squat Crusader church, and into the misty parklands of Jesus Green and Stourbridge Common just beyond. The Cam was waiting for them there in the coming dawn, the silent silhouettes of swans cutting across its velvet surface.

Samantha was starting to cherish her daily hour on the river—the grimy smell of it, the clank and chunk of the oars in their gates, and the lovely puffs of mist that rose from Stuart's mouth in steady rhythms with every stroke he took. And then it was back to town, straight to the Department in their river-soaked clothes. They were with the archaeology team by nine o'clock and bumping along in either van or Jay's small rental fifteen minutes later, Cambridge's skyline shrinking in the morning mist.

Wardy Hill continued to surprise. A massive structure had once been there, it was clear: a great, round enclosure secured behind a mighty double wall. At breaks, Samantha would sometimes walk the shadows of its long-gone ramparts in sober silence. She marveled that something so mighty could disappear so entirely, leaving only fragments.

Lots of them, though. The eaves gullies were still turning up potsherds—more, Clare said, than almost any site in the Fens. And now bits of metal were coming out of the units as well: nails and filings and a couple of delicate Iron Age rings. Ignoring Oona's glare, Samantha studied the jewelry again and again, taking them out of the finds bags and turning them over and over in her hands.

Who had owned them? she wondered. Could they have belonged to Boudica herself?

And, if there was a moment where Oona wasn't looking, she would slip a finger through a ring and let her imagination wander.

At day's end, Samantha would go back to Cambridge under the spell of the day's discovery, hurrying to King's College to catch the Evensong service in the most beautiful building on Earth. If she was lucky, Graham Aubrey would have a solo. If she were luckier still, their eyes would meet as he sang it—the holy, heavenly music directed straight at her. They'd share a shy hello afterward in the forecourt, braving the teasing of Graham's friends as he repeated his invitation to come visit him at home and she again gave her vague acceptance. And then she'd head off to dinner with her cheeks flushed red, knowing the boy still liked her.

With her own activities keeping her busy, she was less bothered that Evan spent his evenings with the Iceni Society, engaged in the same boorish antics that Cambridge students had wrought upon the townspeople since the university began. She knew in the morning she could escape all that, leaving behind the regimented bustle of the last eight hundred years for the age-old freedom of the Fens.

The rhythm continued, day after day. Her daily adventures were safe but thrilling, and Samantha's vague new worries were layered over by stratum upon stratum of science and fun.

Until the morning that someone tried to kill her.

———

It was quiet out on the water at dawn. Some secret Iceni Society event had gone on late, late, late into the night before and no one was eager to row. At Stuart's suggestion, she commanded her crew to paddle at quarter stroke near the beginning of the Long Reach, and she took comfort in the gentle silence all around her.

As the Cam swished around the boat beneath her, she glanced across the snow-spotted meadow. The grassy expanse, the tranquil river, and the low-rising sun gave the impression of untouched wilderness, even though Samantha knew that humans had been here too, shaping and working the land for centuries upon centuries, back to the time of the real Iceni and their valiant Warrior Queen.

A swan glided near the boat, making the picture complete. But Samantha knew enough to steer clear. On an earlier outing, Evan had tried to smack one with his blade, and the enormous bird had reared up in the water and chased them, its nostrils thrumming, an unworldly hiss issuing from its beak.

"For Boudica!" Stuart had cried, and only then was the laughing crew able to outpace the swan. Today, Samantha gave the bird wide berth, and Evan eyed it warily as they left it far behind.

Samantha called, "Easy there," in the shadow of the Railway Bridge, and the rowers laid their blades flat to skitter atop the water. In the Cam's flooded state, there wasn't much space between the surface and the bottom of the tracks. Their voices echoed off the beams of steel above.

"Bit knackered this morning, boys?" the Viscount called from the bow.

Samantha smiled at the teasing. She may not have been privy to all of the Iceni's secrets, but here on the river she was one of them—their leader, in fact—and they were hers to command.

"Stroke's not keeping a steady rhythm," Kasim complained. "Lost his tempo somewhere in the pub last night!"

But as the boat continued its slow, unpowered glide, her eyes floated upward.

A figure was leaning over the rail above them, dark against the lightening sky. Samantha couldn't make out the features of the face, obscured as it was by a dark, heavy jacket and a ratty knot of scarves. Even so, she could feel the intensity of the stare and sense a deadly malice.

*Cálmate.*

The rest of the world around her lost its sound. The laughter of the rowers seemed to hush, and the birds stopped cawing on the riverbanks. This person wanted to be seen.

"Carry on, Archaeo Cox?" asked Stuart, but his voice sounded distant, unaware.

Only Samantha faced forward, and only she could watch as the shrouded figure set two large buckets on the rail, an arm's reach apart, and tipped them slowly over. Twin ropes of blackish liquid oozed out, meeting the surface of the Cam with an extended, ugly plop.

"Guys," she managed, her voice uncertain. But there was nothing she could have done to predict what happened next. The river current carried them forward, just between the tarry streams of liquid, and there was no time to steer them clear. The substances drizzled over the oars on both sides of the boat, coating them in thick stripes as the boat made its way downstream. Only then did the crew realize that something wasn't right.

"What is that?" asked Stuart.

"Oi!" said Gog or Magog. "Who's up there?"

There was a flash of brilliance on the rail as Samantha's seat drew even, and two crumpled pieces of paper floated downward, both ablaze. She heard a hiss as the flames met the surface of the water and a crackle as the oil took fire. And then the realization struck her. Someone was trying to set the boat alight.

"Start positions!" Samantha cried.

But before the rowers could slide forward in their seats—before many of them had even heard her—the River Cam threw up two angry walls of flame, one on either side of them.

"Hurry! Start positions! Go!"

This time they complied, burying their blades into the water at a frantic, jumbled pace. But they were no match for the speed of the blaze as it chased them up the twin slicks of tar. Samantha felt its heat as the fire flanked the stern—so intense that she had to close her eyes.

"Bloomin' hell!" Stuart shouted, as his oar caught fire. Evan's went up an instant later, and then the others up the boat's full length. But still they rowed, the fire hissing with each blade's entry to the water but never going out.

Samantha gripped the sides of the boat, noting the terror on the faces of the rowers before her.

"Faster!" she shouted, feeling the heat across her cheeks.

But speed wasn't the problem now. Though they had left the twin strips of flame behind, their blades still burned. And no cry for Boudica could put those fires out.

"Unlock your oars!"

Her rowers followed her shouted orders at once, unscrewing the long poles from their riggers and pushing them away and clear. The boat rocked violently side to side without the balance of the blades, but the stunned rowers fell forward in their seats anyway, exhausted.

"Crikey!" the Green Man managed, as the eight burning pyres drifted away and sputtered out along the banks.

"An animal activist, I'd wager," gasped Kasim. "Even these horrid swans have their human supporters. Don't ask me why."

But Samantha had the creeping sense that their attacker had no interest in the swan.

"It was a prank, if you ask me," said Stuart. "And a bloomin' good one too."

A prank? Samantha thought. No, this was far too extreme—even for rowdy Cambridge.

"Either way," Evan said, "I now officially hate rowing."

And as the rest of the boat allowed themselves some nervous laughter, Samantha held back. A buried memory had been triggered by the person on the bridge: the muscular frame, the snakelike way he held his head. And suddenly she knew exactly who he was.

But no. Of course she didn't.

And she spent the morning trying to convince herself it wasn't possible.

———

The ride to the site that morning was a raucous one. The panic on the Cam turned more jovial in its retelling, with Stuart and the others applauding the audacity of the unknown prankster. Any remaining fear among the Iceni rowers was edged out by academic one-upmanship.

"One of the Hellenistic boys, I reckon. That was Greek fire, that was."

"Bollocks, Magog. Greek fire's not even Greek," said Kasim. "It's Byzantine."

"It's Roman, in point of fact," the Viscount said. "Hasn't anyone here read Theophanes?"

The next few days settled back into comfortable repetition, eroding Samantha's certainty and easing her troubled mind. The incident on the Cam could indeed have been a very mean-spirited prank. Maybe she was just being paranoid, after all. Maybe her nerves still hadn't recovered fully from Peru.

The familiar Cambridge rhythm slackened on Christmas Eve, when Clare allowed the students the opportunity to travel home for the holiday. And the Suttons would be traveling as well—to celebrate in Salisbury with Clare.

It would be the best Christmas ever. Clare had promised Samantha a tour of her hometown and all its surrounding landmarks: mysterious Silbury Hill, the Roman spa town of Bath, and the mystical stone circles of Avebury and Stonehenge. So Samantha threw an extra notebook into her Union Jack backpack along with some clothes, knowing she'd have so much to write down.

Too excited to wait for her brother, Samantha hurried alone through the Porters' Lodge and bid Tom a merry Christmas on her way outside. A light snow was falling, making magic of a gray afternoon. The world was alive with promise. She reached the Department at a run and spied the professors waiting by Clare's big orange car.

"Evan's coming!" she cried. "He's just finishing a phone call."

But then she stopped. Jay was frowning, and Clare's eyes were wide and red. They had been fighting.

"Change of plans, kiddo," said Jay, with a sad smile.

Clare wrapped her in a warm embrace.

"Maybe next year, Samantha," she said, opening her car door. "Happy Christmas."

Samantha and Jay trudged back to the college in silence. This was all Jay's fault, of course. That he and Clare disagreed on Wardy Hill's Boudica connection was not the only problem. It was that Jay approached the issue with his trademark humor. But Clare had no patience for it this time, not when her career was concerned.

Boudica was coming between them.

---

Jay seemed eager to give Samantha and Evan a Christmas to remember. He took them out for pizza, followed by a movie at the Grafton Centre mall. Samantha and Evan had seen it before—it had been in American theaters months earlier—but still it was a welcome release. And as a final treat, Jay tried to arrange tickets to the Christmas Eve concert at King's Chapel.

"Sold out," he said, coming in from the snow. "Even the waiting list's full."

Samantha tried to hide her disappointment. She had wanted to see the choir again and craved the comfort of Graham's glorious voice.

Instead, she called home. Her parents had a conference to go to the whole of Christmas Day—something called "Maintaining a Healthy Work-Life Balance"—and tonight, Christmas Eve, would be the only chance to wish them a happy holiday.

"Where's the phone, Evan?" she asked, when the scheduled hour arrived.

"Oh, do you mean the *emergency* phone?" he answered. "What's the emergency?"

So Samantha used the phone in the Porters' Lodge instead. Tom showed her how to dial and stepped into the back office to give her privacy.

"Find any dinosaurs yet?" asked her mother, clueless as ever.

"No," Samantha sighed. "Not yet."

"Samantha, please try not to bother your uncle," said her

father, conferencing in. "Bringing you along last summer turned out to be such a hardship for him."

"And do what your brother says," said her mother. "He's old enough to look after you."

These comments were too backward to correct. Her parents still didn't know her, and maybe they never would. So she made her empty promises, wished them merry Christmas, and handed the phone to her brother.

Samantha spent the rest of the evening in Trinity Hall's Middle Combination Room, a cozy lounge with warm red walls. As Evan made another emergency call home to Annie Cartano and left a threatening message on Keith Barrett's voice mail, Jay told Samantha about his days as a student at Cambridge—the jaunts with Clare to London, York, or Henley, and the occasional field trip to Oxford, which he still called "The Other Place" in mock disgust. These were his fondest memories—stories Samantha knew already, some by heart—and each involved Clare Barrows.

It was clear how much he missed her. Jay grew a little sadder with each telling. And he didn't mention Boudica once.

———

But the Warrior Queen returned to Samantha's dreams that night regardless, conjured like some vengeful spirit by her deepest thoughts alone.

The chariot burst from her swirls of sleepy darkness to tear across a mist-cloaked plain. Again, Boudica's face was Clare's, but grim instead of friendly and set with dark resolve. At her feet her children huddled, their faces familiar too. They would witness the cold justice of their mother. They would see their vengeance served.

Boudica gripped a spear in one hand and the reins in the other, channeling the rage of her black steeds toward the looming city walls. The Iceni host charged all around them, tens of thousands strong. They knew their target well: Camulodunum—that garish insult in wood and stone. Here the Empire sent its soldiers to retire, to grow old on Iceni labor and fat on Iceni lands. But these conquerors of half the world were no longer in fighting shape. Their confidence in easy victory had left them weak. And with the active legions away on other matters, there was no one to defend them.

A cry of alarm and the smell of smoke came from the citadel as the Iceni forces stormed the walls. Around the royal chariot, the townspeople wailed and waddled toward the temple. Boudica eyed each one. Two would be captured for eventual sacrifice to Andraste in the water between the worlds. The rest, perhaps, she'd spare. With hundreds of hostages, Rome would have no choice. She'd have her land back from them and all her honor too.

The acrid smoke stung her throat, and she drew a long sip from the ornate tankard at her side. She dismounted and paced the temple steps as the town burned down around her. Watching the citizens clutch their valuables, Boudica's anger flamed anew. Who were these Roman intruders?

Who gave them the power to break their sacred oath and offend the gods? And by what authority did they steal the birthright of her children and shame her before her tribe?

But then the wronged queen's eyes alit on something that would not burn. Some*one*, really, for the bronze statue was the most lifelike that she'd seen. From its wrinkled lip and sneer of cold command she knew it was the emperor in sculpted form, holding court before the temple built to honor him.

*So they made you a god*, she thought. *Can you save your mortals now?*

There would be no hostages today.

Her first order was followed in near silence—the metal groaning just a little as the statue's head was wrenched free. But when her forces stormed the temple, it was all of Rome that seemed to scream.

As the dream began to fade, Samantha watched the Queen stride into the midst of the slaughter, holding the metal head aloft as the Iceni voices cried in triumph. But Samantha felt the Queen's most secret sorrow—her longing for Prasutagus, her confidant and king.

———————

Samantha woke on Christmas morning with someone of her own to long for.

She biked toward the boathouse through the deserted town, stopping short where a line of slender houseboats strained at their moorings near the Jesus Lock—the blue

*Merlin's Beard*, the yellow *Ferret*, the slate-gray *Hereward the Wake*.

"Oi, Samantha!"

Graham was on the last of the narrowboats—the *Agrippina*, painted a noble scarlet. He was clad only in a thin T-shirt and shiny tracksuit trousers, and was clearly shivering as he held open the door to greet her.

"Happy Christmas," he said.

"Merry Christmas," she called back. "Is this your boat?"

"Of course it's ours. Whose else?" he said. "Lord Catesby gave it to us when we moved over here from Coveney. Now come on. I'm letting in the damp."

The cabin was cozy, warmed by a small stove and decorated, a little sloppily, for Christmas. But the long room was so narrow that it was difficult to maneuver through it, especially with all the boxes and shelves that lined the walls.

"There's more space toward the stern," Graham said, and ushered her farther inside.

To Samantha's relief, Ned Aubrey was not there. But that made her nervous for other reasons. She had never been alone with a boy before. At least not like this.

Graham's room was more of an alcove, a bed and a dresser hemmed in by the surrounding furniture. She didn't know where to go.

"You can sit on my bed," he said, then added. "Or there, on that crate. My dad will be back in a bit."

Graham's face had gone a little red.

"Right," he said, as Samantha settled onto an upturned box. "I want to show you something."

He pulled another crate into his space. It was very, very heavy, marked only with "June–August" and the year.

"It was a good summer," he said. "We went out almost every weekend."

He tipped the box out onto the floor, and Samantha gasped aloud.

Before her was a pile of artifacts: medieval love tokens, stone loom weights, hammered coins in plastic sleeves, potsherd after potsherd, and dust from the ceramics that had been pulverized by the weight of the heavier objects.

"The metal detector doesn't pick up the stone or the ceramics, obviously, but we find all sorts of things poking around."

"Are these all from one site?" she asked, her voice an involuntary whisper.

"Oh, no! We went all over this summer. Near Cambridge, of course, but also up near Peterborough, and Lincoln, and one day as far down as Kent."

"Does anyone know you have this stuff? Anyone official, I mean?"

"Nah. We could report them to the county office, but we never do. My dad doesn't like the government types knowing our business."

Samantha frowned.

"Do you even keep notes?"

"Don't have to! My memory's an iron box." He plucked

a small green object from the pile—a hammered metal triangle attached to a loop. "Found this in Spaulding, near a machinist shop. Thought it was modern, at first, but my dad says it's Viking! And this." He picked up a long smooth rock. "A whetstone. Found it near Coton." His face skewed into a frown. "Or was it Comberton? Well, doesn't matter. My dad will remember."

Samantha's mood had darkened. While Graham and Ned Aubrey had been prowling the English countryside last summer, robbing it of its history, she had been risking her life in Peru to stop just that sort of thing from happening.

"But it *does* matter," she said as calmly as she could. "If you don't know where something was found or what was nearby, it's basically useless. You have to be trained to do archaeology. You have to know something about how it all works."

Graham laughed.

"My dad thought you'd say that. You're like a hoddy-doddy scientist, he said, after we saw you up at Wardy. He hates scientists. More than he hates the government, even. He says that they talk down to everyone, that they're a bunch of high-learned robbing buggers who think they own the past."

She felt her face go red.

"Please don't take it personal," Graham said, realizing his mistake. "And anyway, that's not what I think. I think archaeology is brilliant."

But the warmth of the fire had lost its charm. She

looked at the sad pile of artifacts on the floor—meaningless now, as far as science was concerned. The thrill of her visit was gone.

"I think I should go."

Graham's eyes flew wide open in pleading.

"But there's something I still want to show you!"

He rummaged in the next box, pulling out a small cardboard container. Inside, wrapped in tissue paper, was a coin of polished silver. Graham held it out to her, but when she did not take it, he took her hand and gently unfurled her fingers.

She did not want to look at it, to show any kind of interest whatsoever. It was stolen goods, as far as she could tell. Taken not only from science, but from out of the story only archaeology could tell.

"Look, Samantha. Look!"

She almost pitied him. He meant well. He had no idea of what he'd done. But Graham's cheerful face was so excited, so open. And so she looked.

The coin was small, its design off center. On one side was a pig in profile—stamped so close to the edge that part of the animal was missing off the side. Its hair bristled in a fringe—like the crest of some rooster. And on the other side was a horse in mid-gallop, spindly and weird.

"Guess where this one's from?"

Samantha sighed.

"I don't know, Graham. Do you even remember yourself?"

He smiled, mistaking her angry tone for teasing.

"This one's from Wardy Hill. Right from where you're working."

This got her attention.

"How old is it?"

"About two thousand years," he said, his eyes twinkling. "It's Iceni, Samantha. Could've been in Boudica's own piggy bank."

The name caught her off guard. Boudica, yet again.

For all their work and all their worry, was *this* the proof she needed? Was this what she'd need to convince Clare that the Warrior Queen had something to do with Wardy after all so she'd alert the Heritage Office? Could this single coin save the site from its owner? And could it close the rift between the two professors?

"I'd like you to have it, Sam."

But this was too much.

"I can't."

"Course you can." He closed her fingers around it. "It was mine, and now it's yours."

Samantha studied it again.

"I'll borrow it, but only to show my uncle. And then I'll bring it back. "

"I won't take it!" said Graham. "It's a gift. It's Christmas, after all. The coin is yours to remember me by."

She relented and slipped the cold metal into her pocket, feeling exactly like a thief.

I have to show it to Jay and Clare. But they are going to be mad I took it from Graham in the first place. The only possible way I'll convince them is if I first.

FRONT

BACK

I forgot about the door to nowhere. I guess I just never thought I'd actually have to use it!

"THAT THE FEET OF THE BODY HAD BEEN TIED TO THESE STAKES NO ONE SEEING IT COULD DOUBT FOR A MOMENT. IT MAY BE CONCLUDED THAT THE EXECUTION OR MURDER TOOK PLACE...

[copy rest later]

**Camulodunum** =
  Modern day Colchester

**Verulamium** =
  Modern day St. Albans

**Londinium** =
  Modern day London

I'm **POSITIVE** there was someone in there with me. At first, I just thought it was my nerves, but I SAW

# CHAPTER 11

She would share the coin with the professors, Samantha promised herself. But she would have to educate herself first, secretly, after hours. She would have to come prepared.

There was little reason for locked doors during the Winter Holiday—at least from the College's point of view. Tom maintained strict control of the only entrance, and other than the bedders and a few college staff, traffic in and out was light. Evan had noted with some glee that Trinity Hall's own tiny chapel was left unlocked and bragged that he had even played "Chopsticks" on its organ. If this was true, Samantha figured, there was a chance that the college's Old Library was left open as well, and that she could sneak in some research unobserved.

On Christmas night, Evan's call to Annie went longer than usual, and his pleas were not having their usual effect.

"Just wait until I get back," he was begging, when Samantha listened at her door. "Don't go out with Keith again until at least we've had a chance to talk."

It wasn't clear if Annie relented or Evan just gave up, but it was after midnight when he finally went to bed. Looping the string of her notebook over her head, Samantha crept from their room in total darkness and in the closest to silence the building allowed. But for every creak of her footsteps on the sagging floorboards, other noises sounded from rooms that were supposed to be empty—squeaks, bumps, and the groans of ancient wood.

Her thoughts turned to what had happened some days before on the River Cam—that prank, if it was a prank and not attempted murder.

*Cálmate*, she told herself.

The Old Library was reached up a steep staircase from the North Court, then through a short corridor lined with the bare stone of the college's original construction. To guide her, Samantha had only the soft green glow of the EXIT signs and the shiny sparkle of a disco ball from the nearby Junior Common Room—left over, she figured, from a party at the end of term.

The shimmering lights danced across the ancient oak door, but it took a while for Samantha to see how to open it. It was unlocked, she quickly realized, but could only be entered by folding back a metal panel and releasing a hidden pin. At last the aged door swung inward, and Samantha slipped inside.

She dared not risk the overhead lights, or even her flashlight right away, opting instead for the thin moonlight that streamed through the many delicately paned windows.

The floor creaked mercilessly here—the boards long and arced like the deck of a galleon. Before her, along both walls, were rows of age-old bookcases, alternating tall and short, and capped by decorative finials.

Across from the entrance, a glass case threw back the reflection of the moon. Peering close, she noticed a jumble of bones inside—a human skeleton—and the glint of metal chains. She could just make out a faded label that explained how the bones were discovered shackled to two wooden stakes. Hundreds of years ago, or more than a thousand, this person had been chained in place and left to die.

She shivered. Cambridge and its skeletons. This would have seemed just a little out of place at the county library back home.

Two computers sat just inside the entrance, but Samantha decided against turning them on in case some electronic record would be made of her visit. Besides, they probably required a password, like all the other computers she had seen since her arrival. She would have to use the archaic card catalog instead.

Boudica would be in the Bs. She went for the drawer marked Blix-Burgess and yanked it open. The letters on the cards were tiny. She switched on her flashlight, then held it between her teeth so she could find the card she was looking for:


BOUDICA/BODICEA/BUDDUG:
SEE VOADICEA

Samantha smiled to herself, her lips curling up around the flashlight. Even in a library the Warrior Queen wasn't easy to locate. She slammed the drawer shut. The sound echoed through the darkened room, taking on a strange character in the distant corners.

Or was that another noise altogether? A cough? Some footsteps? An opening door?

She shook off her apprehension. The card for "Voadicea" directed Samantha to a specific row and shelf, but she realized that she would have her choice of five or six crumbling volumes. She pulled down a particularly dusty tome and was about to take it to a nearby table when she felt a powerful yank. Attached to the book was a rusty metal chain, leading all the way back to a rod in the bookshelf. This must never have been a lending library. The books could not be removed.

So she stood, her breath rising in billowing clouds through the moonbeams, looking at one book after another with her flashlight in her teeth.

Boudica's capital had indeed been Thetford, she read, just as Tom had said—closer to the great coastal flats where the Iceni collected the salt that made them rich. But they would have known the Fenlands well, and they would have taken note of Wardy Hill's natural defenses.

Samantha switched to the Roman accounts of Boudica's rebellion. As she read, the historical characters took on their familiar forms in her imagination. It was Clare again that she saw as Boudica, leading her army around the heel of England, rallying her own Iceni and the neighboring kingdoms to her cause. And it was Catesby who heard of the uprising and ordered his Governor General back from another front of battle to crush it.

As book after book described Boudica's campaign of revenge, Samantha felt her kinship growing. She too had been lied to. She had been wronged by the people she trusted most. And as the bloody campaign coursed across the land, Samantha understood that Camulodunum, Verulamium, and tiny Londinium, now London, wouldn't have been enough. Boudica would have needed to face the Roman Governor General himself to settle things once and for all.

Samantha closed the book and replaced it on the shelf, stirred by the story she had read. But her archaeological mind was triggered as well. Surely there would be some physical proof of Boudica's revolt, given all the killing and destruction involved. What had archaeology turned up so far, if it had turned up anything?

She walked back to the card catalog, eager to read more, and for a moment her flashlight played across the skeleton in its case. Had this person been an Iceni? Had he been executed to set an example?

She located the card for "Iron Age Archaeology" and was about to find the appropriate shelf when she spotted dancing lights across the floor: the disco ball from the Junior Common Room. The library's door must be open. But she clearly remembered shutting it behind her and managing the complex mechanism of its latch.

She froze, sinking slowly to the floor beside the skeleton in its case. Had someone followed her inside? She heard the creak of the floorboards and strained to hear if they took on a more human rhythm. But there was nothing. Just the dull thud of her own heartbeat behind her eyes.

*Cálmate.*

And then, across the central aisle, she noticed another door. If there was someone in the library with her, waiting for her in the dark, it would be good to put a second barrier between her and her pursuer. She took in a long breath, then darted low to the opposite wall.

For several agonizing seconds her hands fumbled with the ancient latch. Its hinge was stuck, as if it hadn't been opened in centuries. She pressed hard with her fingers, prying and straining until the metal finally gave way and the door flew violently outward.

The outside cold hit her in a powerful gust, and she took a dizzying stumble backward. Above was the moon, its light surprisingly severe. Far to the right was the shining River Cam—just over a low brick wall. Immediately before her was blue-black nothingness, just a long fall into the icy rose beds below.

She had seen this door before, she realized. It was the one Jay said had connected a bridge to the Master's Lodge some centuries before. It was no use to her now. And as the wind slammed the ancient door shut, she retreated back inside, ducking into the cover of a bookshelf.

*Cálmate.*

She waited in stunned silence, straining for any sound. Was that her heartbeat, or were those footsteps coming across the planks? Was someone creeping closer in the dark? Did they think she had left the room, and were they going after her in pursuit? She shrunk low to the ground and waited, beating back her terror with long and measured breaths.

And then she heard the outer door fly open again with a bang, and a wailing, anguished cry. In the grip of her own fear, she thought it might be her own and threw her hand across her mouth to cover it. The wind rammed the door again and again against the brickwork, and she squeezed her eyes tight. Was she imagining the whole thing? Was this just an artifact of her summer in Peru and its lasting strain upon her psyche?

There was only one way to find out.

Samantha crept again toward the gaping doorway, eager but terrified for a glimpse. Outside, dark against the moonlight, windswept trees cast writhing shadows across the snowy lawn. But she saw—or thought she saw—human movement out there too, skirting through the darkness of the hedges.

This was all her shattered nerves could handle. She turned and ran the other way: through the Junior Common Room and North and Front Courts and to the questionable safety of her room.

She went to work the next morning in numb silence, fingering the Iceni coin in her pocket.

Of course she should tell her uncle what had happened the night before—of the figure in the library and how it had come after her to do some kind of harm. Or how she'd thought that had happened, anyway, and how Jay's failure to keep her safe last summer still scarred her troubled mind.

But she quickly ruled it out. How would she explain why she was in the library? Why was she researching Boudica, against Jay's specific instructions? Worse, how bad would he feel if he found out that he had put her in danger once again? And how could he protect her, anyway? She decided to wait to tell him what had happened. At least until the workday was done.

The day's labor turned out to be hard, painful, and unpleasant. A warmer night and colder morning had left a lid of frozen mud across every unit floor, rendering the screens almost useless once again. Heavy Fenland soil clung together in fist-sized chunks, studded with bits of ice. The dense mud was so heavy that Samantha could not lift a full bucket of it by herself. Across the ringwork, Evan was also having trouble, and the first time he managed to lift his pail high enough to tip it into the screen, the metal lattice buckled under its weight, tearing from the wooden frame with a loud metallic rip.

"Okay, everyone," Jay cried out, "Next person to break one of my screens sings 'The Star-Spangled Banner' at the Ridge & Furrow!"

And so the team's own hands became the frames, their fingers the metal lattice. They squeezed each clod of frozen mud until their palms ached from the effort and burned from the cold.

Kasim and Stuart had the worst of it. They had set up a garden hose to rinse the potsherds of their sticky clay, and their fingers had turned a painful purple. And while the finds that emerged in this manner filled bag after bag, Samantha knew that there were other secrets still embedded within the frustrating lumps, and that there would not be time enough to retrieve them.

Clare was back from Salisbury, and Samantha could tell things between the professor and her uncle had improved in her absence. But not entirely. Clare smiled a little less warmly at Jay's bad jokes, and Jay seemed to choose his words more carefully. Samantha wanted so badly for them to be whole again, like before, when love or even marriage seemed possible. They needed something to bind them, a discovery to celebrate together.

It wasn't a serious offense, she reasoned. The Aubreys had found the coin here, after all. Not *exactly* here—and that fact continued to bother her—but what was one artifact in a project like this, where the site's destruction-by-theme-park was imminent, and a full hour could be spent plucking fish bones from a clot of frozen mud? And besides, it was worth it. The tension between them had to be fixed for the good of the project.

So, that was partly why she did what she did as the

workday came to an end. It couldn't have been easier. Left alone to tidy up as Stuart packed away the tools, she reached into her pocket, plucked out Graham's Iceni coin, and tossed it to the muddy ground.

But at once she felt the weight of her guilt. She couldn't do this. It was wrong and she knew it. She bent to pick it up again.

"What's that, Sam? Give us a look."

The warm female voice startled her and arrested her retrieval of the coin. She turned, trying her best to hide it with her boot. But a second surprise made her step back, and the coin glinted still, even in the shadows of the winter afternoon.

It was Oona Jessel, just beside the unit.

"Oh," said Samantha, squinting up at her. "I…I thought you were Dr. Barrows."

Oona's thin lips stretched into a mirthless smile.

"Did you? How very peculiar."

It was strange to see the sole female student outside among the units and their adjacent piles of mud. Usually, she ensconced herself in the lab all day, halfheartedly sorting ceramics and scaring the others away with her chilling rehearsal of lines.

"So," she said, her crisp accent returned. "What's that you've found?"

"Nothing," Samantha said, and Oona cocked her head. "I mean nothing very interesting…it's just a little piece of metal."

"O wonderful, when devils tell the truth!" Oona recited, then held out her hand. "Come on. Let's see it."

Samantha relented. She had no other choice.

"Well," Oona said, her voice hard and mocking. "This will please your uncle."

"Let's wait to show him," said Samantha. "I'm not totally sure what it is."

Oona stared at her.

"Well, I am. Catesby insists that his students be able to distinguish Roman coinage from those of the vanquished. This is a silver boar-horse C type. First century. Iceni."

Samantha felt sick.

"Oh, don't be stupid," said Oona. "I'll give you full credit."

Even worse, Samantha thought. Regret tumbled over her like the cold and sticky mud. But there was nothing she could do about it now. And as she watched Oona show the coin to the professors, she sank guiltily to her knees.

I can't believe I did that. I really can't I wish I could take it all back. Now, everybody is talking about Boudica, non-stop. Also, awful Oona and Clare seems suspicious I have to fix this somehow

CASTLE HILL

O QVID TVÆ
BE EST BIÆ

There's been a second attack. This time we wer super lucky. We were on our way to and if Jay hadn't all been badly hur.

BALLISTA

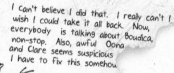

# CHAPTER 12

"Guess your thief of a boyfriend missed one, Samantha."

Evan was relentless with his teasing as they drove to the site the next morning, but Samantha was too beset by rolling fogs of fear and shame to give him much thought. What had seemed like such a good idea now haunted her, and it was becoming harder and harder to come clean.

Samantha had been given credit, as she'd been promised, and the whole team was quick to congratulate her. But it was Oona who'd showed the coin around and received most of the praise.

"What a triumph," Kasim had said. "We've got her on our side!"

"I knew it," Stuart had chimed in. "We'll make Oona one of us yet!"

Now, it was clear that the discovery of the Iceni coin had completely changed Jay's mood. He was absolutely buoyant at the wheel this morning—belting out bits of

Sinatra and the strange old ballads he remembered from his student days.

"Bring me my bow of burning gold!" he sang. "Bring me my arrows of desire!"

In fact, on that morning of the attack, he was as happy as she'd ever seen him.

It happened on Castle Street, just past Castle Hill. Automatically, Samantha and Evan leaned far over as they always did, trying for a peek of the odd little hillock between the buildings on the Cam's northern bank where a castle had stood to control the crossing. There were no fortifications left these days, but it was easy to imagine a tiny garrison atop the rounded green hill, keeping a wary eye on the traffic below.

"It was Norman," Jay said, as the hill flashed into view between the modern offices of a telecom company. "Built when the French invaded, a thousand years ago."

"Was there ever a battle?" Evan asked, his voice betraying mental images of knights, swords, and catapults.

"Oh yeah." Jay's exuberance was building. "The garrison was built to quash rebellions, and this part of the country has had more than its fair share of those. Here. I'll show you."

Jay stomped on the brake, causing his young relatives to lurch forward in their seats. He just wanted to give them a better look, but instead he probably saved their lives.

A movement caught the corner of Samantha's eye,

something arcing through the air at an uncomfortable speed. But before she could see the projectile clearly, she could hear it—a whistling sound growing closer.

"Uncle Jay!"

And then the road ahead of them exploded in a shower of stone and pavement. Bits of it hit the windshield, sending out webs of tiny cracks. Samantha threw her arms over her face, and she heard Evan shouting from the back.

"What was that?" said Jay. "You guys okay?"

They nodded. They hadn't been hurt. Not yet. A second attack might still be coming, though, and they might not be so lucky.

But Jay didn't seem to consider this possibility.

"Stay here," he said, swinging open his door and stepping out onto the road. He didn't seem in a hurry as he dropped to his knees on the tarmac, examining the large round stone still spinning in the gutter.

"Well, well."

"What is it?" Evan asked through the open door. "A cannonball?"

Jay stood, looking out across the road.

"Something like that."

Samantha followed her uncle's gaze, tracing the projectile's path backward over the small parking lot and through the trees to its origin at the top of Castle Hill.

"I'll be right back," he shouted, and took off at a jog. But Evan was too alarmed to wait and hurried to follow.

After a moment's hesitation, Samantha did too, her clawing fear making it easy to keep pace.

Up the hill they ran, keeping to its winding path. The view from the top was of all of Cambridge, its roofs and steeples dark against the rising sun. But their attention was fixed on the spidery wooden contraption that crowned the peak. It looked like a giant slingshot, and its bowstring still hummed from its recent use.

"A *ballista*," Jay said. "A Roman missile launcher. This looks like one Catesby had us build when I was a student here."

A weird coincidence, Samantha thought. But Evan had noticed a scrap of paper beside the modern ancient weapon, pinned to the earth with a stick. Scratched across the page in heavy pen was a series of letters:

O   QVID TVÆ
BE   EST   BIÆ

She stared at it, trying to sound out the strange syllables inside her head. But then her uncle laughed aloud.

"It's an old Roman riddle," he said. "'Above' is *super* in Latin. So you could read this as *O SUPERbe quid SUPERest tuae SUPERbiae*. If I remember my vocabulary, it means something like: 'Conceited man, will anything remain of your arrogance?'"

Was this a threat? Samantha wondered. But her uncle just chuckled, seemingly impressed.

They descended the hill and climbed back in the car, where Jay resumed his singing: "Bring me my bow of burning gold. Bring me my arrows of desire!"

Ballistas, bows, and arrows. Once again, her uncle was laughing in the face of danger, Samantha knew, but still it felt like he was laughing at her and her concern.

"Someone's having a little fun with us," Jay said.

This was too much.

"*Fun?*"

"Come on, Sam. I'm sure you've realized by now that Cambridge has a long, healthy tradition of elaborate pranks. This is fairly typical, actually. A not-so-subtle message from the Lord Professor or one of his friends."

He seemed eager to change the subject.

"Now sing with me. 'Bring me my spear: O clouds unfold! Bring me my chariot of fire!'"

She didn't join in as he requested but sat up straight in her seat, the verse triggering a buried memory. She saw in her mind the flaming wreckage of a bus at the foot of a remote Andean cliff-face. And her thoughts turned unwillingly to its sole American survivor.

"But it almost killed us," Evan cried, as alarmed as she was by their uncle's nonchalance.

"Almost dented the car, maybe. As unpleasant as Catesby is, he would never want to do us harm."

"Maybe," said Evan, his eyes still wide with fear. "But someone else might."

Jay's smile did not reassure them.

"Who would possibly want to hurt us, Ev? Who in the whole wide world?"

Samantha knew. And from the look on her brother's face, it seemed that he did too.

———

But all the talk at the site that day was of the Iceni coin and its likely link to Boudica. Thrilling new questions fueled the project. Had the Warrior Queen lived on Wardy Hill, after all? Or was she buried here, along with the treasures of her reign? Samantha winced at each excited theory. Planting the coin had been like sowing a seed, and there was nothing she could do now to beat back the growing excitement.

It relieved her somewhat that Clare was still cautious, unwilling to let the find disrupt the tasks at hand.

"We have a job to do," she reminded the team over lunch. "Leave the oohs and aahs to the metal detectorists."

But it was too late. The promise of further Iceni discoveries distracted even the most vigilant eye. Mundane tasks began to lose their appeal, and methods went suddenly sloppy. A discovery for the ages was waiting up at Wardy—and they would be the ones to find it.

Evan, especially, was a lost cause. The morning's attack had had a strange effect on him, and he set to work with a sort of desperation—burrowing and tunneling into the earth in search of the next big find. Jay was susceptible too. When a twisted metal coil was pulled from a profile, he quietly proclaimed it to be Boudica's brooch. The discovery of some cow bones amounted to Boudica's banquet.

And while his voice was joking when he said these things, and his face held a carefree smile, Samantha knew what lay beneath it. Finding Boudica at Wardy Hill would do more than show up Catesby; it would revive her uncle's whole career.

She frowned, surveying the mania that she'd caused. It was now the winter of the Warrior Queen, and it was all Samantha's fault.

———

That night she dreamed of Boudica, hell-bent on revenge.

She saw a city burning: Londinium—Samantha knew, with the strange certainty of dreams—the huddled beginnings of the modern British capital. Boudica's army had grown. Other tribes, even ancient enemies, were bound to her by their shared hatred of the Roman invaders. Now she was their queen as well.

Samantha's mind followed Boudica as she sped through the fiery streets, carrying the metal head of the emperor high above her own. The sight of it enraged and enlivened her forces, and a great cry went up among them as they tore the buildings to pieces. But the Warrior Queen was not satisfied as the night sky flickered orange and red. She wanted Roman blood, not Roman brick, and most of the town's residents had fled before she'd arrived. Someone must have come to warn them.

Andraste deserved a proper sacrifice for all the fortunes she'd bestowed. And so Boudica took more time than usual with the few Londoners who remained—branding them with iron, flaying their skins, slashing them to pieces, and leaving their heads, openmouthed, as offerings in the brook that fed the town.

A surprise attack and elegant Verulamium fell next in fitful dreamtime, its lavish streets choked with blood and fire. Samantha could see Boudica circle the ruin in her chariot, wrapped in winter wool. But she wanted more. She craved the Governor General's death. And so Boudica ordered her swollen army north and west, and toward his coming legions.

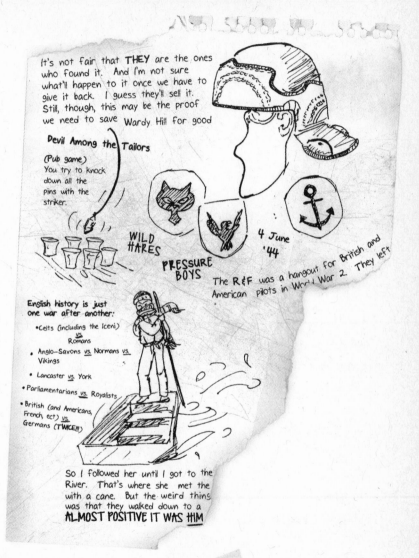

It's not fair that **THEY** are the ones who found it. And I'm not sure what'll happen to it once we have to give it back. I guess they'll sell it. Still, though, this may be the proof we need to save Wardy Hill for good

**Devil Among the Tailors**

(Pub game)
You try to knock down all the pins with the striker.

WILD HARES

PRESSURE BOYS

4 June '44

The R&F was a hangout for British and American pilots in World War 2. They left

English history is just one war after another:

- Celts (including the Iceni) vs Romans
- Anglo-Saxons vs Normans vs Vikings
- Lancaster vs York
- Parliamentarians vs Royalists
- British (and Americans, French, ect) vs Germans (TWICE!!!)

So I followed her until I got to the River. That's where she met the with a cane. But the weird thing was that they walked down to a **ALMOST POSITIVE IT WAS HIM**

# CHAPTER 13

Real enemies found Samantha the next day, wending their way up Wardy Hill in a phalanx of glittering red.

The morning had been a productive one. While a south wind hit the hill with the ferocity of a charging army, emptying the sky of its usual hot-air balloons, the warmer weather made digging easier. Samantha and Stuart had completed a unit in the site's inner ring and begun another in the eaves gully of Structure VI. Her trowel met no resistance through the semisoft mud. The repetition lulled her into a convincing serenity and she made a kind of game of it, slicing each curl away at its base and hacking it apart, first with her right hand and then with her left. Soon, she had uncovered a single jet bead, a pair of chalk spindle whorls, and a stone object that looked to be used for grinding. Clare was thrilled by the finds. They showed, she said, a vast trade network, linking Wardy to other Celtic people throughout the land.

Then came the big red buses.

There was a flurry of conversation among the Iceni as the hulking vehicles turned from the nearby village to head up the gentle grade. Who would be sightseeing way out here? Was it simply a lost group of tourists looking for Ely's great cathedral? Or birdwatchers, perhaps—eager for a sight of a merlin, crake, or the rare night heron of the Fens?

But then Samantha spotted an antique car trailing behind them and knew that something else was going on. These people were here with Catesby. They had come for Wardy Hill.

"Bloomin' hell," said Stuart, and the Iceni laid down their tools to stare.

The scarlet coaches came to a stop with a hiss beside the pillbox, and a line of people poured out. All were men and boys. Some were dressed in camouflage, others in hunting jackets or the thin, slick tracksuits of their favorite football clubs. When the compartments in the belly of each bus were opened, out came a quantity of gear: large canvas bags, coolers, and grocery bags of snacks. A stereo was turned on immediately, spilling loud American rock tunes across the peaceful Fens.

The assembly fanned out along the edge of the road, staking down canopies and setting up tables and chairs. Only when the group began to unpack their bags did it become clear what their purpose was. Each had a metal detector in his hand.

"Oh, this is just bloody fantastic," said Kasim.

"Is this a bloomin' joke?" Stuart asked.

Samantha realized what was happening a moment later. Catesby had organized a metal detectorist rally, right in the middle of an active excavation.

Jay threw down his gloves, his shovel, his trowel, his hat. Anything he could throw, he threw, hurling each item to the ground in anger. And then he marched across the field to confront the Lord Professor.

Catesby was in the middle of an announcement when Jay reached them. From her position, Samantha could only catch snatches of Catesby's sleepy voice and the somewhat raucous laughter of the crowd. But Jay's voice was firm enough to be heard across the field.

"Is what it looks like, Cairn?"

"It's Sir Cairn, if you please," the older man replied, ignoring the substance of Jay's question. "At least in front of the public. Must keep up appearances, and all that."

"You've gone too far this time, letting these people come here. Way, way too far."

"These *people* are my guests," said the Lord Professor. "When work begins on Vivant Romani in one week's time, my Wardy will be closed to them as well. I do hope you will accommodate them as best you can, Sutton. Mustn't be elitist, must we?"

It was with disappointment that Samantha saw another pair preparing—the Aubreys, father and son. Ned was busy calibrating the machine while Graham stood glumly by. The boy looked up, and for a moment his eyes met hers. But he dropped his gaze, ashamed.

Catesby left then, pleased with the chaos he had caused. And as his car puttered away, the metal detectorists dispersed, heading across the site in twos. They made no effort to steer around the team, sometimes dipping their instruments into the units themselves.

"Oi!" shouted Kasim, as one pair neared his area. "Mind the sidewalls at least, will you?"

The man only laughed and turned to his compatriots.

"Some nerve this brown little fellow has, gents. He wants to save our English heritage from ourselves!"

This Stuart wouldn't stand for. He threw down his screen to come to his friend's defense.

"You pikey ned! Sod off!"

"Pikey?" said the man, his face breaking into a smile. "I don't think anyone has ever called me that before. I'm a professor of neuroscience at Oxford, my Scottish friend. Who, exactly, are you?"

Stuart took a stride toward him, but a faraway cry stopped him cold.

"Oi!"

Samantha set down her trowel. It was Ned Aubrey's voice. His excited tone was noticeable even through the blasting wind.

"Everyone, come quick! Me boy's found something you're not going to believe."

Suddenly all the detectorists were running, eager for

a glimpse. But the pronouncement emptied the students from their units as well. Even Oona joined the group, stepping outside the pillbox lab for the first time in days.

The Aubreys had taken their search downslope from all the others, where the sweeping curve of the ancient droveway led back away from the Fens. The crowd made for them through the wind, leaning against it like stakes against a charge of cavalry.

"Bloomin' hell," said Stuart, when he reached the unit at last, and the assembly echoed his sentiment in a chorus of "brilliants," "bloodys," and "blimeys." Glinting up at them through the gravelly fill was a hammered piece of metal. Only half the object had emerged so far, but what the Aubreys had uncovered gave a sense of its overall shape. It reminded Samantha of a hunter's cap, but wrought of iron, tin, and bronze. The raised nubs up and down its length would have deflected the slashes and thrusts of swords and spears, and the wide flap along the visible side would have shielded the warrior's left cheek and jaw from injury.

Ned Aubrey knelt astride it now, his thin lips strained in a grin. Beside him, Graham couldn't meet Samantha's angry glare.

"Medieval, innit?" Aubrey asked nobody in particular. "From a knight?"

The Viscount shook his head, too awed by the discovery to consider his audience.

"No, not a knight. That's a Roman cavalry helmet. First century, AD."

"Maybe it's more war booty," offered Kasim, "Brought here after one of Boudica's raids."

Clare broke her silence at last.

"Let's not go down that road again, shall we?"

"Maybe not Boudica herself," he said, "But the booty idea is something to consider. We're right beside the ancient water line here, and a war trophy would have made a powerful offering."

In all the speculation, Aubrey had lost interest. His attention was back on the helmet, and he was using both hands to pry it from the earth.

"Stop," said Jay. "Please, please, stop. We need to take photographs, make measurements, ensure that we record everything that we can."

There were some laughs and some hushed insults from the metal detectorists around them. A great treasure had been found and lay waiting to be claimed by its discoverer. No one was going to let some foreign archaeologist intrude.

"Don't worry yourself, Yank," said a triumphant Aubrey. "I pride myself on being a reasonable man. You can have the helmet, soon as I pry it free. And then it's yours to study…"

His thin lips cracked into a smile.

"…for the rest of the afternoon."

Samantha felt her pulse begin to race. It wasn't much time, but it might be all they needed. Surely, a find like this would bring Catesby's project to a halt at once. Had Graham just saved Wardy from its owner? And even she could not keep Boudica from her mind.

The helmet sat on the table in the middle of the Ridge & Furrow late that afternoon, laid out on a piece of protective rubber foam.

"Even Catesby will admit that it's spectacular," Clare said, as she and Samantha examined it together. "And if anything will affect his plans, this is it."

The rest of the Iceni were in a riotous mood. Stuart and Kasim had cleared the floor for an improvised game of Devil among the Tailors, using a unit string and plumb bob for the striker, and empty pint glasses for pins. Jay had joined in with equal gusto, and laughed and clapped along with the group as his first attempt sent shattered glass across the floor.

Samantha was too engrossed with the helmet to give the mischief much notice. The right-side cheek flap had been twisted and torn away, telling of agony and death. Her mind filled with the horror of war, the wild brutality of Boudica's uprising.

She looked away and up to the pub's low ceiling. Between the oaken beams, burned into the yellowing plaster, were numbers, names, and nicknames—"Pressure Boys," "The Wild Hares," and "4 June '44."

"What are those?" she asked Stuart, when he came to place his empty pint glass on her table.

"Last wills and testaments," he said. "The markings of the soldiers stationed here in the Second World War—both Brits and Yanks. Did it with their cigarette lighters before they shipped out. Some never returned."

It was a sobering realization. Whether it was the Icenis and Romans, or Saxons or Normans, or Nazis, Americans, and Brits, war was another of England's traditions, how things had always been done.

The portraits of long-dead fellows stared out on the revelry in quiet judgment. But Samantha shared the corner with living eyes as well, distracting her from her research. Oona was at the other small table, her black clothes rendering her invisible in the shadows. All that could be seen was her cold, blue stare. And she was muttering again. Must be going over her lines, Samantha thought. But then she noticed the phone pressed to the actress's ear as some whispered conversation reached its end.

The door burst inward, crashing against the wall and sending a blast of icy air across the joyous crowd. A nervous hush fell across the team as Catesby barreled in. Beside him strode Ned Aubrey, his yellow teeth bared in a cruel smile, his flat plaid cap clutched in his long, stained fingers.

The Lord Professor pried off his comical earmuffs and shuffled to the central table, approaching the helmet like a pilgrim to a shrine. Evan shrunk away.

"My," said Catesby, and lifted the object from its place. "My, my, my."

Yes, Samantha thought, it's yours. British law said as much. Catesby could do with it whatever he wanted.

But Samantha didn't expect *this*. Catesby held the helmet above his head for a drawn-out moment, and then brought it reverentially down atop his mop of hair. It was a self-coronation. And, to Samantha's horror, the professor had become the emperor of her nightmares.

"Well?" Catesby barked, and issued his loud, wet laugh. "How does it look?"

Samantha scanned the small assembly. Only Oona was smiling.

"So what happens now, Cairn?" asked Jay. "Clearly we'll need more time."

Catesby shook his head.

"Bad news on that front, old boy. My developers have moved the date up again, I'm afraid. They'd like to lay the foundations as soon as the ground has thawed. "

Their murmur of horrified gasps widened Catesby's smile and Aubrey's crooked grin beside him.

"How much time?" asked Clare.

"Another week should be sufficient for your project, I would think," Catesby replied. "What say we conclude by the time of my regatta? That way, you all can focus on the festivities."

With that, the Lord Professor strode to the door, the Roman helmet still atop his head. There was a hushed pause before the volume rose again, the happy sounds of moments before replaced by howls of outrage.

And that's when Oona stood, donned her coat, and threaded her way through the tables to slip out into the cold.

---

The chaos in the Ridge & Furrow was so intense that no one noticed Oona's departure. No one but Samantha. For reasons she couldn't quite explain, she pulled her own jacket on and followed.

Outside the pub, snow had fallen, snow on snow, so that the whole world seemed muffled and quiet. To the left, Samantha could see the tracks made by Aubrey and Catesby on their way south to the Department. But a more delicate trail led to the right, to the north and out of Rose Crescent.

The temperature had dropped again and the city was quiet, remarkably so, with only a few townspeople braving the wind and cold. Oona's trail north was easy to trace through the city's historic core.

Before long, Samantha met the major thoroughfare that led to the Cam Bridge. *A* Cam Bridge, anyway, as a sequence of them had spanned the river here for more than 2,000 years. Oona was nowhere to be seen. Samantha stopped for a moment, sucking in the searing cold air and watching the thin stream of townspeople hurry through the darkening hour toward home.

She spied a stationary figure on the bridge before her, staring out over the ice-flecked water. It was Oona. Samantha just hadn't recognized her.

The student had transformed herself en route—her severe elegance had somehow become a more casual kind of beauty. She had gathered her prim haircut into a short ponytail, unbuttoned her tight black coat, and relaxed her hurried gait. Even her face was different—new makeup made her flushed and healthy looking instead of the usual ashen pale.

The effect was complete when a car pulled up beside her and Oona's mouth widened into a warm smile. A distinguished, older woman emerged from the backseat. She used a sturdy black cane, and her white fur coat matched the color of the snow, exactly.

"It's so nice to meet you. In person, I mean, after all our talks on the phone."

"And you," said the gentlewoman, shifting her cane so that she could shake Oona's offered hand. "As I've said, Catesby and I have had our differences, but this is an important occasion, and I am prepared to help you honor it however I am able."

Oona looked convincingly touched. It was strange to see her so warm.

"I am delighted to hear it. Now then, shall I lead the way?"

Samantha ducked behind a snow-topped car, expecting them to walk back into town. But to her surprise, Oona led the woman around the foot of the bridge, down a stairway to the river, and into a waiting punt. It was an odd place for a meeting. But a poleman was ready for them, prepared to steer them along the Cam.

"Please mind the gap," Oona said, offering the woman a hand.

Samantha looked around for a place to hide so she could hear whatever happened next. But the river was a tidy one these days, controlled by locks and hemmed in by concrete banks, and there was no way to approach without being seen. Instead, she crept low to the center of the bridge, straining for whatever snatches of conversation she could hear as the punt passed by beneath her.

"I apologize for holding the meeting like this," said Oona. "I just wanted to make sure we wouldn't be overheard. And to give you some good Cambridge fun, of course."

Her voice sounded strange—and it wasn't just the echo between the bridge and water. Gone were the actress's crisp London vowels. They had been replaced by the earthier sound of some other region. What part was she playing now?

The poleman gave a flick with his pole, and they floated away upstream.

"I know my request is slightly unorthodox," Oona continued. "I hope this won't cause you problems."

"It shouldn't, if you're as cautious as you promise," said the gentlewoman. "And as I said, it befits the occasion."

"Thank you, m'lady," said Oona, her altered voice fading down the river. "What I need from you is this…"

Samantha stood now, trying to listen as the boat drifted around the bend, past the colleges of Magdalene and St. John's. But just before the punt disappeared from view, the poleman gave a sharp look backward.

Samantha froze. She knew this man. It was the same one she'd seen on the Railway Bridge before he lit the Cam aflame. On Castle Hill too, she realized, and in the Old Library itself. He was garbed in the same green army jacket, the same black hat pulled low over his eyes.

But this time, he hadn't expected to see her. His scarf was looser than before, thrown casually around to warm him, not to disguise his face. This wasn't Ned Aubrey; she was sure of it. This was someone much, much worse.

The "X" of scars was seared into her vision. And even after the boat had disappeared from view, she couldn't stop her hands from shaking at her sides.

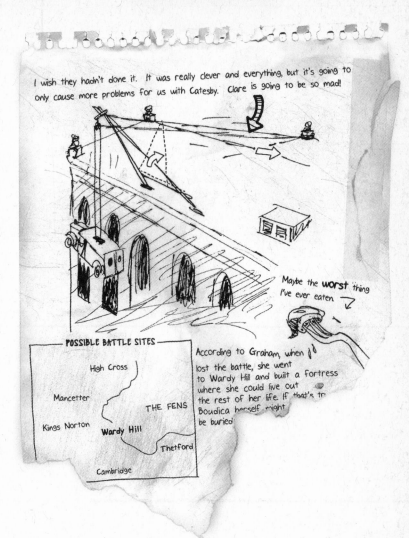

I wish they hadn't done it. It was really clever and everything, but it's going to only cause more problems for us with Catesby. Clare is going to be so mad!

Maybe the **worst** thing I've ever eaten

POSSIBLE BATTLE SITES

High Cross

Mancetter

THE FENS

Kings Norton

Wardy Hill

Thetford

Cambridge

According to Graham, when sh̶e lost the battle, she went to Wardy Hill and built a fortress where she could live out the rest of her life. If that's tru̶e Boudica herself might be buried

# CHAPTER 14

**B**y the time Samantha retraced her steps to the Ridge & Furrow, Jay was gone. He wasn't in his rooms in the college either. Only when she checked Trinity Hall's back lawn did she find him at a picnic table, bent over his books in the cold.

"He's here, Uncle Jay," she gasped. "He's followed us to Cambridge!"

Jay looked up from his research, annoyed by the interruption. Samantha knew why. The stakes were so much higher now—with Catesby's approaching deadline and the growing list of finds. That he had chosen to sit outside meant he was trying his best to concentrate.

"What are you talking about? Who?"

Samantha couldn't bring herself to say the name, but Jay read her face correctly.

"Adam Quint? No, Sam. No way."

"But I saw him!" she went on. "Just now, in town. He's up to something, he and Oona. They're going to try to hurt us."

Jay closed his book and leaned back in his wooden chair.

"Oh, Sam. Come on. Adam Quint? Why would he come here? Why would he bother? He's in a tough spot, in terms of his degree. He hadn't finished his research in Peru, remember, and has to start his research over—almost completely from scratch. He doesn't have time to worry about his old professor or go all the way to Cambridge, of all places."

Samantha did not agree. The seared "X" across Adam's throat and jaw may have reoriented his priorities. She was here, and so was Jay. That was reason enough to come to England.

"*Cálmate*, Sam. Okay? I'm under the gun now, and Clare is less and less willing to help me. Please, can I get back to work?"

There was nothing she could do. So she met his aggravated look and nodded, then turned to leave him in the cold.

———

Revenge was called for, the Iceni decided. But Catesby's latest outrage required something far more than a caricature in snow.

The plan was hatched late that night at an Indian restaurant between hurled handfuls of korma and naan. Samantha was not invited. As Evan continued to remind her, she was not an Iceni and never could be. She was just a girl, after all, and "there are hundreds of years of tradition to consider…"

When she awoke next day, Evan was already up and gone. She would have to bike to the river on her own for rowing practice. Tom gave her a nod as she walked through the Porters' Lodge, then returned to the tabloid newspaper he had spread across his desk.

Outside, the morning had not yet broken, and new snow crunched beneath her feet. But when she stepped out into Trinity Lane, Samantha could tell that something was off. There was someone blocking her path.

"G'morning, Archaeo Cox. Practice is canceled this morning, I'm afraid."

It was the Green Man, smiling broadly in the middle of the narrow lane. What was he doing here? He was due at the boathouse in fifteen minutes, along with Samantha and the rest of the team. But then, far ahead she spied the disheveled Viscount, his back to her, rubbing his arms for warmth. The two of them seemed to be acting as lookouts. What sort of trouble was Stuart planning now?

"What's going on?"

"Some mischief, a dash of madcappery, and a little monkey business, besides. I'd go back inside if I were you, get a kip in before breakfast. It's almost New Year's Eve, after all. You'll want to be rested for whatever celebration you've got planned."

"Come on," she said, stuffing her freezing hands into her pockets. "What's up?"

The Viscount laughed with such gusto he almost slipped on the ice.

"The perfect question, Archaeo Cox. Look and see for yourself!"

Samantha followed the upward thrust of his chin. Some sort of shadow swayed above them, blocking out the lingering stars. In the faint light of the street lamp, Samantha could make out the glint of metal, the matte black of rubber, the shimmer of grille, and the twinkle of bug-eyed headlights. It was Catesby's antique car, rising slowly through the air.

"He keeps his keys in the ignition," the Viscount said. "Must not think anyone would dare to take it."

"Steady," she heard above her, in Stuart's gentle whisper.

"Wait," came Evan's strained response from some unseen corner of the roof. "My hands are slipping."

It was the most audacious prank Samantha had ever seen. The top of the Senate House must have been seventy feet off the ground, and the car was already about halfway up.

"Ready?" Stuart asked. "Okay, now pull!"

There was a series of grunts, in three or four voices, and the car surged upward once more. A rope had been passed through the windows, front and back, then looped through a pulley rigged to the building's roof with a triangular metal frame. Another rope dangled so that Kasim could guide the car from below. But still it swung, threatening the ancient masonry on both sides of the passageway.

"Not always easy to find parking in this town," said Kasim, keeping an eye on the swaying hulk. "We're giving his lordship the perfect spot."

"It is awfully iconic," the Viscount agreed.

Samantha stared.

"He'll kill you!"

"Us? But we have nothing to do with it!" said the Viscount. "We're out on the Cam with you!"

"A scratch crew from Churchill College is borrowing our blades this morning," Kasim explained, proud of a plan that was clearly his own. "They're leaving their ridiculous pink ones on shore. Everyone will think that they're us out there. No one will know the difference."

There was a creak above them as the vehicle jolted upward once more, and then a clunk, a string of swearing, and laughter.

"All right up there?" Kasim asked.

Stuart's face, cold and red, leaned out over the passage.

"Evan's slipped, is all. Nearly cowped it off the side."

"Is he okay?" Samantha asked.

"Yeah, Sam. He's fine. Colorful vocabulary your brother has, though. Never heard someone say 'sodding' and 'blooming' and 'fiddlesticks' all in the same sentence. Or with such vigor."

Everyone flinched when a clatter was heard up the alley. But it was just Gog and Magog, pushing a strange contraption in the direction of the Archaeology Department.

"They're taking his Lordship a replacement," the Viscount explained

It was an Iceni-style chariot, made of cardboard and rollicking across the cobbles on two warped bicycle tires.

"Final pull, boys," Kasim said, and again Samantha looked up.

This would be the last, yes, but it would be trickier than most. The team would have to pull the car not just up, but over and onto the Senate House roof. There was a groan as the rope strained against the winch, and she caught her breath as the car swung wildly, a wheel glancing against the stonework of the balustrade. But then Catesby's pride and joy was at last at rest and parked in the worst spot in the world.

———

"Have a good morning, guys?" Jay asked his niece and nephew when he met them at the Department. "I hear it was *uplifting*."

Samantha frowned. So he must have been in on it too.

"Anyway, Sam," he went on, "there's a surprise waiting for you at the site today. Our loss might just be your gain."

"What do you mean?" she asked. But Jay only smiled in response.

She didn't have her answer until the team's vehicles pulled up at the pillbox, and she saw Graham Aubrey waiting.

"You have Catesby to thank for this," said Jay, as Samantha tried to check her wide smile. "With the new time limit, we need all the help we can get."

She got out of the car and trudged forward, her backpack over her shoulder.

"All right, Sam?" Graham asked her.

It was the typical British greeting, and by now she knew how to respond.

"All right," she said. "Are you helping us today?"

"Today, tomorrow, and every day until the project's through! My schedule's free now, since the concert is over."

"Then where's your metal detector?" asked Evan. "Where are all your criminal friends?"

Graham didn't seem bothered by the insult. But his face grew tight and serious when Jay began to address him.

"If you work with us, you follow our rules. Finds get bagged and sorted, not taken home to keep. Okay?"

"I do understand, sir. Lord Catesby explained it all to me already."

"Good," said Jay, smiling again. "Well then. Sam, why don't you partner with Graham today? Stuart can work with me while you show Graham the ropes. If you don't mind, I mean."

Jay knew very well that she didn't mind, and she felt her face go a little hot from his teasing. But she was able to give a casual nod.

"Let's go, Graham. I'll show you everything."

The boy hauled his backpack over his shoulder and followed Samantha to the unit she and Stuart had opened the day before. It was just how she'd left it—its profiles sheer, its floor flat and even—a perfect rectangle, sunk into the earth.

"Brilliant," said Graham when she'd finished. "Can I climb down?"

"Yeah," she said, pleased by his deference. "Just be careful of the sidewalls."

There was room enough for both of them on the floor of the unit, but only just. As Samantha slid in beside him, their shoulders touched, and they both laughed—embarrassed.

But then Graham grew quiet. He took his gloves from his hand and stroked the earth at their feet, tracing the contours with his fingers.

"You did this?" he asked, and she nodded.

"Bloody hell, it's smooth," he said. "You don't want to see me try this!"

"I do, actually," said Samantha. "But you'll need the right tools."

At this Graham grinned.

"I've brought me own."

He opened his backpack and poured a clattering heap out onto the unit floor. Samantha saw at once that these were not the tools of careful excavation, but the implements of a treasure hunter—all serrated scoops and thick metal probes—coarse tools for coarse digging.

But there was a sort of trowel in the pile and she plucked it out. The blade seemed longer than she was used to and skinnier—designed to gouge artifacts out of the earth.

"This'll do the trick," she said, and blushed again. The phrase seemed overly American.

They set to work. Samantha let Graham take the first turn with his trowel. He moved self-consciously, more accustomed to digging pits whenever his metal detector beeped. But he was open to her advice—almost desperately so—and summoning a bolt of courage, she even took hold of his sleeve and guided his hand across the unit floor in a smooth, even stroke.

This unit was full of pottery—the same, utilitarian stuff that they had been finding here for weeks. But it was like Graham couldn't see them, forcing his trowel through and brushing them aside.

"Wait, Graham. You've got to slow down."

She called his attention to each sherd, explaining each piece they came across as best she could—which one was a piece of a bowl, which a chunk of jar or beaker.

"Were these Boudica's too?"

His sudden question startled her, and her reply was harsher than she meant it to be.

"What do you mean, 'too?'"

"I mean, along with the bucket you found of hers. And…" his voice dropped to a whisper. "…my Iceni coin."

She shook her head.

"We don't know that, Graham. In fact, we don't know that Boudica was here at all."

Graham laughed.

"You might not, but I do, and so does everyone who lives nearby."

She looked up and out of the unit, scanning the site for Clare. She was more committed than ever to following the professor's instructions, to letting the archaeology speak for itself. But Clare was nowhere to be found. In fact, Samantha realized, she hadn't seen her all day.

"Okay," she said. "What's the story? What's Wardy's connection to Boudica?"

Graham's face cracked into a wide grin.

"She's buried here, you muppet! This is where she came to die."

Samantha shivered. But it wasn't from the cold.

"I thought she died in battle."

"No! Samantha. You don't know the story at all, do you?"

He told her how Boudica had raced to meet the Roman legion, building her army as she went. But the Governor General had swept down to meet her, his seasoned troops prepared to take on her ragtag Iceni throng. And then Graham told her of the speech she'd made to her assembled troops and how she'd let loose her hare—an old Celtic practice—to guide the course of battle.

"Her hair?" Samantha asked, remembering how the Warrior Queen was described as a redhead, with wild locks flowing to her waist.

"No, a hare. You know, like a big rabbit?" He put his fingers above his head to show a pair of ears.

"Anyway, it didn't help much. Her troops were trounced. Obliterated."

"I knew all that."

"You didn't know about the hare. And that's the best part. And what happened after the battle—where Boudica went next."

"Wasn't she killed?"

"No. Not in the battle. One story is that she took her own life. Another says she got sick and died."

He grinned.

"But that's not what we say 'round here."

Graham was every bit the showman that Jay was, mindful of the power a good story could wield.

"The hare she released before the battle? It was an offering to the Iceni goddess Andraste. Some people think it was to ask for help, to show her the best way to confront the Romans. But in our version—the local version—Boudica's hare led her toward home, to where she was out of danger, and where she could live to fight another day."

He took out his trowel, scratching out a map in their unit's perfect floor.

"This here is Thetford, where Boudica's palace might have been. And over here are High Cross, Mancetter, and Kings Norton—all possible sites of the final battle. Leaving Andraste out of it, if Boudica wanted to make her way back to her own territory, she would've needed to skirt the south part of the Fens. And all the while she and her surviving forces would be looking for higher ground where they could hole up."

He plunged his trowel into the center of the map.

"Wardy Hill. Where the hare finally came to a stop, the story goes. A good choice too, I reckon. Fens on one side—no one's getting through them—and a good long view of the mainland on the other. Good place to come after taking on the whole Roman Empire, I would reckon. Here she and her surviving people could live out the rest of their lives in peace."

Samantha thought for a moment, silent. Hare or no hare, there were a lot of "if's" in Graham's story, to say the least. But *if* Boudica had survived the battle, and *if* the survivors had stopped on their way back home, the rest of the theory made sense.

Was this what the archaeology had been saying all along? Did that explain the lack of Roman goods, even into the Roman period? Were the helmet and chopped-up skeleton the grisly souvenirs of that final battle? And the stave of the bucket—a typical burial item—had that been placed in or near Boudica's grave, when the Queen had eventually died?

Maybe this was Boudica's refuge, after all. So said Graham. So said local legend. And so said Jay, more or less, even if he'd never been that explicit. And while the artifacts didn't say it, not exactly, they seemed to fit the story well enough.

Samantha's imagination could be restrained no longer. She was convinced. The Warrior Queen had lived out her final days on Wardy, and she was waiting for Samantha to find her.

———

They worked that way until noon, side by side on the frozen unit floor. Graham was improving, hour after hour. His work with the trowel—once a spastic series of gouges and pokes—had grown even and smooth. He took his time at the screen as well, squeezing the clods of frigid clay between his fingers for any artifacts he might have missed.

But what she liked most was his company. She loved the way he pursed his lips as he worked and the way he brushed the hair from his eyes—now free of the gel she hated. And she loved how he sang, the whole morning long:

*Oh mother, dear mother, I have had a strange dream,*
*Young William lies floating in a watery stream.*

Samantha placed her trowel aside to listen.

*Dear William, my William, do not adventure in,*
*For there's death and false waters in the lakes of cold Fen.*

She felt a chill go up her arms.

*Oh where was he drowned, where did he fall in?*
*For there's death and false waters in the lakes of cold Fen.*

The old song was true, Samantha thought. There was death here on Wardy Hill. And strife and heartache too. But now she had a friend to face them with.

———

They were so wrapped up in their work that they missed Jay's shouted announcement that it was time for lunch, and

Kasim had to come to retrieve them. They were the last to reach the pillbox, and Stuart gave her a congratulatory wink.

She grabbed the bag lunch from her backpack and looked for a place to sit down. But the team was too big to fit in the lab at any one time.

"Up here," Graham said, and they stepped back into the cold. He plucked the lunch bag from her hand and placed it lightly onto the pillbox's roof beside his own.

"Now climb up, Samantha," he said, knitting his fingers together.

She did as she was told, letting him heft her up and over so she could clamber onto the flat concrete slab. Graham pulled himself up behind her.

They sat side by side, their feet dangling off the edge. She opened the paper bag, pulling out a packaged coronation chicken sandwich, the usual small hard apple, and packet of steak-and-onion-flavored crisps. Graham set out a spoon, a napkin, and—finally—a small plastic tub with an aluminum lid.

"Sorry about the smell," he said, as he ripped the packaging clear.

It hit her immediately—a sharp, fishy stink like tuna, almost, but ten times stronger.

"Don't worry about it," she said, trying not to wrinkle her nose.

From the label on the foil, she saw that the handsome boy beside her had for lunch something called "jellied eels."

She had heard of the dish before—something Jay had

told when she was very, very little, and that Evan had repeated again and again in an attempt to turn her stomach. Even now, she remembered the details of their preparation—how the squirming creatures were cut into sections, boiled, and left to cool—the proteins in their bones firming the water into a firm, gelatinous, block.

"My dad loves them," Graham said, still apologetic. "It's an honest man's food, he always says."

Samantha smiled. She needed to do something to make the boy feel better.

"Can I try one?"

He smiled, surprised, and handed her his fork, then held out the plastic pot so she could help herself. The nearness of the dish burned her nostrils, and it took some effort to pry a section loose of its gelatin casing and pop it in her mouth.

"They're better with chili sauce," said Graham.

"No," said Samantha, trying hard not to gag. "It's fine how it is."

It wasn't that bad, to be honest—not after the first shocking bite. The eel itself was rubbery but tasted fine. It was the chunks of clear gelatin that were the challenge—a fishy taste in what felt like a dessert. But she managed to choke the whole thing down.

"Jellied eels go back centuries here in the Fens," said Graham. "Your Boudica probably ate them long, long ago. The whole place must've been crawling with the buggers then."

"They're eels, Graham. I don't think there was much crawling involved."

He laughed, and they finished their lunch in quiet conversation. Pressed close together, they looked down the gentle, rabbit-dotted slope to nearby Coveney village and past it across the Fens. The usual mealtime clamor rang out below them, rising and falling through the bunker's lookout slits. In Samantha's excitement, though, and in the beauty of the winter's day, the racket seemed to fade completely: overcome by wind and birdsong, layered over with the sound of her own heartbeat. And once or twice, she thought, of Graham's.

———————

Tom stopped her in the Porters' Lodge as she returned to Trinity Hall that evening, pulling her from her pleasant thoughts.

"Your uncle with you, miss?"

She shook her head.

"No. He's still at the pub with Dr. Barrows, working. He said he'd be back late."

Tom considered this a moment, then slid something to her across the desk. A book—one that her uncle had brought with him—old and tattered and losing its spine. It was a copy of the *Annals of Tacitus,* the ancient Roman text that recorded part of the Empire's history, the Boudica story included.

"It's an unfortunate bit of business, I'm afraid. The

bedder nicked it from your uncle's room. I caught him with it on the stairs."

Samantha froze.

"This bedder, what does he look like?"

"Like a bad memory, miss. He's been sacked. Won't be coming around here anymore. And even if he does, I'm changing the locks. No need for you to worry about it."

But Samantha worried all the same.

———————

The wrong Aubrey was waiting for them at Wardy Hill the next morning.

"Back again," he said, leering at Clare as she unlocked the pillbox door. "I'm your lucky charm."

"Nah," Jay answered, shouldering a pickax. "We've had better luck with your son."

The thin man's mouth thinned to a cruel, predatory grin.

"See here, mate. My boy came home last night, banging on about how he'll be a scientist one day, an arkkie, just like Doctor Jay Sutton! Wants to go to America, he says! Wants to study under you!"

Samantha watched her uncle's face turn red, even as he managed a smile.

"I'll tell the admissions office to keep an eye out for his application in a few years."

Aubrey's long arms closed the gap between him and her uncle in an instant and slammed Jay hard into the laboratory's concrete wall. Jay's pickax fell to the ground.

"You keep away from my son. You hear me?" Aubrey spat, his hands bunched around Jay's collar. "Lord Catesby gives us a good life here. We don't need nothing from the likes of you."

There was the honk of a horn, and their eyes turned to the road.

"Ah," said Aubrey, dusting off Jay's arms and shoulders. "Here's his lordship, now."

So Catesby had gotten his car back, after all. There had been work crews outside Samantha's window all night long erecting a massive crane. And now the Lord's prize possession screeched to a stop beside the site, looking a little scuffed.

The Lord Professor stepped onto the road, and three other men got out of the car to join him. They all carried clipboards and rolls of blueprints. Each wore a hard hat—an odd precaution, Samantha thought, on a barren, featureless hill.

"Don't mind us," said Catesby as he led his workers around the fence. "There are only six more days until we break ground on Vivant Romani. We have a few final measurements to take."

The engineers fanned out, taking readings, reviewing their plans, and probing the frozen soil with rods.

"This is the exact center of the park," she heard one say. "The Imperator's main support will be just over here."

Right where she had found the bucket stave, Samantha realized darkly. If Boudica was buried on Wardy Hill, she may well have been where the engineering team planned to drive the roller coaster's central posts.

They wandered over to the pillbox.

"This we can leave, if you like," said another member of Catesby's crew. "We can always incorporate it into the toilets."

"No," said Catesby. "That won't do at all."

For a moment Samantha thought he was planning to save this reminder of British heroism from such an inglorious fate. But then he spoke again.

"I require the hill itself, gentleman, as nature made it. A tabula rasa. Ned, will you be a good fellow and lend a hand?"

Clare shouted out and Jay threw down his tools, but they were too late. Aubrey hefted Jay's pickax over his shoulder, then brought it crashing into the side of the historic building. The impact exposed a hidden seam in the concrete, and a panel of concrete came dislodged. Another blow would knock it loose and collapse the entire structure.

"Wait!" Clare cried. "Our finds are still inside!"

Ned gave Catesby a sidelong look, asking silent permission to take a second swing.

"My sincerest apologies, Doctor! What an awkward misunderstanding," said the Lord Professor, as the excavation vans pulled up and their doors flew open.

"We must be patient, Ned. There are only five more days."

And then he turned toward Jay, his hand up, his stubby fingers spread.

"Five."

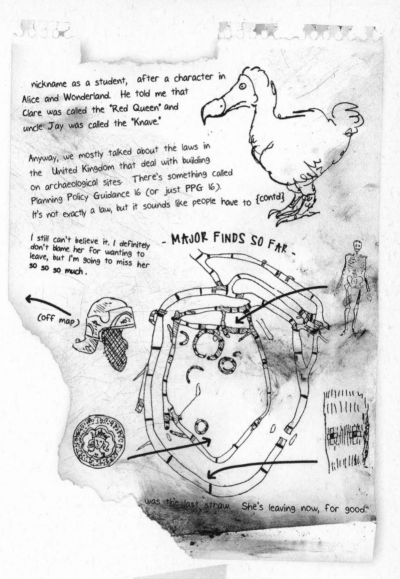

nickname as a student, after a character in Alice and Wonderland. He told me that Clare was called the "Red Queen" and uncle Jay was called the "Knave."

Anyway, we mostly talked about the laws in the United Kingdom that deal with building on archaeological sites. There's something called Planning Policy Guidance 16 (or just PPG 16). It's not exactly a law, but it sounds like people have to {contd}

I still can't believe it. I definitely don't blame her for wanting to leave, but I'm going to miss her so so so much.

- MAJOR FINDS SO FAR -

(off map)

was the last straw. She's leaving now, for good.

SSFNb2-WH: 15

# CHAPTER 15

A stapled stack of papers was waiting for Samantha when she returned to her room. Jay must have printed them out that morning when she was on the river and slipped them beneath her door.

"NATIONAL HERITAGE ASSET LISTING AND DESIGNATION APPLICATION," it said across the cover, and remembering her conversation with Stuart some weeks before, she at once knew what Jay wanted her to do. If Wardy Hill was put on the list of protected sites, it couldn't be touched—even by the owner of the land.

She flipped through the pages, bitter that her uncle was once again involving her in something that he shouldn't. But Jay was right and Clare was wrong. There was a link between Wardy and Boudica; Samantha was sure of it. And if no one else was willing to stand up to Catesby, the job would fall to her.

So for the rest of the evening and late into the night, she

sat in the brightest corner of the Ridge & Furrow with the forms spread out before her.

"Homework," she explained when people asked, but she made sure to cover the papers until they had moved on.

The paperwork was as complicated as Stuart had warned her when she first arrived. The form asked for things like the latitude and longitude of the site, and its postcode and national grid reference. These things Jay would know, but he wasn't anywhere to be found. Clare too—but Samantha didn't dare ask her.

The rest of the application Samantha filled in with gusto, eager to prove that the site was of "national importance," as was required. Where the form asked for information on how rare the site was and explained that sites with "with few known comparators are more likely to be scheduled," Samantha wrote that Wardy Hill had been home to the mighty Warrior Queen Boudica at the time of her death—and that *no* other known site could boast that. Where the form asked for information on the site's potential to "contribute to our knowledge through further study," she explained that the study that had been done so far pointed to a warrior queen.

The final question may have been the simplest, but it was the only one that gave her any pause: "Is the heritage asset currently at risk of demolition, alteration, removal, or salvage? If so, please identify that risk."

She breathed deeply, picked up the pen, and wrote the following out in full:

Lord Professor Cairn Colin Catesby, Baron Catesby of Coveney.

It felt good to finish the application. It was, at least, a try. But only when the envelope was sealed did she notice the small print on the instruction page, explaining that applicants could expect to wait at least five months before receiving a response. Her heart sank. By then, Wardy would be leveled, and park-goers would be screaming along the Imperator's twisting tracks.

"You finish whatever it was you were working on?" Jay asked that evening, as they walked home from the pub that night. But Samantha refused to play along.

"It's too late," she said. "Might as well throw it in the trash."

"Rubbish," said Jay, affecting a decent impression of Catesby. "Rubbish! Give it here."

With a long, tired sigh, she uncinched her backpack and pulled out the thick, white envelope. Jay borrowed her pen to scrawl a few words above the address in his messy, boyish hand.

ATTN: THE DODO

"This'll get it to the top of the pile. The Dodo's an old friend."

Samantha knew that "ATTN" stood for "attention" and that using it in the address would direct the envelope to a particular person. But who? Jay didn't elaborate. And when Samantha slid the envelope through the slot for

London courier in the Porters' Lodge, she was still wondering how a person called the Dodo could be of any help at all.

———

He stood waiting for them the very next morning, the last one of the year. He was a thickset man, and his unruly red hair seemed to move independently of the gentle morning breeze. An ill-fitting suit hung lopsidedly over a shirt that had come partially untucked, and his tie was knotted with all the refinement of a monkey's fist. His goofy grin completed the look, all big teeth and gums.

"By my lovely lady Queen!" he said.

"By our stalwart, steadfast sovereign!" Jay answered.

Another Iceni, Samantha realized, as the two laughed and embraced. Jay stepped back, giving his friend a once-over.

"Good to see you, Dodo. It's been a while."

"Ages! And my, have you been busy!"

Samantha frowned. Was he talking about what had happened in Peru? Had word gotten out? But the way that the Dodo was looking at Samantha and her brother made his meaning clear.

"No, no." Jay laughed. "These are my niece and nephew. But I guess they might as well be my own kids. Guys, this is Simon Daub, from the Heritage Office."

"A pleasure," said the Dodo, and Samantha could tell that he meant it. "Your uncle is a sort of hero of mine. And a onetime rival. How is Doctor Barrows, anyway?"

Jay grew uncharacteristically awkward.

"You can ask her yourself," he said.

Clare was rounding the corner now, holding court among a few of the Iceni.

"No," whispered the Dodo. "You two?"

"Hello, Simon," Clare said, before Jay could reply. "What on earth are you doing here?"

"I'm popping along with you, it seems," said Simon. "Site evaluation."

Clare's eyes narrowed.

"For scheduling? Which site?"

The Dodo chuckled and held up his clipboard to show her.

"*Your* site, I'm discovering now. Wardy Hill, Coveney, Cambridgeshire. I had a mysterious call to go into work early this morning, and the application had already arrived by rush delivery. I came straight away."

Clare's face had darkened. She glared at Jay.

"This is all we need, Jay Sutton. Thanks for that."

But Jay shook his head.

"You've got the wrong Sutton, Clare. But I'm glad that Samantha took the initiative. Someone needs to stand up to his lordship. Someone's got to save the site from him."

Samantha flushed a deep and angry red. She had been used. And now Clare would be mad at her for taking her uncle's side. Catesby would be furious at her too. And dangerous.

Clare sighed.

"It's not your fault, Samantha. You haven't done any-thing wrong."

But her exhausted voice said otherwise.

"And you two," she said, turning on the Dodo and Jay. "Watch yourselves. This isn't some Iceni Society prank. Jay's career's at stake, and mine as well."

Dodo was quick to assure her.

"There will be no mischief, monkey business, or mad-cappery, Clare. I will make my determination on the evi-dence alone, not on my friendship with Jay."

"Nor your history with Catesby?" asked Clare.

"Ah," said the Dodo. "That I can't guarantee."

And he and his old friend erupted with laughter.

—————

"Listing is a tricky business," the Dodo said, as the car sped north through the frozen flats. "We can't save everything, of course. And it takes a lot these days, with the politics the way they are. We have to be very choosey."

"But this time Boudica's involved," Samantha said.

Her anger had ebbed a little. There were larger issues at stake than her uncle's manipulation. This was her chance to save Wardy Hill for science. And for Boudica too.

"I read your application, and if what you claim proves true, I think there'd be little argument of Wardy Hill's national importance. But finding a link to Boudica— real, supportable proof—will be like finding a needle in a haystack."

"This haystack seems *made* of needles," said Jay, swerving around a patch of ice. "High-status items, Roman war booty, Iceni coins…she's there, Dodo. And with your help, we're going to find her."

"And if so, we'll drink to her eternal remembrance. But I will be objective, Jay. I have to be. I want you to know that."

Jay only smiled.

"You just wait, Dodo. We'll make a believer out of you yet."

————

As soon as they stepped from the car, the Dodo's paperwork went flying, borne aloft by an Arctic blast of wind. With Samantha's help, he spent the first fifteen minutes on-site plucking forms from muddy spoil heaps and out of frozen puddles. By the time they were finished, and by the time the pages were safely corralled under the clamp of his clipboard, the Dodo's suit was a rumpled mess, and his wind-plastered hair looked like it would never be the same.

Samantha had submitted the application, so it was decided that she would be the one to give him the tour—pointing out the lines of the ringwork, the contours of the eaves gullies, and the sources of all the major finds. The Dodo was silent until she led him into the pillbox and showed him where those finds were kept—the coin that Graham had given her, the stave, the chop-marked bones, and photos of the Roman helmet—which was now in Catesby's hands. Clare looked on, displeased.

"Your uncle was right," said the Dodo. "This haystack may be more needles than hay."

Samantha felt a quiver of hope.

"You will have to keep me informed of any new development," said the Dodo, examining the coin up close. "It might not take much more."

He caught Clare's exasperated frown.

"I retract that," he said. "That was most definitely off the record."

But Clare had heard enough. She looked at Samantha, her eyes full of disappointment, and sadly trudged outside.

———

Clare's College was Clare College, a fact both that Jay and Evan found endlessly amusing.

"Clare is a good fit for Clare," Jay had joked, far too many times. "That much is clare."

"Which Clare?" her brother would ask. "Clare's Clare or Clare's Clare?"

Even Samantha agreed that it was a perfect match—and not just the name alone. Clare College was like Trinity Hall's slightly older sister, its graceful brickwork abutting Jay's college to the south and spanning the river with one of the university's most beautiful bridges. But that night after dinner, as Samantha entered the other college's gates and slunk through its Porters' Lodge unseen, she was too troubled to give much notice to its beauty.

It was time for Samantha to level with Clare Barrows. Boudica's enemies were closing in, and she needed the young professor on her side.

She didn't know where to find her, though. She entered the great Old Court and looked around, her eyes drawn to a faint glow across the cobbles. Across the snowy space a door was open, marked "Buttery," and she made her way toward it. But nearing the arch she halted. There was an argument in full swing inside. She could hear Clare's sharp voice and her uncle's, cold and unyielding. He too must have come to make his case.

Samantha slipped inside and then down the narrow staircase she found. The voices grew louder, bouncing in strange angles off the vaulted ceiling.

"You know how much I need this, Clare. You know what's happened with my job back home."

"Yes, Jay. I know precisely. That's exactly why I invited you here, if you remember. This was to be your chance for redemption."

Samantha sat quietly on the steps, hidden behind a pilaster, as her uncle's voice went on.

"But that chance is here on Wardy, not with Cairn. He'll never hire me, especially not now. What I need is a discovery. Something important. It's the only way my university will take me back."

Take him back? Samantha thought. What was Jay talking about?

"Jay, this isn't it. Wardy Hill is not your ticket."

"What is it, then?"

"A modest Iron Age settlement, nothing more. A place where people gathered in some number as the world left them behind. People who couldn't adapt. People who were on their way out."

"People like the Iceni after the coming of Rome," Jay said. "People like Boudica."

"Come on, Jay. This is the conclusion you draw from some bits of disarticulated bone? A sole bucket fragment? We have the helmet, yes, but it's so far away from the enclosure that I'm not convinced of any relationship. And we have a single Iceni coin—which, I might add, strikes me as particularly odd."

"What about the stories in the area, of Boudica and her final refuge? Oral history is a legitimate line of evidence, Clare."

Samantha had heard Jay share this view before, how archaeology corroborated the age-old migration stories of tribes in the American Southwest, for instance, and vice versa. Now she nodded in the dark, hoping this argument would hit its target.

But Clare wasn't looking for a fight. Her voice grew gentle.

"Jay, I would love it if Wardy had something to do with Boudica. I really would. Finding her would be the fulfillment of a childhood dream. But we're archaeologists, remember? We tell the artifacts' stories. It's not their job to tell ours."

"Yes, Clare. We're archaeologists, and we're good

at what we do. But we're both at the mercy of someone who's not."

It must have been Clare who now slammed something hard, the shock of it ringing off the ceiling.

"Is that what all this is about? Your petty little rivalry? This is not just about putting people's cars on roofs, Jay, or your wounded pride. This is my career we're talking about—all I've ever worked for—and you seem more than willing to put it all at risk."

Jay must have stood then, his chair screeching against the floor. But Clare went on, enraged.

"Cairn's my boss, if you haven't forgotten. And once Vivant Romani is open for business, I'll bloody well be the first in the queue."

There was a loud bang. Jay must have kicked something—a metal trash can, or the leg of a table or chair. And then there were angry footsteps, heading her way. Samantha had nowhere to hide. Her uncle's reddened eyes met hers as he charged past her up the stairs. And when Clare trudged by some moments later, deflated and drawn, Samantha knew that something good had ended.

———————

Clare did not invite Samantha to join her, but she did so all the same, following the British professor through the darkened college in tense, uneasy silence. She stayed several paces behind as they left the majestic Old Court, and when they passed over the Cam on Clare College's bridge, she took special note of the wedge famously missing from one of its stone ornaments. That's how she felt now: unfinished, incomplete.

"Not now, Samantha," Clare said, as they trudged through the snowy Fellows' Garden. "Please. I need to be alone."

But Samantha pressed on after her—across Queen's Road, through the second Porters' Lodge, and into Clare College's western campus. They didn't speak as they entered the inner courtyard, and Samantha almost lost her on a turning set of stairs. But when she came to the top, Clare was waiting and held the door open for her to enter.

The professor's lodgings were every bit as warm and cheerful as Samantha had expected. Photographs covered the walls and lined the big stone mantel: some with Clare in Paris, Rome, and Lima; one with Jay in their student days, King's Chapel in the background; another as a skinny teenager, dressed as an archaeologist from the movies; and another with Samantha in Peru.

Samantha sank into a plush orange sofa, waiting in silence as the archaeologist prepared two cups of tea. A suitcase was open on the floor and mostly packed. Clare had already been preparing to leave.

"I do love Cambridge," she said now, as she handed Samantha her mug. "But I love getting away from it too."

"You're going?"

"I am, Samantha. Yes. Home to Salisbury until the new term starts."

Samantha felt a tear well up, hot and unwanted.

"Why?"

Clare did not respond, but Samantha knew the answer anyway. She had been forced to make a decision. And for Clare, the choice was a clear one.

As they finished their tea in silence, Samantha drummed up her courage. This might be her last chance to ask her the question that had been troubling her for weeks.

"Is Boudica there, do you think? Is she really up at Wardy?"

Clare was quiet for a long, long time, then sat down beside her and pulled her in close.

"I'd like to think so, Samantha. I really would. But that's probably not something that archaeology can answer. Your uncle is just chasing a ghost, I'm afraid."

Clare squeezed Samantha's knee.

"But that's his choice now. I've given up. So come on, then. Off you go. I need to pack my things."

She stood and pulled Samantha to her feet. But Samantha had another question, and her voice broke as she voiced it aloud.

"Will I ever get to see you again?"

Clare's eyes softened.

"I'm sure you will, Samantha Sutton. You'll be a professional archaeologist yourself, soon enough. We'll work together, you and I. We'll be a team."

The answer cheered her, but it wasn't the only one Samantha was looking for.

"And what about my uncle?"

This final question Clare declined to answer. She put

her arm around Samantha for a long minute and held her close, without so much as a word. And then she ushered her quickly toward the door.

———————

Samantha spent the next two hours walking through the age-old city on her own, lost in troubled thought. The few people who remained in Cambridge were now preparing for the New Year, and she saw straggling bands of teenagers out in the streets, shivering in their party clothes. The group of King's College choirboys was among them, lounging beside the ice-choked Mill Pool. When she spotted Graham in their midst she immediately turned around. He couldn't see her, not like this, with her face all red and her hair stuck to her cheeks from crying.

But it was too late.

"All right, Sam?" he said, jogging up alongside her.

"All right," she managed.

His smile was so warm and friendly. If he had noticed how upset she was, he was hiding it well. Or maybe he was just sparing her the embarrassment. But there was a quaver in his voice, and she realized that he was nervous.

"Um, listen, Samantha. I was wondering if you might fancy meeting me tonight?"

She hesitated. All she wanted was to curl up in bed and hide. Clare was gone. Catesby was ascendant. And, if her suspicions were right, her worst enemy in the world was here in Cambridge and eager to do her harm.

But then she looked over to where Graham's friends were sitting, watching his every move.

"Sure," she said glumly. "Okay."

Relief coursed across Graham's face.

"Brilliant. I'll meet you just outside King's, then? Half past ten?"

She nodded and set off toward home. It was a date with a boy she liked. Her first date ever. And there was no way the timing could be worse.

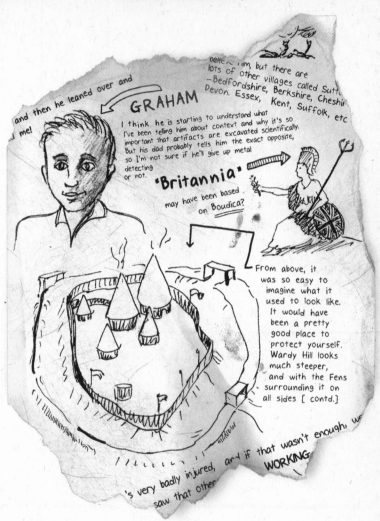

and then he leaned over and
...d me!

belie... ...im, but there are
lots of other villages called Sutt...
—Bedfordshire, Berkshire, Cheshir...
Devon, Essex, Kent, Suffolk, etc

**GRAHAM**

I think he is starting to understand what
I've been telling him about context and why it's so
important that artifacts are excavated scientifically.
But his dad probably tells him the exact opposite,
so I'm not sure if he'll give up metal
detecting
or not.

"Britannia"

may have been based
on Boudica?

From above, it
was so easy to
imagine what it
used to look like.
It would have
been a pretty
good place to
protect yourself.
Wardy Hill looks
much steeper,
and with the Fens
surrounding it on
all sides [ contd.]

's very badly injured, and if that wasn't enough, w...
saw that other

WORKING

SSFNb2–WH: 16

249

# CHAPTER 16

Samantha got ready to meet Graham in secret, eager to avoid Evan's teasing and craving just a little time alone. She was in no mood for flirting. But she did have questions that Graham could answer. His father and Catesby seemed to go a long way back. What did Graham know of the old professor? And had an American student come to Cambridge? One with a ghastly red scar?

When the moment came, though, and she saw him waiting for her in the snow-dappled glow of the street-light, there was nothing on earth that would make her ruin the moment.

"Do you trust me?" Graham asked, as soon as they met.

The question caught her off guard. Was he going to offer up some answers on his own?

"Why?" she asked.

"There's something I want to show you."

Graham stood in front of her, looking her square in the eye.

"So do you trust me?" he asked again, and Samantha couldn't help but nod.

He took her gloved hand in his, surprising her so much that she almost jerked away. It was the first time she'd held hands with a boy, but Graham seemed so confident and comfortable that her shock soon faded. By the time they'd reached the gates of King's, it almost felt natural, except for the bolts of energy each shift of his fingers sent rippling up her arm.

They entered the age-old college, bundled in their coats, the gentle snow dampening all the city's night-time sounds. The great face of the Chapel loomed above them, majestic even now. To her surprise, he led her to a small door in the side of the church, far away from the public entry. Somehow Graham produced the key from his pocket.

"Where'd you get that?"

"Nicked it from the chaplain. But I don't lend it to the other choristers. I only use it to explore."

With a smile, he pushed in the door to the church's dark interior.

The great Chapel was theirs, all alone. She had never imagined that she would see it like this. The lights were off. The soaring stained-glass windows were lit only by the snow-draped lamps outside, their colors muted in gothic silhouette. She could just make out the sweet, dark smell of the day's incense, which mingled with Graham's scent of earth and wool and lavender soap.

He let go of her long enough to strike a match against the cold, white stone and light a candle he had borrowed from a table near the entrance. Now, the walls and windows flickered, giving glimpses of carved dragons and hounds and, above them, cities long vanished and fleets of ships sunk long ago.

"This way."

He led her to the front of the church, where another old key opened another old door. There the grandeur ended. Now they faced the bottom of a stark stone staircase, spiraling upward and out of sight.

"Follow close," said Graham. "Mind your step."

Samantha pressed herself to the wall and clung to the narrow rail, growing dizzy as they twisted up into the darkness. Each stair narrowed in a wedge shape toward the central column, and she had to watch the placement of her feet. Once, she slipped and almost fell, and only Graham's firm grasp kept her from tumbling backward.

Higher and higher they went until the cold hit them, hard and sudden. Samantha could tell that they had reached a long, red-brick corridor, open to the outside on the left through a series of glassless windows. To the right, arches led into the eaves, the in-between space between ceiling and roof.

No one was ever meant to see this, Samantha thought. This layer of the past was suspended in the air, like archaeology upside down. The coarse, rough-hewn level was so at odds with the chapel's otherworldly appearance below.

But Samantha was at home in places like this. And, she was satisfied to note, Graham seemed to be too.

He opened a final door at the corridor's end, and they were outside, the stars of the northern sky laid open and brilliant above them.

"I've wanted to take you up here since I met you, Samantha. Even at night, it's the best view in the city."

"Won't someone catch us?"

Graham laughed.

"Who'd be mental enough to climb up here in the middle of winter? Who besides us, I mean?"

They stomped up the creaky old stairs to the peak of the roof and took in the awesome view. There was the belfry of Great St. Mary's, stolid and stately, even in the midnight shadows. In the other direction, the river glinted, a thin veil of ice across its surface. And to the north, the bulk of the town, from where the faint sounds of New Year's revelry were swept away by the blistering force of the wind.

This was as good a time as any.

"I have something for you." Samantha said, pulling a present out from under her jacket. At once she regretted the wrapping. The tabloid newspaper she had used showed a ridiculous headline splayed across it in big letters—YOB EATS MATE'S GUINEA PIG PAL. She regretted having wrapped it at all.

"A gift for New Year's?" Graham asked, with a smile. "Kind of you, Samantha."

"It's just a field notebook," she said, even before Graham

had ripped the paper free. "I thought you might like to have one. Now that you're doing *real* archaeology, I mean."

It was just like hers—an extra she had brought from home—and she had threaded a cord through the spiral binding so that Graham could hang it from his neck like she did.

"Cheers, Samantha. It's perfect."

They stood until they could stand the stinging wind no longer, then walked back down to the protection of the balustrade. Graham sat down close beside her. Very close. His warmth was welcome.

"Do you like it here, Samantha? Are you enjoying your time in England?"

"Yeah," she said. "Mostly."

This was her moment. Now she could ask him about Catesby and Adam, the Greek fire, the ballista, about his own father and what he might know. But instead, to her embarrassment, she began to cry.

"It's okay," Graham said. "Tell me."

Samantha's feelings poured forth—about Clare leaving and Jay's irresponsibility, about Oona's strange behavior and the old enemy she thought might be closing in on her and her uncle. But when she was finished and she looked to Graham for comfort, she found something else instead.

"Cor blarst me. Are all American girls like you?"

"What do you mean?"

He looked at her, full-on.

"Samantha, you're only twelve!"

She frowned.

"So what? You're only thirteen!"

"No, what I mean is—you're so serious! I feel like I'm with an adult sometimes when I'm with you. There are enough grown-ups around to deal with all this. These are their problems, not ours."

"But I need to be strong," she said. "For my uncle's sake."

Graham only smiled. "Oh, you're strong, all right. Strong-willed, strong-headed. You're just like Boudica."

"No, I'm not."

The comparison felt wrong. It was Clare who was supposed to be the Warrior Queen. She was the one who should have fought back against Catesby's invasion.

"But Sam. You're not alone in this," he went on. "I can help you. After all, even Boudica had her Pasa… Prasta…Parsta…"

"Prasutagus," she said.

He had already leaned in to kiss her on the cheek. It was very light, lasting only a second, but the warmth of his breath and the touch of his lips lingered on and on and on. When it was over, and when their faces pulled apart, Samantha couldn't think of what to say. Graham was quiet too, all his bravado gone. They sat grinning in the electric silence.

"I don't think you would want to be Prasutagus," she said at last. "He dies, you know, pretty much at the beginning of the story."

At once she wished she hadn't said it. It was an awkward,

unfunny joke—something her uncle would have said. But she didn't have the charisma that Jay did to pull it off.

To her relief, Graham laughed aloud.

"Well, her general, then," he said.

Here too Graham was wrong. Boudica led her own troops. Samantha almost said so aloud. That was the whole point.

But she decided to let it go. Across King's Parade, the bells of Great St. Mary's began to clang, ringing midnight in with peals of bronze.

A new year had begun, pushing Boudica even deeper into the past.

———————

But in Samantha's sleep, the Warrior Queen lived still.

Her dream that night chased Boudica from behind, charging north and west from Verulamium's smoldering ruins along the island's principal road. But they were slower than the Queen would have liked. Her army was still larger now, more difficult to manage and hampered by dozens of bound Roman captives for sacrifice to Andraste. Her soldiers were weighed down by the fruits of their pillage. She herself kept the head of the emperor's statue at her feet, as well as the helmet of a Roman officer she'd struck through the cheek with her spear.

But this was not the time for regret. In the narrow valley ahead waited the entire Roman horde, all glinting metal and scarlet robes. Leading them was the Governor General, and beside him stood the emperor of half the earth.

*Well, this isn't accurate*, Samantha thought, even as she dreamed. *Those two were never there, not together, anyway.*

She saw that Boudica's face was Clare's once more. And it was Catesby the Emperor who faced them across the field of battle, as imperious as ever. But the soldier at his side wasn't Aubrey this time. There, in the garb of the Governor General, was Adam Quint, the burnt "X" upon his throat and jaw as red as his flowing cape.

A goddess's prophecy was needed now. Boudica drew out from her robes a shuddering hare—Andraste's messenger on Earth. No Iceni spoke, or Roman either, as she set the animal on the frosty ground. For a moment it huddled there, too frightened to move, until with a shudder it bounded away, off to the left side of the field of battle. Left was lucky. So the goddess was on their side.

She hefted the emperor's head high once more, and with a bloody roar her host began its charge. But as Boudica's horses swung wide across the furrowed turf, and as the Queen raised her spear to throw, Samantha saw the Roman legion form a perfect, lethal wedge. And she knew at last that this was a fight they could not win. Their ragtag army was no match for career soldiers selected for their abilities from all over the Roman world.

Death was near. There was no escaping it. And as the Romans charged in close formation, she heard Boudica's fearsome, final scream.

———————

It wasn't until the team had assembled in front of the Department on New Year's morning that Jay broke the news. Clare had left the project, he announced, and there would be no work that day. Now that he was the project's sole director, he needed time to make a plan.

"I know this is another fresh start, guys, and I'm sorry. Especially with only four days left to go."

But no one seemed upset by this. In fact, to Samantha's sorrow, the excavation team almost welcomed Clare Barrow's withdrawal.

"She was getting to be a right downer," said Kasim, as the group dispersed. "She slagged off the Boudica theory without a second thought."

Stuart, at least, defended her.

"She was just being cautious. And I don't blame her. Linking Wardy to Boudica would not be something you'd want to get wrong. You'd be a laughingstock. It's the sort of thing that could destroy a career."

The students scattered, Evan among them, and Samantha was left alone with their uncle.

"We need a break from all this, don't you think?" he said. "You and me?"

No, she thought. What he needed was space to do some work. Samantha remembered what Clare had said about her uncle's shaky knowledge of British archaeology and his lack of expertise. Without her here to guide him, he was completely out of his depth.

But Samantha saw that his face was drawn and worried now, his usual confidence dimmed. Restoring his spirit would have to come first.

"Okay," she said. "A very short break."

Cambridge distracted Jay from his troubles and put him in a talkative mood. His memories poured forth as he pointed out the scenes of his various student escapades along the King's Parade. That was the café where he and Clare would go after class and fight about some new archaeological theory. That was where a tour bus had struck his bike, and he'd sprained his wrist and ankle. And here was where his final marks had been posted—in Cambridge fashion—for all the world to see.

"But your grades were good, right?"

"The best," Jay grinned. "Despite Cairn's best efforts to fail me."

They had a quick lunch at the Copper Kettle, and Samantha jumped to her feet as soon as they'd paid the bill.

"You should get to work now, don't you think?"

Jay smiled.

"You're worse than Clare."

But he seemed to relent. They climbed into his rental car and took their usual route out of town. Jay talked incessantly as he drove, telling Samantha of his plans to get back at Catesby and save the site from destruction. They were one and the same, and she knew they would never work. But she let him talk. She let him talk and talk and talk, without uttering a single word.

It was only when the car turned right instead of left that she said something.

"This isn't the way to Wardy Hill."

He smiled.

"We're not going to Wardy, Sam."

They drove a few miles farther into a compact, cozy village. It was like many others in the Fens—with its gabled brick houses, pretty steepled church, and striking absence of trees. But there was something different about this place. Something almost familiar. And when Jay pulled up alongside a neat little cemetery, she was curious about what he might say.

"Samantha Sutton. Welcome to Sutton, Cambridgeshire, England."

"Our ancestral home?" she asked.

"For one of our family lines, anyway," said Jay. "This is a part of who we are. This is from whence we came."

Samantha let it sink in.

"And the town is old," her uncle went on. "Old enough to be recorded in William the Conqueror's Doomsday Book. And two centuries earlier, there are stories about how a king saved it from a Viking invasion. Our ancestors were also here then, I'd assume, swords in hand, ready to fight off the Nordic raiders."

"And before that?"

"And before that too. And back and back and back."

"Back to Boudica?"

Jay turned to her.

"Could be, Sam. That's right. Which means it's our own past we're trying to protect. For us—for me, at least—it's personal."

Samantha nodded. She understood. And as the bells of the tiny church struck noon, she wondered if Iceni blood flowed in her veins and some small part of the Warrior Queen too.

"Now one last surprise," he said. "But I'll need your brother for this one. We'll go back to town and pick him up."

Samantha shook her head.

"No. Really. You need to get back to work."

Jay grinned.

"Sam, this *will be* work. The very best kind. What we need is a fresh perspective."

––––––––––

Jay's strides quickened as he approached the launch site, and Evan and Samantha exchanged a nervous glance as they raced to keep up.

Their balloon was still on its side, the stark white nylon billowing with blasts of hot air. As three of the flight crew gripped the ropes and stays, Samantha could make out the swelling design—a seated woman, a forked trident in one hand, a shield in the other. She wore a golden helmet, its visor open, her gray eyes fixed with grim resolve.

"Is that her?" Samantha asked. "Is that Boudica?"

"No, kiddo. Her name's Britannia. The English version

of our Uncle Sam. Or, well, maybe our Lady Liberty. But you're not the first to notice the similarity between Britannia and the Warrior Queen."

The fabric rose and rose, growing taut, taking shape. And then one of the crew let loose the fire, a bright spear of orange in the winter's steely light. With a lurch, the woven willow basket righted itself, waiting for them to board. Jay's walk became a jog.

"You guys are going to love this."

Samantha eyed the darkening sky. The clouds were darker than she had ever seen them, and a chilly wind whipped up from the Fens.

"It's safe?" she asked, barely keeping pace. "With the weather, I mean?"

He smiled.

"I've flown in conditions much worse than these—snow in Cappadocia, heat in the Massai Mara. You should have seen the sandstorm I went through in Wadi Rum! And nothing happened to me there. The only thing I had to show for it after was the sand in my ears and the smile on my face."

The pilot greeted them as they walked to the gondola. She was a young woman, pleasant and plump. She clearly found Jay handsome. Samantha noticed that the pilot seemed flustered as Jay strode toward the balloon, and when he said a friendly hello, the young woman flushed red.

They climbed aboard. Samantha had to take Jay's hand as the basket shifted and pivoted on the ground, straining to take flight.

"Right!" the pilot said. "I understand you had a particular destination in mind? Let's see if the winds cooperate!"

She reached above her head and released the fire in a long, continuous burst.

Samantha felt the balloon begin to rise. It was a gentle movement at first, but there was a lurch and a bump as the crew released the stays. Then they were through the surface breezes and gliding higher, as soft and silent as a bubble.

The earth was far below them now. Trees, hedges, and farmsteads rushed by, their snowy fields gleaming. The vastness of the Fens was more apparent way up here, its bleakness spread toward all horizons. It would have been a harsh life in Boudica's day, and harsher still for the invading Romans, who lacked the age-old knowledge needed to survive here.

The pilot knew what she was doing. A small panel of instruments told her their altitude and speed. She could adjust their height above the earth by releasing more fire into the nylon balloon or using a second lever to open small vents in the top of the canopy. Samantha looked up, past the apparatus to the balloon itself, white against the coal-black sky. Their course followed Britannia's painted gaze. She felt herself relax a little.

"Can I try?" asked Evan.

"Yeah," Jay said, as eager as his nephew. "Can he?"

It was Jay's charming smile that won the young pilot over.

"All right then," she said. "Just this once."

She showed Evan how to feed the propane into the flame

above, and with a wide smile, he released the valve. A great tongue of flame shot up, like some sky-turned dragon.

"Raaawr," he said. "This is brilliant!"

It was, Samantha agreed, as she felt the balloon rise still higher. And her brother's use of British slang hadn't rankled her at all. Rampton rolled by beneath them, then Aldreth, Hill Row, Wentworth—the pilot calling out the names of each village as they approached. And finally, there was Coveney, and beside it their low, round hill, rising gently from the surrounding Fens.

"Look, guys," said Jay. "We're almost there."

Samantha did look, leaning out over the basket's edge as far as she dared as they whisked along toward Wardy. The perspective transformed the place entirely. An ancient stronghold was appearing below them—or the shadows of one, outlined in the turf. She could make out the ring-works, the remains of the water gate, the round foundations of structures, the causeways leading in and out. A whole citadel took shape in the curved stains of the ground.

"Wow," she said. "It's a fortress, that's for sure!"

"Look," Evan pointed. "Look!"

But his voice was alarmed, not excited. And then she too saw that the site below them was crawling with peo-ple—on a day where the team had been asked to stay away. Samantha had been so focused on the archaeological fea-tures that she hadn't even noticed them. But they were there, arranged in twos and threes, scraping at the earth with trowels and shovels.

"Metal detectorists?" Samantha asked.

"No," said Jay, his face wrinkled in concern. "Those aren't amateurs. They're digging in units. Measuring trancepts. Using screens. That's a full-fledged excavation going on down there."

"How?" she asked. "Whose?"

His face grew dark.

"Mine."

And Jay was right. Samantha saw their own excavation vans beside the pillbox and could pick out some of the Iceni crew: the Viscount, the Cerne Giant, Gog and Magog. Oona was there too, supervising things in her fine black coat. And there was someone else beside her—bedecked in a green army jacket and wrapped in scarves. Samantha watched this figure turn its face upward, and even at such a great height she could sense the cold hatred of the gaze.

"We need to go down there," said Jay. "Now."

He didn't ask the pilot's permission, this time—reaching above his head for the lever and opening the vents in the canopy.

"No!" cried the pilot. "Stop!"

But Jay was too fixated on the scene below them, and he would not let go.

Samantha felt her stomach rise, and her heart along with it. They were descending far too fast. So much air had escaped the balloon above them, in fact, that it was beginning to lose its shape.

"Let go, sir! We'll crash!"

It was already too late. The basket swung to one side as the balloon began to deflate, knocking the Suttons and the pilot into its wicker railing. Above them, Britannia's face was lost in folds and the canvas was slack behind her painted shield.

"Hold on, guys!" Jay shouted, as if they had a choice.

The ground was rushing up to meet them.

"Brace!" cried the pilot. "Brace!"

There were seconds before impact, and Samantha did not know what to do. But as Britannia crumpled down above them, she felt strong arms around her, lifting her in a protective embrace. She closed her eyes.

When the collision came, it came from the side and continued as the basket was dragged away from Wardy and through the mud of an open farm field. They had been saved by a low gust of wind, which had caught their collapsing canvas and dragged them sideways to slow their fall. She felt the arms around her go tighter and hold her even as the basket spilled over to throw them onto the snowy earth.

She pulled free from the arms that held her and struggled to her feet. The pilot was already on the radio, calling out for help, and Jay ran up beside Samantha, asking again and again if she was all right.

She looked to where her brother lay sprawled in the snow, his features racked with pain. It was he who had held her as they plummeted toward the earth. It was he who had tried to save her.

———————

"Addenbrooke's Hospital is more than two hundred years old," Jay said as they sat in the ground-floor waiting room. But the bit of trivia did nothing to curb her worry. Evan was injured—maybe badly so—and it had been her uncle's fault. And something sinister was afoot up at Wardy Hill.

"I'm just saying he's in good hands, Sam. These doctors know what they're doing."

Samantha nodded. The ride back to Cambridge had been excruciating. She had never seen her brother in so much pain. And he had been injured protecting her. She would owe him for that.

A physician came out to greet them. Samantha did not like the look on his face.

"Dr. Sutton? I'm afraid I have some bad news."

Jay stood.

"What, what is it?"

"Your nephew has sustained a very bad break. He may even need surgery. But it's too early, at this point, to know."

"What is it?" Jay asked. "His skull? His spine?"

The doctor looked at him strangely.

"Oh heavens, no. It's his toe. His little toe. I'm sorry. I assumed you knew that his pain was localized to his foot."

Samantha looked at the doctor in disbelief as Jay exploded in laughter.

"He didn't mention it, no. It was just a lot of screaming. But thank you, Doctor. Thanks very much."

"A pleasure," said the doctor, still puzzled by their confusion. "I'll just need an hour or so to tape him up and fit him with some crutches."

"We'll let him rest, then," said Jay, his face growing serious once again. "Now, come on, Sam. We have some questions we need answered."

---

"Sutton who?" came the voice from inside the office.

But Jay was in no mood for bad puns. He shoved the door hard and marched into Catesby's office. The Lord Professor was at his model, studying the mock-up of the Aventine Adventure Wheel.

"Do come in, Sutton. And please sit down. You look like you've had quite a shock."

"What's going on, Cairn?" Jay said, "Who do you have working out there?"

Catesby did not look up.

"I understood that you and Dr. Barrows have parted ways? It's a galley without a captain now. I have all the slaves I need to row, but no one on deck to steer the ship."

Now Jay's face was red and angry.

"You don't like how I'm doing things, is that it? You don't like how I'm getting in the way of your big plans?"

At last, the Lord Professor faced them.

"Retrieving my car came at the expense of the British taxpayer, Sutton. But your wild theories are taking money directly from me. *Tempus fugit,* as I've reminded you before. I thought it might be helpful to bring in someone who would be able to focus on the task ahead of them, and not dream of ancient queens and fairy tales."

"Who?"

Cairn smiled, his tiny eyes gleaming.

"My apologies," he said. "I had been told that you two knew each other."

Samantha froze. It was Catesby's turn for retribution, she realized. But she had never expected this.

A figure no one had noticed stood from behind Catesby's desk, scarves loose around his neck and wrapped in a jacket of army green. He turned to face them with a familiar menace—the wrestler's frame, the scowl-like smile, those mirrored sunglasses, and that military cap pulled low across his brow. And then there were the twin scars—Samantha's doing—stretching from his chin to his ear, and from his throat to his cheek, forming an angry, puckered *X*.

"Oh, Cairn," said Jay, as he saw his former protégé. "This time you've gone too far."

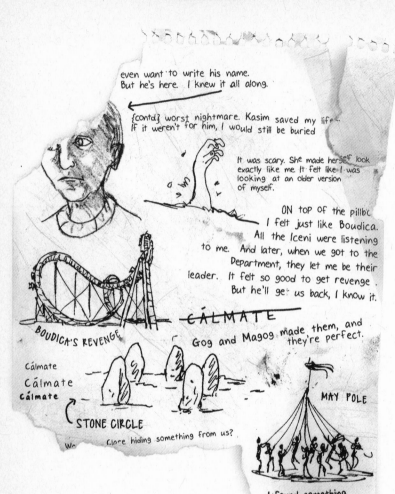

even want to write his name.
But he's here. I knew it all along.

{contd} worst nightmare. Kasim saved my life.
If it weren't for him, I would still be buried

It was scary. She made herself look
exactly like me. It felt like I was
looking at an older version
of myself.

ON top of the pillbo
I felt just like Boudica.
All the Iceni were listening
to me. And later, when we got to the
Department, they let me be their
leader. It felt so good to get revenge.
But he'll get us back, I know it.

CÁLMATE

BOUDICA'S REVENGE

Gog and Magog made them, and
they're perfect.

Cálmate
Cálmate
**Cálmate**

STONE CIRCLE

MAY POLE

We    Close hiding something from us?

I found something
that could save us all.

# CHAPTER 17

**H**ello, Samantha Sutton."

She was still frozen, though, and couldn't find her voice. Before her was the man who'd chased her through Cambridge's alleys, who'd stalked her through the library, who'd lit the Cam on fire, and who'd aimed the deadly ballista at their car. But there was nothing she could think to say to horrible Adam Quint.

"Why, Cairn?" Jay asked. "Why him?"

Catesby folded his arms across his chest.

"He came to me, as it happens. He's spent the last few months in Cambridge in private study, focusing on our Roman past. I've taken him under my wing as a private pupil. Apparently, his former mentor disowned him. Have you ever heard of such a thing?"

Jay's face was paper white.

"That's not what happened."

But Catesby went on.

"He's been working as a bedder at Trinity Hall. I can

barely imagine it. It's a reverse of your American dream. From a PhD course in archaeology to a launderer of linens!"

"And a tidier of rooms," Adam added, jangling a large set of keys. "And an organizer of notebooks when it seems like it should be done."

Samantha's eyes went wide. So he had been in her room and had rifled through her things. And he had left her the threatening riddle on the page—the Pompeii graffiti repurposed for his ends.

"But I'm here to fix all that," said Cairn. "To restore him to his rightful place. Now that your slovenly friend from the Heritage Office has expressed some mistaken interest in my property, the excavation must continue. It should please you to have a new director, Sutton. I think you'll have a lot to learn from him as your project reaches its dusty death."

"Oh," said Jay. "We'll have lots to learn from each other."

———

There were three days left to dig—three more than Samantha would have wished. She couldn't face Adam. Not again. But she knew she had no choice.

It took Evan two tries to rouse her from her bed the next morning—the second with a flick of cold water from the tap. She was relieved that he was cheerful, after the shocking events of the day before. But he didn't have to go to the site today. Not with his new crutches and a broken toe.

"I'll keep busy, Archaeo Kid," said Evan. "I have some calls I need to make."

So Samantha and Jay were alone on their way to Wardy, and her uncle was lost in his own misery almost the entire time. Only when they began the final climb up the gentle hill did he turn to look at her, waiting for an answer to the question she had been too distracted to hear.

"You okay, Sam?" he asked again.

She nodded.

"Good, kiddo. I'm going to need you."

He would. It was clear on their arrival that Jay would need all the help he could get. Samantha spotted Adam Quint before stepping out of the car. He wore the same green army cap and mirrored sunglasses he had had in Peru, augmented with his new heavy jacket and knot of ratty scarves. He looked sure of himself in his role as site director, ordering the Iceni team around. Oona stood smugly beside him. How long had these two known each other, Samantha wondered? And which of Wardy's secrets had they already shared?

As Jay and Samantha headed for the lab, two of the Iceni came over to greet them.

"We had no choice," Stuart said. "The Emperor came into the Ridge & Furrow and said he'd either send us back here or send all of us down."

"Send you down?" asked Jay. "Expel you? He can't."

"We weren't sure, to be honest," said Kasim. "He is a lord, after all. And none of us were keen on finding out if he had that particular authority."

Samantha went back outside to mingle with the others. Adam paced among them like a general before a force of timid conscripts, twirling his knife-sharp trowel. He had made no effort to cover his scars today, and they glistened red and angry, their ragged edges still singed black. And when he neared her, Samantha shrank away, sure she could smell the stink of scalded skin.

The site fell silent as Jay trudged from the pillbox—the Iceni straining for some sign of hope.

"Okay, Adam," said Jay. "How do you want to do this?"

Adam stared at his old professor, but then just turned his head and spat. And when he spoke, it was to the entire assembly—as if Jay Sutton wasn't even there.

"Listen up. I need one person per unit, at a unit per hour. We have a lot of wasted time to make up for, so let's get moving."

Samantha watched as the team hurried to follow his commands. Everyone seemed desperate to meet the grueling pace of Catesby's new commander general. It was clear that Jay had lost control of the project.

Three days, she thought. She could manage that. Soon, she would be home in California, biking with Janet and Jeanette Pitt-Rivers to school, or reading in her favorite chair in the library—maybe trying fiction for a change. Her Uncle Jay would patch things up at his university by the Bay, and life would return to normal.

Just three more days.

*Cálmate*, she told herself. *Relax.*

She retrieved her tools from the pillbox and set off toward her unit. She had been working near the ringwork's land gate, where a tangled mess of ditches and gullies showed how the inhabitants of Wardy had defended themselves at the fortress's weakest point.

But someone was in the unit already today, hacking away at her perfect floor with a pickax and using the shovel to hurl out clumps of earth, unscreened.

Oona.

It was strange enough that the actress was out in the field working, not sorting sherds at her table in the pillbox. But once again, Oona had transformed herself. Her smart, black coat was replaced by a parka of royal blue, and she had gathered her hair into a pair of braided pigtails. A notebook swung from her neck with each stroke of her tools, hanging by a knotted length of cord.

Apart from height and hair color, Samantha Sutton was staring at herself.

"Uncle Jay! Uncle Jay!" the imposter mocked, in perfect Californian English. "I'm in my own unit already! What should I do?"

Adam snickered from the adjacent hole, hacking away.

"What are you doing?" Samantha asked.

"Who me?" said Oona. "Hurrying things up a little. Seems that *I've* been going a little too slow."

Samantha bent to pick up the clipboard at her feet and scanned the current level form. Her own name had been written across its top, but not by her. Apparently

Oona's talent for impressions stretched into handwriting as well.

She realized what they were up to, impressions aside. If Catesby was asked—by the Dodo, or by anyone else—the forms would document how the units had all been dug to a reasonable depth, and that all the archaeology had been sound. No one would be able to prove otherwise.

The braids and the notebook were just a cruel, unnecessary extra.

Samantha found an unclaimed unit far away from the others, where there was a break in the ringwork's outer ditch. Clare had been working here, she remembered, and the walls of the rectangular hole was already shoulder high. The depth beckoned her. If Samantha knelt on the unit's smooth floor, she'd be free of further mocking, even as her uncle's former student took up position nearby.

She set to work. Crouched low, her arms in steady motion, she even felt a semblance of peace. Some of Clare's kindly presence seemed to linger in the unit. The peaty air itself seemed warm as well, carrying with it the sweet smells of decomposing vegetation. Was it this smell that alerted her to the danger—the aroma of moss and damp, growing stronger? Was it instead the strange wet whisper from the southern profile? Or was it the menacing human shadow that signaled the unit's imminent collapse?

In any case, her instinct was triggered just in time, and she threw her arms up to protect her head as the walls fell in. The weight of the earth drove her down, filling her ears with a wet sort of thunder. Then there was a gasping sigh of the soil settling and the lonely silence of a tomb.

She couldn't move. She certainly couldn't see. And she feared she couldn't breathe. But the pocket of air between her face and upthrown arms would be enough to keep her alive, at least for a minute or two. She waited, holding the panic at bay. Surely someone had seen it happen. Surely someone would come to her rescue. Adam had been right there. A man of his powerful build could reach her with a few strokes of his shovel. It would be the easiest thing in the world. Or it would be, if he wanted to.

And then the panic came.

She drove down with her arms and legs, trying her best to stand. The weight was just too much, and every movement collapsed the space before her mouth. She could taste the soil that would kill her on her lips.

She heard a muffled roar and a distant, chunking thunk, thunk, thunk. Within seconds, a new kind of pain erupted across her back. But it was fleeting—the glancing blow of a shovel's edge. She choked for breath as the mud around her face was scraped away, and then her arms were free, her legs, her feet. She felt herself dragged up and out and laid flat upon the ground.

"What happened?" Jay shouted, as she finally opened her eyes.

She looked around. Kasim still held the shovel in his hands. It had been he who had rescued her.

"He did it," he said, jabbing the blade at Adam. "He buried her!"

Adam turned to glare at him, and Oona laughed her tittering, newfound laugh.

"I saw him!" Kasim said, flinging down the shovel in anger. "You have to do something! He just tried to *murder* your niece!"

Jay took a step toward his old student. His voice had a quaver to it now.

"She's a kid, Adam. She's twelve years old. If you have to hurt someone, hurt me. But leave my niece alone."

Adam closed the rest of the gap between them so that they stood there chest to chest.

"Accidents happen, Dr. Sutton. You know that." He pulled his scarf away from the seared $X$ on his throat and jaw, releasing the stink of scalded flesh. "She knows that too. But does everyone? Do your employers back home know just how accident-prone you are? How you bungled the situation in Peru? How you put your students in jeopardy? They might see it as a liability."

Jay opened his mouth, but nothing came out. The Iceni glared on, helpless as well. With his connections to Catesby, Adam had control of them too.

"Are we done here?" Adam asked. "Can we all get back to work?"

Samantha watched Kasim retreat to the pillbox, cradling his head in his hands with disbelief. She saw her uncle, shamefaced and defeated. If things continued this way, there would be nothing left of the site at Wardy Hill, and nothing left of her uncle either.

It was time for a new tactic, she decided. She would need to lead a rebellion.

---

The second day of Adam's leadership was almost as terrible, even if no one was buried alive. Kasim and the Viscount arrived to find their unit full of horse manure. Samantha's held a rabbit, dead and skinned. Then, around mid-morning, the Green Man's shovel split as he stomped down on it, gashing his leg from ankle to knee. The head of Magog's pickax flew off on the backstroke, striking Gog hard in the shoulder and sending him sprawling into his spoil heap.

These were no accidents, of course, and no one believed they were. Though the team said nothing in Adam's presence, Samantha knew she could form a loyal army now.

The opportunity came at the midday break. Her uncle had invited Adam to a pub lunch in the nearby village—a final attempt to arrive at a truce. But Oona had gone along as well, and the whole team watched Jay struggle to keep up with the malevolent duo as they made their way downhill.

Samantha had to act. Using the crack in the pillbox wall as a foothold, she climbed to its roof and stood there, her heart pounding as she held up her hand. She had to wait for a few moments until the team took notice. But when their defeated eyes met hers, she steeled herself and forced aside the last of her misgivings.

"I…I want to say something."

"Not more bad news, is it?" asked the Viscount. "I don't think I'd be able to handle it."

There were murmurs of agreement.

"No. But you're right," she said, surprised by her own confidence. "We've put up with a lot. All the new deadlines, the metal detectorists coming through. The Emperor's even had some of us attacked: the Greek fire on the river, the ballista on the road, and yesterday, here on the site, when I got buried alive."

She had everyone's attention now. A pair of rabbits eyed her from behind the group. Even they seemed to hang on what she would say next.

"But we can't be afraid of him," she went on. "There's more of us, aren't there? And we're braver too. Every day we're out here, trying to do our jobs. We're not back in the Department like Catesby is, sitting by the fire while Adam and Oona do his dirty work."

She felt her nerves creep in with her mention of those names. It took the last of her courage to continue.

"I…I know I'm a lot younger than you guys. Probably some of you think I'm just a little girl. And that's okay. I get that. But I have a plan to get back at Catesby, and I'm going to need you to help me."

She heard her voice go hard.

"I say we take the battle to him."

There was a long silence as the Iceni looked at each other, and Samantha half expected them to turn and walk away. What was she thinking? she wondered. She was no leader—not of people almost twice her age. She stooped to lower herself back down.

But then Stuart let out a fearsome roar.

"For Boudica!" he cried.

"For our stalwart, steadfast sovereign!" the Cerne Giant added.

"For our lovely lady Queen!" yelled the Viscount in response.

Just beneath her at the edge of the pillbox, Kasim thrust his own fist in the air.

"And for Samantha too!"

She stood straight again and smiled. And for the next few minutes, cries for Samantha and the Warrior Queen rang out together across the Fens and sent the rabbits running.

———————

She asked them to meet her late that night at the Silver Street Bridge. The Ridge & Furrow would not be safe from Catesby's spies.

"No Evan?" asked Stuart, as the group assembled.

"Not with his foot," Samantha said. "Too dangerous."

"Pity, that. This is Iceni business, pure and true."

They reached the Archaeology Department just before twelve. Downing Street was empty of cars and bicycles, and all was quiet. But even so, they moved along as silently as they could. In darkness, the cheerful redbrick loomed black and forbidding, shining where dripwater had frozen in the carvings on its face. They came to the entranceway and stopped. The gate was locked, just as Stuart had predicted. It had to be her to do this. She was the only one small enough to slip between the iron bars.

"I'm going in," she said.

Stuart flashed an encouraging smile.

"Good luck!"

She squeezed through the gate, feeling the cold metal through her jacket and against the side of her face. Then she was through, inside the courtyard. She pulled her winter hat on straight.

Kasim pushed Samantha's backpack through behind her.

"Third window over," he said. "It should be open."

She took off at a jog, bending low. One, two, three from the right she counted as she crept across the frozen grass and through the bushes that lined the building. Using the hedge, she climbed up and gave the window a gentle push. This was her last chance to turn back. But she wriggled through the opening feet first, landing with a bang atop the Lord Professor's hardwood desk. And then she headed straight for the model, uncinching her backpack as she went.

In the moonlight, the twisting tracks of the Imperator gleamed on mini–Wardy Hill. One by one she withdrew Gog and Magog's new creations, laying them out on the edge of the table. And then Samantha set to wiping Roman Britain from the face of the small-scale earth.

She began with little Trajan's Column, yanking it from its balsa moorings. She replaced it with a miniature maypole, bedecked with ribbons and surrounded by prancing, tiny Celts. Next she ripped the circus away—its tiny plastic chariots popping loose from their tracks—and substituted a Neolithic stone circle. She removed the entire panel on which the Forum sat, reducing it to natural wood. And at last she tore the Imperator free and put in its place a new roller coaster: the merciless *Boudica's Revenge*.

When she was finished, she hurried across the room and toward the open window. But she stopped when she reached Catesby's desk. A piece of paper there caught her attention. She picked it up, holding it to read in a shaft of moonlight. It was a letter, but it wasn't addressed to Catesby.

*Dear Dr. Barrows,*

*It was a pleasure to meet with you. As discussed, the accompanying shipment encloses catalog number P&EE 1965 12-1 1. I release it into your custody and trust that you will guarantee its security until it is returned.*

*It is a fitting tribute you have planned for Catesby. I do hope that this meets your needs.*

She couldn't make out the signature but saw from the letterhead that it had been sent from the British Museum in London. She read the letter again, and then again—the giddiness from her small-scale raid beginning to dwindle.

What did Clare know, exactly? Was there something she'd kept secret?

With new anxiety overlaying the old, Samantha placed the letter back where she'd found it, then climbed onto the desk, slipped through the window, and ran through the moonlit court. She would tell the others of her victory, she decided, but would hold Clare's mysterious secret close.

———————

Clare came to her in her dreams that night, taking the form of Boudica once more.

She knelt there on the field of carnage, defeated and alone. It all was over—the rebellion crushed, her fury withered to despair. Iceni lands were Roman now, the Iceni Roman subjects.

As the heat of battle sputtered out in pools of blood, the Governor General found her. She steeled herself, waiting for the slicing sword to take her head. It never came. Instead he fixed her with his cross-scarred grin and flung a vial at her feet. She tried to find her voice, to curse him with the power of just Andraste. But he had wheeled on his horse already and trotted off before she had a chance to respond.

Boudica plucked the vial from the earth. Poison. She recognized its sickly gleam. In their imperial arrogance, her conquerors had expected her to follow the Roman custom. But she was no longer a threat, and Rome did not care if she lived or died. They had left the choice to her.

Her decision seemed an easy one. No matter the depth of the dishonor, suicide was not the proud Icenis' way. But the Iceni were no more. She kept the vial, just in case.

The General's legions regrouped, leaving the valley to the vanquished. The Queen stood to survey what remained. Her chariot was near, her terrified children still inside it. Her bag of Roman spoils sat close by. Andraste still was owed her due. Boudica heaved a butchered Roman over a wounded horse and wended her weary way among the dying and the dead.

She saw the survivors rising. Arrows stuck from torsos, bare skin blackened by streaming blood. But their faces showed their loyalty. She was still their stalwart Queen, and they stood awaiting her command.

The hare appeared before them at the mouth of the valley, emerging from the tangled bodies of the faithful. One ear seemed damaged and blood smeared its fur—but it was alive, and there was still spirit in it as it scampered away toward home.

Boudica heaved the metal head of the emperor high and issued her one-word order.

"East!"

And so, the survivors followed Andraste's messenger. For days and days, they limped after it, east and then south and then east again, until the ground grew soft and wet and opened to the marshes of the Fens. The hare's tracks ended where the water began. Before them was a gentle hill on the horizon, just at the edge of the great vast swamp.

Boudica could protect her people here. A fortress would be built on this low hill, and she and her surviving people could grow old and die within it. Unless they were given the chance, of course, and could begin their rebellion anew.

---

It was the project's final day, and the Iceni mood was as tense as ever—more tense, perhaps, as they awaited Catesby's regatta that afternoon and braced for his revenge for their attack on the model. Surely, he had discovered the damage by now. And surely, he would retaliate.

But if Adam had heard anything about the miniature Vivant Romani, he was careful not to show it—issuing his orders with the same aggression as the vans unloaded and the team shuffled over for assignment. Samantha followed his barked instructions, and Jay did too, watching Adam's every move. Something bad was going to happen. Samantha just knew it—and was almost envious of the injury that kept her brother safely back in Cambridge.

Then, with an hour remaining in the entire project, it began to snow. The heat from the brazier beside Samantha's unit acted like some sort of force field, melting the swirling flakes before they ever hit the ground. But as the snowfall thickened, the fire itself grew weak, smothered by the growing blizzard.

The snowmelt was too much for the soil to absorb. Her unit held a puddle an inch or two deep, fed by the rivulets that streamed in from the profiles. Now, as Samantha worked her trowel through the frigid water, each stroke sent ripples across the floor like waves across a wild sea.

She herself was soaked to the skin. Her royal blue jacket—the good one from the camping store in Sacramento—seemed to have given up, and she felt the freezing tickle of melted snow across her shoulders, back, and arms. Somehow her boots had also failed her, and her feet squished every time she changed position in the unit.

She took a quick glance at the pillbox across the road and the light that glowed from its gun slits. How she wished she could take shelter there and warm herself with some hot tea and biscuits. But Oona was inside, and Adam too, celebrating their victory and the project's early end.

And besides, there was still some work to do. Even now, Samantha thought with her last bit of hope, there might be something here to bring to the Dodo and save the site forever.

"Fifteen more minutes!"

Jay's voice was easy to pick out from the center of the ringwork. It was all the Iceni needed, and she saw them climb from their units, indistinguishable with their tightly cinched hoods and low, defeated slumps. Only she and her uncle continued to work.

Something within her snapped. It was all her fault that things had turned out this way—all because of that stupid Iceni coin. She had failed her uncle and Clare and Boudica too—who, it turned out, had probably never seen this place. Samantha had put an idea in Jay's head—a wild, exciting, pointless hope—and the price had been his love life and his job.

She flung down her trowel in disgust.

But instead of the wet slap of water or the slurping suck of mud, the impact brought a loud, metallic zing. And a spark, lighting up the inside of the unit like a firework. It was so sudden and so brilliant in the gloom that it knocked Samantha back onto her gloved hands.

She rocked forward. Whatever she had hit was big and unyielding. Samantha took off a glove and gave it a poke with her bare skin, feeling metal, freezing cold. But this wasn't some corroded piece of steel or lump of rusted iron—her finger could trace some fine details in the metal beneath.

This would require a more delicate approach, she realized. A trowel would scratch something like this, no matter how gently it was applied. But she would need to work quickly. She pulled a fresh sleeve of chopsticks from her backpack and snapped them apart, then used one of the soft wood tips to push coils of wet mud from the intricate metalwork.

Whatever the object was, it seemed primed for discovery. The mud came off easily, as if it had clung to the surface for hours, not centuries, and as if the artifact itself was yearning for freedom.

"Five minutes, kiddo," Jay called out across the field. "We have a boat race to get to."

Samantha worked as fast as she could, her face inches

away from the gleaming metal surface. Only when the object poked up out of the earth did she allow herself to take a full look at it. And what she saw then almost sent her scrambling from her unit.

It was a human face—or a perfect, metal reconstruction of one. There, in blackened metal, were the looping curls, big ears, imperial brow, and sharp nose of some Roman emperor. Two empty, angry eyes stared up at her, casting an ancient scorn. It looked a lot like Catesby.

"Uncle Jay!"

He jogged toward her across the long white field.

"What is it, kiddo?"

But then he caught sight of the artifact in the unit and his mouth fell open too. They stood together in silence. She knew the face that stared up at them. It was unmistakable. She had seen it in books on Britain's early past, in pictures of busts of marble and terra cotta, and in profile on ancient Roman coins. This was the emperor himself— the man who had sent his legions to invade Britain in the first place, and who had struck that false and fateful treaty with the Iceni's mighty king.

But that wasn't all, Samantha thought. This was the statue from Camulodunum's Temple, destroyed by Boudica and pillaged by her forces. The head was the ultimate trophy: the spoils of the Warrior Queen's first major victory and the beginning of her valiant quest for vengeance.

"This is everything, Sam." Jay whispered. "This is exactly what we needed."

And she knew he was right. So Wardy had been Boudica's, after all, and this was all the proof they needed.

Just then the pillbox door opened, spilling light and raucous noise across the gloomy Fens. Adam was coming their way. There was no time.

"Do it, Sam," said her uncle, and made a sweeping motion with his hand.

He was right. There was only one option. So she used the trowel to bury the head again under globs of freezing mud.

SSFNb2–WH: 18

# CHAPTER 18

The afternoon was a strange time to be rowing, Samantha thought. She was so used to the predawn practices that it felt like a morning sport. The sight of all the other boats unnerved her, as well as the thin crowd that had gathered on the bank to celebrate the country's newest Lord.

But it was the thought of an ancient emperor and his heavy, newfound head that quickened her pulse. They had what they needed now. Wardy Hill was safe. Jay Sutton was saved. And Boudica, the Warrior Queen, was finally avenged.

Today the world would celebrate Catesby. Tomorrow it would put him in his place.

She would enjoy this.

"All right, Archaeo Cox?" asked Stuart, as she entered the boathouse.

"All right."

She decided to pretend that nothing was out of the ordinary. Jay would be taking Evan's place inside the boat, her brother's broken toe keeping him from rowing. She led her crew in warm-ups, ordering them to do their star jumps and fireman's carry exercises, just as she'd been told. And all the while she studied her uncle carefully, relieved to see him acting as if everything was normal.

They were on the river just before two. Stuart had managed to find rowers to fill more than a dozen boats to race that day, even in the dead weeks between the terms. They rowed upriver to their start positions in a long and orderly row, the blades of their colleges colorful and shining.

"Easy there," she said, and her crew obeyed at once, letting the flat of their blades skim against the surface and slowing the boat to a stop. Evan stood with his crutches on the riverbank, looking a little ignored.

The Cam was too narrow for traditional racing. There were some places where two boats could not fit side by side, let alone twelve. Instead, the crafts fell into a randomly determined line, bow to stern, waiting for the signal before they would explode across the water, trying to smash the boat ahead before the boat behind could ram them. It seemed violent, barbaric. But it was tradition. And traditions didn't have to make sense.

Nothing could have prepared her for the sound of the first warning cannon. It was a thunderclap, jolting the whole world with its vibration and shattering her heightened nerves. Even its echoes caused their own ripples across the water.

They had four minutes.

"We've got this, Samantha," said Stuart, flashing her a

nervous smile. She hadn't told him what she'd found, or Kasim either. Now, his pale Scottish knees were shaking above his socks. What is it from the cold, she wondered, or plain nerves?

She adjusted her microphone, aware that her words would be heard not just by her own crew but by the bystanders on the towpath and the boats ahead and behind.

Jay winked at her now from the seventh seat, but she had to look away.

"All right, everyone," Samantha said, going through the motions. "Number off please, from bow."

Her hands were trembling. And from the way the rowers said their numbers, she could tell that they were nervous too.

"Ready, Sam?" asked her brother from the shore.

She nodded, and watched as he pushed the boat away from the bank with the end of his crutch.

One minute remaining, and the warning cannon roared again.

"Let's get a good, strong start, guys," she said. "Keep your eyes on stroke and seven. Lengthen on my call."

"Don't run us into the bank, Cox!" shouted the Viscount from the bow seat, resulting in a nervous chatter. "Aim for the boat ahead!"

"Quiet, please," said Samantha, and her voice was flat and firm. "Focus."

"Thirty seconds," said Evan, and it was impossible not to begin a countdown in her head.

*Twenty-nine, twenty-eight…*

"Wait!" shouted Gog, in the fifth seat. "There's something wrong with my footplate."

"Mine too," said Magog, behind him.

*Twenty-one, twenty…*

Samantha could see that something was wrong with the straps that fastened each rower's foot to the boat. But there was certainly nothing to be done about it now.

*Fifteen, fourteen…*

"Go to start positions, Sam," said Jay, trying to sound calm.

"Start position!" she cried.

*Eleven, ten…*

"My feet are stuck," the Viscount shouted from the bow, and Samantha could have sworn she heard laughter from the bank.

*Seven, six…*

"Sam?" asked Stuart, wide-eyed. "Are we ready?"

She opened her mouth to answer, but then the cannon went.

The boat heaved forward, eight pairs of legs straightening at once, then bending again, breaking the forward motion into little jolts.

"Lengthen!" she cried, relying on what she'd memorized in practice. Everyone on the bank seemed to have a whistle, and it was too loud to think properly above the shrill, incessant noise.

They were making good speed into First Post Corner, slowing only slightly as Samantha maneuvered them into the Gut. The gap between them and the boat ahead seemed to be closing, and a quick look behind her confirmed that their pursuers had not gained. The problems with the boat seemed to be stable, for now.

There was a commotion downriver, in front of them. Two boats up, a Downing rower's oar had caught in the water, pushing him backward in the seat and jamming his blade awkwardly in its rigger. They could be bumped easily now by the Darwin boat, which would send Downing and Darwin to the bank. Samantha would have to hurry, or there would be a two-boat gap between her and her next closest target.

"All right, guys, power for ten!" she cried. Stuart responded immediately, plunging his blade in the water and powering it through with great and terrible speed. Samantha felt the pace quicken and the space before them close.

And then something popped loose. It was the Green Man's oar, ripped clean from its rigger. Another angry shout and the Viscount's, too, broke free and was left in their choppy wake. They were down two rowers, leaving six to do the work of eight.

"Keep going, Sam," said Stuart, between gasps. "Make them work for it!"

And so she did.

"Keep going!" she cried. "Row!"

The crew took her commands to heart and somehow managed to move the boat through the water at almost the same speed. But behind them, the next boat also surged forward, finding encouragement in the pair of bobbing oars in the water.

"We're holding them off!" she shouted. "We can do this!"

There were whistles on the bank, growing closer and closer together. A bump was imminent. But there were other noises too: shouts of worry and warning.

"Careful, Samantha," shouted her uncle. "There's something going on ahead."

She could see it, now: an unexpected shape, low on the water and bearing down on them like some Jurassic predator. She craned her neck, hearing the angry protest of the riverbank crowds. And then she recognized what was heading their way, threatening a head-on collision.

Samantha would know it anywhere by its cherry-red paint and pure white trim: the narrowboat *Agrippina*—the Aubreys' floating home.

Samantha had to think quickly.

"Bow side," she cried, "rowing on. Stroke side, back it down. Ready…one…and two."

The boat pivoted in the water.

"Now, everyone, three quick strokes."

The team reacted instantly—a living machine—powering from the middle of the river toward the safety of the empty bank, desperate to get out of the way.

But when she looked ahead, it was clear they hadn't even managed that. The narrowboat had closed the gap and hadn't turned to miss them.

"Samantha?" said Stuart. "He's still coming."

She heard the rip of Velcro and saw the Green Man struggling with his footplate. The boat lurched to the side, its balance thrown off. She heard the sound again and saw Gog and Magog tearing at the straps around their ankles, desperate to get out of the boat in time.

"Hold on to your oars!" Samantha cried. "You'll make us tip!"

But the gap was closing now, and it was every rower for himself. In a rush, they emptied from the boat, leaping to the shore or into the freezing water, leaving only Jay, Stuart, and Samantha stuck in their seats. The boat was listing heavily to one side. If anyone stood—or even moved—they risked capsizing.

"Get out, Samantha!" shouted Stuart.

"But it'll flip over."

"Go, Sam," cried Jay. "Now!"

Moving as gingerly as she could, Samantha unplugged her microphone and rose shakily to her feet. But her movements were too slow. It was too late.

The *Agrippina* caught them at their midpoint, slicing through the thin wood and smashing into the concrete shoring of the bank. Samantha tumbled forward among the rails and seat slides, then rolled over the edge of the boat and onto the frigid land. Jay and Stuart followed behind, gasping in a pile on the bank.

Instinct told Samantha who was behind this, and impulse prompted her to look up. There, far in the distance on the river's opposite bank, she saw scarves and a heavy coat, the glint of mirrored sunglasses, and an army hat pulled low. All she could see of the face was a half-satisfied grin.

————

That night Samantha could not find comfort in her usually cozy bed. She needed sleep, but sleep just wouldn't come.

The afternoon had been hectic and terrifying. There had been doctors on the riverbank, examining all the Iceni rowers for signs of hypothermia. There were police too. Samantha overheard one of them explaining to his fellow officers that the key was still in the *Agrippina*'s ignition and that its throttle had been tied in the On position by a piece of threaded twine.

"Bloody animal activists," they murmured to one another, but Samantha knew better. The culprit's motives were vengeful but did not involve the Cam's cantankerous swans.

But what kept her up was not the day's regatta or tomorrow's Vivant Romani celebration, planned for ten o'clock. No. What agitated her wakeful mind was the head of the emperor back up at Wardy, lying half exposed to the elements. The thin slick of mud she'd used to hide it could easily be swept away by rain. And if some metal detectorist decided to return on his own that night to wand the area under cover of dark, she couldn't imagine the sound of the resulting squawk.

There was no other choice. She would have to retrieve it now.

Samantha did not stop to wake her uncle. He had his

own plan now, he'd whispered to her over a tense dinner. It was designed for maximum effect: to shame his old rival and crush his hopes in public. He would wait for the groundbreaking ceremony—when the Lord Professor's celebration was in mid-swing. But Samantha knew that things couldn't wait. The risks were just too huge.

Still, she could not do it alone. Stuart, she decided, her old friend. Stuart was the only one who could help.

It was pure luck that Tom was away from the desk—making tea, most likely, in the small office in the back. The door squeaked as she opened it, and she crossed the room in three steps—then out into the shadows of Trinity Lane before the porter could see who'd come and gone.

It was snowing heavily. Only now did she check her watch. It was 10:50—far too late to inquire after Stuart at the Porters' Lodge of his own college without causing suspicion. So she made her way to the Ridge & Furrow through the driving blizzard, bounding along the now-familiar lanes and hoping he would still be there.

She was in luck. Inside the pub she found Stuart and Kasim, pouring their regrets out to each other over steaming mugs of tea.

"Samantha?"

"What on earth are you doing here?"

There was no time for full explanation.

"I need to get to Wardy. It's an emergency. I found something today—something major. And if I don't get it now, there's a chance it'll be lost forever."

The students looked at each other in wonder. But it was a mischievous look—and it showed their eagerness for a final adventure.

"Right," said Stuart. "I'll drive."

"For Boudica!" said Kasim, his eyes afire.

Samantha nodded, but her mouth was grim and tight.

"For Boudica," she said. "More than you can possibly know."

―――――――――

"What is it, Samantha? What did you find?"

But Samantha did not answer them as the van raced through the whirling snowstorm. The thudding of her heartbeat was too loud. There was a chance that she was already too late. She threw the door open before they came to a full stop, her backpack across her shoulders.

"I'll be right back," she said, and stepped out into the blizzard.

She didn't need a flashlight—she knew the site too well—and her step was confident as she ran across the pitted field. She pulled out her trowel and a pair of brand-new chopsticks, eager to put them to use. But then, mid-stride, she caught herself. Something ahead was wrong.

There was a muted glimmer before her—so dim and so fleeting between the snowflakes that she thought at first that it was a trick of her eyes. But then she saw it again: the dull glow of a low-power headlamp, its beam covered to produce only the faintest of lights.

"Nighthawks!" she started to shout.

But a dirty hand covered her mouth before a word escaped.

"No," said a voice. "Don't."

She thrust her elbow back, fast and hard, and felt the grip go slack. One more blow, and she was able to wriggle free. Her opponent had dropped the headlamp in the struggle. She lunged for it, yanked it away, and trained its beam on her attacker.

Graham Aubrey.

She should have known.

She had knocked the air out of him, and he couldn't yet find his voice. She whipped the light back and forth. He was alone. But he was not empty-handed. A heavy sack sat by the edge of the unit—her unit—and she knew what it must contain.

"…mistake…" Graham was gasping. "…please…"

She pushed him, hard—an impulse she couldn't control—and he fell backward into the hole at her feet.

"Samantha," he said. "Wait."

"Wait?" she said. "How could you? I taught you everything! Everything! I thought you understood!"

She was crying. The betrayal was too much.

"Quiet, Samantha. Please. My dad's parked in the village, just below. He'll hear you. And then we'll both be in for it."

"What are you doing?"

"I'm saving you," he said. "You and your uncle, both."

"How can you possibly say that?"

"Samantha, please, I can explain."

The boy at her feet was talking now, his confession tumbling out. It took every ounce of her patience to let him speak.

"Catesby's entire fortune is in Vivant Romani. And with all the engineers and planners involved, each day of delay is costing him more. If construction doesn't start immediately—tomorrow, actually—he'll have to abandon the project altogether."

"Go on," she said. "I'm listening."

"Having Dr. Barrows do the archaeological assessment was supposed to have avoided this. She's Catesby's employee, after all, and if she raised any objections, he could take steps to control her."

"But not my uncle?"

"No, Sam. Catesby has no sway over him."

Graham moved to climb out of the hole. But Samantha stood to block him.

"Not yet," she said. "Keep talking."

And talk he did, faster and faster, seeming almost eager to be free of his secrets.

"The early finds scared him. It looked like there might be something important up here, after all. Oona Jessel kept him informed, but it wasn't enough. He had to get rid of your uncle."

Now Graham's voice dropped low.

"That's why that American bloke came. The scary, mental one."

"Adam Quint."

"Right. Quint. He was supposed to scare your uncle—
*you*, actually, since Catesby reckoned your uncle would
want to protect you, quit the project, and take you home."

She frowned. The chase through town, the Pompeii
graffiti, the Greek fire, the ballista, being buried alive, and
today's incident upon the river—Adam's final chance to
do his old professor some lasting, bodily harm. Anyone
would have assumed that Jay would've tried to protect her
from these things. So would she have, once.

"But that Quint fellow did more than he was asked,"
Graham said. "Catesby can't control him. He's bloody
dangerous."

Samantha studied him. Graham looked scared.

"So what's your job in all this? What did Catesby want
you to do?"

Now Graham's voice got quieter still. He seemed too
ashamed to look at her.

"Catesby's other idea. His second front, he liked to call
it. 'It would be easy to give a final push,' he always said. 'To
finish what was started in Peru.' He wanted to humiliate
your uncle, to destroy what was left of his reputation."

Samantha shook her head.

"But it isn't working. We keep making discoveries.
Wardy Hill will save my uncle's career. Boudica herself was
here, and now we have the proof."

"No, Samantha."

Graham's voice was a shaky whisper.

"Sir Cairn *wanted* your uncle to find Boudica here. He wanted him to tell the world that the Warrior Queen's final stronghold had been found."

"But why?"

"Because he would be wrong."

Samantha felt dizzy.

"They're fake?" she asked, "The finds are all fake?"

Graham shook his head.

"They're real, actually, but two of them aren't from here. I found that Iceni coin out near the town of March."

She swallowed hard. That had been the artifact that had linked the site to Boudica. And everything else she and her uncle had just inserted into the story in their minds—the cut-up bones, the helmet, the ornate wooden bucket. Clare—practical, careful, clear-headed Clare—had been right all along.

"I'm sorry," Graham went on. "Really I am. My dad does anything Catesby asks, and I thought this all was sort of a game. That was before...before I liked you. That's why I'm here now—to set things right."

But she felt no warmth for the boy now. His admission only stung.

"What about that?"

She pointed at the sack.

"From the British Museum. Out on loan."

And then it all made sense. Oona's meeting on the river—where Adam had pushed the punt along the Cam. The actress had been posing as the young professor. Her impression had been perfect. And that's why the letters in Catesby's office had been to Clare, authorizing the transaction.

"It's what you think it is. Samantha. The statue from Boudica's raid on Camulodunum. Catesby knew your uncle wouldn't realize it as a museum piece. And so if he announces his big discovery to the world, his reputation and career will be destroyed. People would see it as the actions of a desperate man."

"Desperate?"

"From the sound of it, your uncle is very desperate, indeed. His university is investigating what happened in Peru. He may soon be out of a job."

At this, Samantha blanched. Jay had never told her. And Catesby had been right—he would have taken the bait. She knew what she needed to do.

She pulled Graham to his feet and helped him heave the head from his bag into hers.

"I'm sorry, Samantha," he said a final time. But she did not respond. Her fury was checked only by her need to act.

Graham hurried off to misinform his father that the head was not yet found and the trap was not yet tripped. For her part, Samantha had to warn her uncle—before he could announce a discovery he had not made and unveil the find that could destroy him.

———

She said nothing to Kasim and Stuart, and they were silent all the way back to town, no one commenting on the head-shaped bag sitting between them on the floor. Should she tell her brother? He would try to help her, certainly, but he was injured and would only slow her down. She had to tell her uncle, and him alone. And she would have to hurry.

But Jay was not in his room in college. He was not in the Ridge & Furrow either, which had closed its doors some hours before. His car was gone too, Samantha discovered, as she ran past the darkened Department.

Tom stopped her as she passed through the Porters' Lodge.

"Where in heaven's name have you been, miss?"

"I'm looking for my uncle," she blurted out.

"Ah, I wish you would've told me. Should be back in the morning. He's off to pick up a friend. From London, he said."

The Dodo, Samantha thought. Catesby's trap had sprung.

have to get to London

Jay is still up at
now it's all up to m*
Only thing I can do

part of this is my fault
was SO STUPID to trust
it's too late

atesby said
was all a trick
pect that we

| Depart | | Arrive | |
|---|---|---|---|
| 11:30 | Cambridge Station | 12:32 | London Kings Cross |
| 12:25 | Cambridge Station | 13:21 | London Kings Cross |
| 12:55 | Cambridge Station | 13:57 | London Kings Cross |
| 12:57 | Cambridge Station | 13:59 | London King |

if the Dodo decides that the site
the situation couldn't be worse
and now Jay and Clare could be

One thing I know for sure is
If he catches me he will kill

# CHAPTER 19

Rome would rise again at 10 a.m.

Samantha was exhausted from her adventures the night before. She dragged herself across the landing as soon as she was awake, hammering on her uncle's door. There was no answer. Jay was still not back. She would just have to meet him at the Department and explain the urgency of the situation there.

The Iceni gathered around the vans that morning, some wearing suits and ties. As Evan loaned Kasim his crutches for a quick experiment, Samantha pulled Stuart aside.

"Have you seen my uncle?"

"At the R&F with his friend from the Heritage Office. But they should be here soon."

This was not good, she thought. There was too much to explain. She needed to speak with him with no one else around.

But her uncle was not alone when he turned onto Downing Street.

"Hi, kiddo," Jay said as soon as she saw him. "You remember Simon."

"Hello there," said the Dodo. "Your uncle has promised me a day for the ages—but I don't think he's talking about Catesby's bloody theme park."

"Uncle Jay," she said. "I really need to talk to you."

"Later, kiddo."

"Now," she gritted her teeth. "It's urgent."

He excused himself from his old friend and led her a short distance away.

"Come on, Sam. I have to keep the Dodo happy. We have Catesby right where we want him! Today is our day! Victory's in sight!"

He gave one of her pigtails a teasing yank and returned to the Dodo's side. And then she saw the old Iceni friends climb into Jay's car and head off to Wardy Hill together before she could do anything to stop them. All she could do was take her seat in one of the excavation vans with Evan and the rest of the Iceni and follow the caravan of invited guests into the vast and hostile Fens.

The crowd gathered in the center of the site, the unfinished units still gaping upward at the sky. Chairs had been arranged in a large semicircle, two or three deep on the snow. Along with the other Iceni and Catesby's team of Romanists, Samantha recognized many in the crowd from the metal detectorist rally some days before. Catesby sat in a seat of honor in the middle of the great space, stealing glances at Jay. Ned Aubrey stood beside him. Lurking nearby were Adam and Oona—cracking their evil, private jokes. They knew what was coming too.

"I want you close, Sam," said Jay. "You too, Ev. Right up by me."

As he led them to the front of the audience, and as Evan straggled behind on his crutches, Samantha did her best to alert her uncle. But the Dodo had Jay's full attention, as eager as his Iceni comrade to take down their old professor with news of a glorious find.

"Where is it?" the Dodo whispered as everyone took their seats. "Where is this secret artifact waiting?"

Jay must not have told him exactly what they had found the day before. He pointed to Samantha's open unit, just a few paces away, and the old friends shared a mischievous smile.

The choir shuffled in, Graham leading the procession into the ringwork's center. Samantha couldn't believe his transformation. He seemed almost angelic in his robes, all traces of his activities the night before completely vanished. But when his eyes met hers, she saw how drawn and tired he looked, and how guilty.

"Wonderful!" cried Catesby, as the singers filed into their rows. "Marvelous! What a surprise!"

And it was marvelous and wonderful as the young voices washed over the assembly, swelling out from the ancient space.

*I vow to thee, my country, all earthly things above,*
*Entire and whole and perfect, the service of my love;*

Graham stepped forward for his solo.

*Her sword is girded at her side, her helmet on her head,*
*And round her feet are lying the dying and the dead.*
*I hear the noise of battle, the thunder of her guns,*
*I haste to thee my mother, a son among thy sons.*

There was applause when the song came to an end. And before it had faded completely, Oona stepped forward, wheeling a covered cart.

"My lord," she said, her voice unrecognizable for its cheerfulness—maybe channeling Clare Barrows once again. "It is my great pleasure to congratulate you on your project and to present this gift on behalf of the Cambridge Area Metal Detector Hobbyists Society."

She pulled the cover away with a flourish to reveal a shovel—its blade a polished silver.

"First excavation tool he's touched in years," the Dodo whispered.

"Made of melted-down coin hoards, I bet," Evan muttered, trying to get his uncle to laugh.

But Jay was focused on the scene before him, leaning forward in his chair. He was waiting for his moment. And each bit of congratulations Catesby received made worse his coming fall.

Or so poor Jay believed.

Now Catesby rose with the roar of applause, clapping his own hands along with the crowd.

"Marvelous," he said. "And what a perfect symbol this is of the partnership between the archaeologists and the public, and our shared love and respect for the past."

"Partnership?" Evan whispered, a little too loudly. "Respect?"

The Lord Professor raised a hand and the assembly fell silent.

"We are now beginning a new project, together—one that will celebrate not only the public's love of the past, but the glory of our Roman ancestors, whose gentle invasion marked the beginning of the British people."

He hefted the gleaming spade.

"For the glory of Rome!" he said.

But just as Catesby placed his clumsy foot on the heel of the shovel, and just as the photographers readied their cameras to capture Vivant Romani's beginnings, Jay's deep voice rang out above everything.

"Just a second, Cairn."

Out of the corner of her eyes, Samantha saw Adam and Catesby share a fleeting look of triumph. Jay had jumped to his feet, but everyone else was frozen, startled by the American intruder.

"Stop!" Samantha hissed. "Sit down!" But there was no stopping her uncle now.

"I want to apologize for breaking up this little party," he said, unable to contain the grin that spread across his face. "But Wardy Hill is now a scheduled monument. It's of national importance—international, really—and it's legally protected from construction."

Catesby gave out an exaggerated gasp. But other than his coconspirators, only Samantha seemed to know he was acting.

"On what grounds?"

The Dodo stood now, looking a little flustered.

"What my American friend means to say is that this site is now being considered for scheduling. There is, I understand, a final piece of evidence?"

"There is," said Jay. "And now might be the perfect time to show you."

The audience rose, following Jay and the Dodo to cluster around the unit. Catesby followed. If one didn't know any better, they would have thought he looked bewildered by what was happening. But Samantha did know better and saw the glee behind his furrowed brow.

She fought her way to the front as Jay stepped down to where he thought the head awaited him, pulling his trowel from his pocket and scraping away at the mud with practiced strokes. Adam looked on, ready to pounce at the slightest sound of metal on metal. But it didn't come.

"Just give me one second," Jay said. But the crowd around was growing restless, their bewilderment changing into anger.

"Bloody Yank," someone shouted, and then other insults followed—most of them much, much worse.

"It was here, though," said Jay. "Right here."

Catesby's angry scowl revealed the same thought, precisely. He was staring at Oona. She had been charged with this final, cruel prank and she had failed him.

"It was here, though," Jay said. "The head of the emperor's statue! The one Boudica brought to Wardy."

Catesby's wicked smile broke through now, a glaring mismatch with his angry words.

"Aha!" he said, returning to his script. "You've been caught out, Professor Sutton. You and your accomplice."

From his inside coat pocket, the Lord Professor withdrew a single folded page. Samantha recognized it as the letter in Catesby's office—the one addressed to Clare.

"You and Dr. Barrows have been very busy. Very busy indeed. You have approached this country's most prominent museum, asking for artifacts under the guise of supporting me and Vivant Romani. But all the while, you have been working to destroy it."

Dodo looked on, confused. Jay's mouth was open too.

"What? No…"

"Samantha!" cried Evan. "What's happening?"

She knew, and she knew what soon would follow. When the unit proved empty, a search would be made of her uncle's rooms, and then—immediately after—of her own quarters just next door. But when they found the head of the emperor, it would be Jay who would take the blame—a desperate man with his career in tatters, a motive obvious to everyone.

And then it would all be over.

She had to act quickly. As Catesby shouted his lordly orders, and as the bewildered crowd milled about in panic, she looked for someone who could help her. She needed to be taken back to Cambridge to collect the head of the emperor and then to escape the university town. But Jay was chest to chest with his former student, shouting in his grinning face. Stuart and Kasim were doing their best to restrain him. There was only one person who could help her now.

"Evan!"

Her brother stood apart from the chaos, perched on his crutches, his face bewildered.

"You've got to help me," she cried.

This seemed to break through his confusion, and he hobbled after her to the line of parked cars. Catesby had not learned his lesson, clearly, as the Lord Professor had again left his keys in the ignition of his precious antique.

"You drive."

Only now did Evan realize what his sister was asking.

"I can't, Samantha. I'm only fourteen."

"You have to. It's our only chance."

She saw her brother steel himself, then open the car door and maneuver into the seat, pulling his crutches in after him. She went around to the other side and climbed in.

"I don't have a clue how to do this," Evan said.

Samantha ignored him, staring through the window at the milling attendees. She saw Adam back away from her uncle, grinning in victory. But then his gaze turned in the direction of their puttering motor. His face fell. And then he charged toward them across the field.

"Go, Evan. Go!"

And go he did, speeding away from Wardy's Emperor and toward the cold bronze head of another.

———

"All right, miss?" asked Tom, as she flew through the Porters' Lodge. "In a hurry yet again?"

But there was no time to explain things to him. The car engine's was still humming, as Evan waited for her just outside. She had ignored him the whole way over, knowing she could not tell him or enlist his help. He was injured, and he would just get in her way if he tried to help. Eventually, he had given up on his questions and focused on his nervous driving. All he had to do to now was drive her to the train station and take the car back to the Department.

Up the stairs she ran, her quick strides filling the time-worn hollows. Her room seemed deathly still. As quickly as she could, she threw on an extra sweater, changed her gloves for a hardier pair, and collected her flashlight from the shelf. From the hiding place in the hearth, she took all the money she and her brother had, then opened her atlas to rip out the pages she needed.

And then it was time to face the emperor.

*Cálmate. Relax.*

Samantha dropped to her knees, and there he was, Boudica's long-dead enemy, glaring out at her from under the bed. She thrust her fingers into the vacant eyes to drag the horrible thing out into the open. She had forgotten how heavy it was. She was able to stuff it in her backpack, but swinging her backpack over her shoulder sent her staggering across the room. There was a long trip ahead of her, though, and she would just have to manage the weight.

Tom wasn't behind his desk when she came back through the Porters' Lodge. But he was right outside it in the narrow lane, leaning in through the window of Catesby's car, with Evan white-faced at the wheel.

No, she thought. Not now. Of course her brother was breaking the law by driving, but he had probably upset some age-old Cambridge custom too. Tom's dislike of her brother would be their downfall. They couldn't afford the delay.

But as she hurried over, it was clear that Tom was not delivering the lecture that she had assumed.

"There's a good lad," he was saying. "There's a good lad."

And Evan, she saw, was crying. Tom was the one adult who seemed at all interested in their safety, and her brother must have had told him everything—or everything he knew, at least, which wasn't anywhere close to all.

"Go inside and lock your door. Enough heroism from you for one day."

Evan sniffled and relented, casting his sister a guilty look as Tom opened the car door for him and helped him onto his crutches.

"As for you, miss," the porter said then, eyeing her heavy burden. "To the railroad station, is it?"

She nodded.

"Not the police?"

"No," she said, "the train."

She could see him considering her—this small-for-her-age girl with some big-for-her-age secret, and a charming but reckless uncle who was no help at all.

"Right," he said, at last. "I'll take you there, then drive this old banger back to the Department where it belongs."

She clambered in, and they drove off in a silence that surprised her. But Tom was a porter, and he knew how to be discreet. Discretion was his tradition. It didn't have to make sense.

———

"A ticket to London, please. Quick."

The ticket-seller cocked an eyebrow over her spectacles.

"You have your parents with you?" she asked. "Can't sell a ticket to someone your age, love, without some sort of approval."

Samantha looked over her shoulder. Tom had driven very fast all the way to the station. But Adam would guess her whereabouts, sooner or later. She had to hurry, even if it meant she had to lie.

"I'm going to see my aunt. She's expecting me."

The ticket-seller relented.

"I'm sure you understand, love. With your accent, I had to ask. Now, then. London, you say?"

"Yes, please."

A broadcasted voice announced an approaching train to King's Cross. This was taking far too long. Samantha shoved a handful of cash through the opening in the window and snatched up the ticket. And then she ran for the train, choosing a door far down the platform. She shrank low in one of the cloth-backed chairs until a whistle from the conductor warned of the closing of the doors. At last, she could allow herself to breathe. She had escaped and was off to London to prove her uncle's innocence.

A flurry of motion in the station shattered the relief. It was Adam, moving toward her at a sprint. He barreled through the line of people waiting at the café and onto the crowded platform, running up and down the length of the train. He was hunting her—her and her cargo. She slid low to the floor between the seats and saw his frantic shadow pass by.

And then the doors slid closed. Had he been able to board?

"Open up!"

Adam's voice was full of rage. But the rail employee's was flat and calm, used to the daily rage of angry commuters.

"You'll have to wait, sir. The next train is just behind this one, not two minutes north. Now if you please, sir. Remove your foot from the door."

Samantha straightened, eager to see what happened next. But her timing could not have been worse. As soon as she sat up in her chair, Adam was at her window, grinning above his raised red scar.

"See you in London, Samantha Sutton," he said, and slapped the window hard.

actually very famous. Jay should've recognized it.

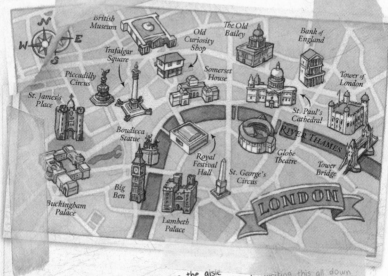

inches away from me right now across the aisle trying to get a hold of my thoughts by writing this all down

It was so strange seeing her in person...well not in person, exactly, but as close as possible. She looks pretty much how I imagined. And she had to be a warrior again today, thanks to me

tricked him, but not for long. And when he finds me,

SSFNb2-WH: 20a

# CHAPTER 20

The time passed far too quickly.

The scenery swept past her window, cold and barren beneath an unforgiving sky. Samantha needed to concentrate, but fear made that almost impossible. The emperor's head sat beside her on the seat, its fearful contours glaring through the canvas.

*Cálmate. Relax.*

She would have only a two-minute head start when she reached the city, so she needed to plan the journey ahead down to the slightest detail. She had to make every second count.

"We will shortly be arriving at London King's Cross," said the recorded announcement, and she hurried for the exit.

She was out and onto the platform before the doors were fully open. The station was crowded with returning holidaymakers, and Samantha did her best to fold herself into the bustle as she made her way toward signs for the Piccadilly Line. She bought a ticket from the machine and boarded the Tube, staying low and out of sight. Adam would know where she was going next. But the doors had sealed shut and the subway was moving. He hadn't found her yet.

Ten minutes later she was outside again, blinking in the cloudy light. The British Museum was just a few streets away. As a few passersby took notice of her backpack, she hefted it high on her shoulders and took off, running as fast as she could and straining against her load.

The great old institution was just as she imagined it would be—grand and austere—all columns and pediments and marble. But she would have no time to enjoy it. She raced through its iron gates and across the large forecourt, relieved to see that the museum doors were open. With no entry fee to pay, there wasn't a queue to block her entrance.

Inside, the Museum smelled of stone and ages—the wreckage of empires, near and far. She threaded through the crowd, looking for any uniformed employee. Within a few seconds, she found one and recited the question she had memorized the whole way there.

"Can I speak with the Curator of Early Britain?"

"Sorry?"

Samantha looked around her, only now realizing that she had stepped inside the gift shop.

"Er…the Curator of Early Britain, please? It's an emergency."

The shop manager frowned.

"I suppose I can ring someone," he said. "Wait here."

Samantha did wait, as patiently as she could, pacing between the tables of books and shelves of postcards, toys, and reproductions without giving them much mind.

But then she saw him—the emperor—staring at her from a glossy book cover. It was, very clearly, the same object that now bruised her shoulders and arched her back. She turned and saw him again. And then again. The emperor stared back at her from printed scarves and pillows, from sketchbooks and mugs, everywhere she looked. A poster of the bust cost £7.99 and gazed at her from the wall across, full of imperial anger and haughty contempt.

So, Samantha thought. This wasn't some obscure artifact she had in her bag. It was a national treasure—one Jay had failed to recognize in his desperation and fevered campaign of revenge. The situation was even worse than she'd feared. She felt dizzy.

"Can I help you?"

An older gentlewoman was standing there in a snow-white coat, clutching an elegant cane. At once, Samantha recognized her as the lady who had met Oona in the punt on the Cam—when Oona was Clare, and when Adam was steering them down the river out of sight.

She tried to speak but couldn't find the words. It wasn't just her uncle that needed protecting, she knew now. Clare was wrapped up in this, as well. The head was on loan in her name, and her reputation rode on its safekeeping. If Clare were blamed for some plot against Catesby, she would be lost as well.

The curator was getting impatient.

"Well?"

"Sorry," said Samantha. "I…I've made a mistake."

The woman gestured with her cane.

"What's that you have there?"

Samantha pulled away.

"It's all right, my girl. Is it an artifact? Something you've brought for me to identify?"

"It's nothing."

"Nonsense. Open the bag so I can see."

Samantha bolted, upsetting stacks of books and post-cards as she ran through the shop, and pushing through the tourists in the foyer to the afternoon cold outside.

She had a new destination now. She would have to get to Clare in faraway Salisbury, and take her Roman cargo with her.

She slid her hand into her backpack, past the face of cold hard metal, until her fingers closed around the phone. Drawing it out, she punched in the numbers with shaking fingers, checking each digit before hitting the green button. But when she held it to her ear, she heard not the ringing of the opposite end, but a pert young voice, obviously recorded:

"You have *less than one minute* of prepaid calling time remaining."

One minute? she thought. Only one? She silently cursed her brother. *This* was an emergency. *This* was what an emergency phone was for.

Now she heard the ringing on the other end—a burst

of two short rings, instead of the longer American one. Samantha paced the steps, upsetting a flock of pigeons.

"You have reached Dr. Clare Barrows, senior lecturer of archaeology at the University of Cambridge…"

The message seemed to go on and on.

"I'm afraid I can't take your call right now, but if you leave your name and details…"

She noticed a man standing across Great Russell Street, waiting impatiently to cross. He was wrapped in a green army jacket and wore an army hat pulled low.

"…I will get back to you as soon as I can."

Samantha heard a beep on the line and spoke as quickly as she could.

"It's Samantha. This is an emergency. I'm coming to find you."

She pounded at the End button with her thumb.

Adam had still not crossed the street. He had definitely seen her, though, and noted the burden she still carried. A wide smile stretched across his scar-crossed face. As soon as there was a break in the traffic, he would come for her and relieve her of her load.

A stream of cars went by unbroken and then a double-decker bus, blocking his view of her as it let tourists off at the Museum's iron gates. Samantha ran for it, sending up a frantic cloud of pigeons. Reaching the road, she launched herself inside, the head of the emperor clanging off the bus's open door. And then she hurried for the stairs to the upper deck.

Before she reached it, though, she heard the driver's angry voice.

"Ten pounds, please."

She whirled. But the driver wasn't speaking to her. Adam had boarded, right behind her. He met Samantha's terrified look with another mocking grin, slid a banknote to the driver, and moved toward her down the aisle.

But the driver wasn't done with him yet.

"A moment, sir. That's ten more for your daughter."

This was her chance.

"He's not my dad!"

But Adam had an answer for that. One that was particularly cruel.

"She's my niece," he said, and gave her an evil wink.

She hurried up the stairs to the bus's open upper deck, trying whatever it took to put distance between them. Despite the cold temperature, only two seats remained— next to each other across the central aisle.

Fate had never been so cruel. She settled numbly into one seat, and a moment later Adam settled into the other.

"Samantha," he said, his voice cold and low. "Niece. You shouldn't run off from me like that."

She shrank away from him, her mind racing. There had to be a way to escape him. She had to think of something.

An amplified voice startled her, booming from the speakers in her armrest.

"Welcome time travelers, young and old and young again! This is Blighty's Bus Tours and Travels in Time!

Hop on, hop off, as you like, just make sure you remember where *and when* you've joined us!"

None of the passengers seemed to listen as the bus pulled away from the curb, wrapped up in conversations of their own as they made their way south and east toward London's historic core. Samantha's whole body was tense as the minutes passed and more of London rushed by. She noticed that a girl about her own age sat directly in front of her, complaining to her mother in a loud American accent about how bored she was. Samantha cringed a little, even in her terrified state. Evan would have liked this girl, no question. Samantha already despised her.

They did share one thing in common, though. Under the girl's seat was the same backpack, cinched at the top and decorated with the British flag. But while Samantha's was dull and streaked with Fenland mud, the other girl's was brand new, its colors still clean and bright.

"We're now entering the City of London," said the voice of the tour guide. "That's City with a capital C. The financial center of all of Europe and where London began."

There was a movement by her shoes and Samantha instinctively jerked away. Adam had leaned across the aisle, probing for the backpack at Samantha's feet. She pushed it out of his reach as the tour guide continued.

"Now, who here has heard of Boudica, Queen of the Iceni?"

Samantha felt her arm go up—an automatic response. She heard Adam's mocking laughter as he raised his own hand high.

"We're now within the walls of what once was Londinium, which Boudica burned to the ground in her revolt of 61AD. It was right by that church there that workers found a pile of Roman skulls—the victims of the attack. But there's a layer of charcoal in the ground all around us, showing just how much the Warrior Queen destroyed. Quite a temper she had! Wouldn't want to be on her bad side!"

The bus turned to follow the line of the swollen River Thames, and they passed one London landmark and then another: domed St. Paul's Cathedral, the reconstructed Globe Theatre across the river, the towering London Eye. Ahead rose Big Ben and Parliament, the most famous monuments of all. By now her panic had overwhelmed her, though—a heavy buzz behind her eyes—and she did not have the time or strength to study them.

But then Samantha's unfocused gaze alighted on something glorious.

Her stalwart, steadfast sovereign. Her lovely lady Queen.

She would have recognized the statue anywhere. It was of Boudica herself.

As they stopped to let off passengers, the figure stood close beside them, just even with the bus' upper deck. The Warrior Queen was mounted in her bronze chariot, her bronze arms raised in righteous fury, a bronze spear clenched in her bronze and gleaming hand. Before her reared two bronze horses, and behind her were her children, safe now in her metal robes.

Adam had seen the statue too, and momentarily redirected his gaze. Samantha watched him study the ancient heroine's feature with a fearsome intensity, as if assessing a vanquished adversary. He seemed almost ready to attack.

This, Samantha knew, was her chance: now, while Adam looked away. She grabbed the backpack from the floor of the bus and stood.

"For Boudica!" she shouted, and heaved her burden high.

Her loud cry startled her fellow passengers. No eyes were on Westminster now. Instead, everyone watched the backpack fly higher and higher, then arc again toward earth.

But the Queen interrupted its path. There were gasps as a strap of the backpack snagged the statue's left hand with a clang, then swung there, side to side. It looked like Boudica herself was doing it, taunting her long-dead Roman foes.

"No," said Adam. "No!"

She cringed, watching the pink "X" throb on his jaw and throat. Would he lunge for her in front of all these people? Or, she hoped, would he take the bait?

He made his decision just as the bus began to move, charging down the stairs and onto the sidewalk outside, then scrambling at the statue's base, looking for a foothold to climb up it.

"My backpack! My brand-new backpack!"

But Samantha ignored the American girl's angry cries as the bus pulled away, and clutched her own burden close until Paddington.

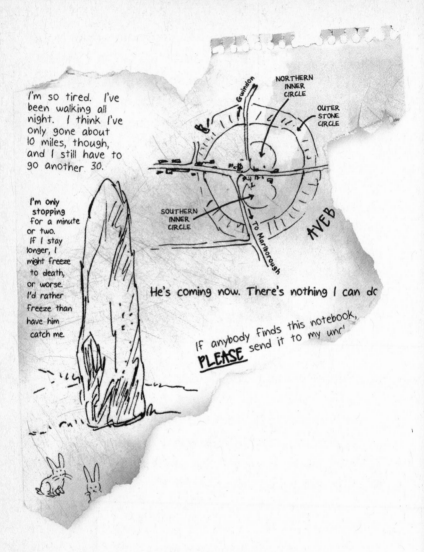

I'm so tired. I've been walking all night. I think I've only gone about 10 miles, though, and I still have to go another 30.

I'm only stopping for a minute or two. If I stay longer, I might freeze to death, or worse. I'd rather freeze than have him catch me.

He's coming now. There's nothing I can do

If anybody finds this notebook, **PLEASE** send it to my unc'

---

Samantha sprinted across the icy bridge, leaving the twinkling lights of the nearby city behind her in the dusk. She wanted so badly to turn and run for them. But between her and Swindon was murderous Adam Quint.

She had not lost him in London, as she had hoped. He must have caught up with her at Paddington, purchased his own ticket, and secretly shared her train. And then he had stalked her through the emptying streets of the small commuter town, waiting for his moment to strike.

They were alone together now, and miles and miles from anyone who could help her. Adam seemed to relish this fact. He followed her, unhurried, his boots crunching on the snow-covered road. Even at a run she could barely increase the distance between them, so great was the weight across her back. But he was waiting to make his move, and when she glanced over her shoulder, she saw that he was smiling.

A thick hedge lined the road on the other side of the overpass, and she plunged through it, eager to put something fixed between her and her pursuer. Even so, she knew it wouldn't stop him for long.

"Really, Samantha Sutton? Hide-and-seek? That's how you want to do this?"

Between the bushes she watched him draw near. He twirled a sharpened trowel around his fingers, reflecting the glint of approaching headlights.

"Please come out. We have so much to discuss."

But he hadn't noticed the car coming, so focused was he on their standoff. And through the hedge, Samantha didn't even see it hit him. One second he was there, pacing on the edge of the road. Then, after a sickening crunch, he wasn't.

The driver slammed the brakes, bringing the hulking vehicle to a skidding stop. Peering through the hedge, Samantha saw the orange door swing open and someone step out to check for the injured young man. But Samantha couldn't spot Adam anywhere. And neither could the driver, who, after several long moments of searching, climbed back into the car and continued down the road.

She sat in silence, trembling from cold now as much as fear. Was Adam badly injured? Was he even still alive? But there was no time to wait and wonder. This was her only chance.

And so Samantha ran.

Forgetting her pain and ignoring her clawing terror, she ran and ran as if an entire Roman legion were on her heels. Seconds became minutes as she labored along the roadway, and the pounding ache in her legs and shoulders became an incessant roar. Minutes stretched to an hour, then two. Adam might be after her still, she knew, and decided to distance herself from the pavement to make her route less obvious.

She pulled her flashlight out and switched it on as she moved away from the country lane and into the moon-lit fields, the better to see the ridges and furrows that threatened to trip her up. But even so, she stumbled on the wild tufts of grass again and again, and caught her clothes repeatedly on the wire fences that marked each property. In some places, the gleam of chalk in the moonlight looked so much like snow that she'd trip over it, expecting something yielding. Her pace began to slacken against her will.

Three hours in and the landscape began to change. At first, Samantha attributed it to her fatigue. But the terrain had become hilly and made her passage harder.

She should press on. She knew it. Adam might still be out there. But a nearby mound offered a place to rest and get her bearings. She collapsed into the snow, holding a dripping handful to her mouth to soothe her searing throat.

In the glow of her flashlight and the glimmer of the brilliant moon, Samantha eyed her backpack. A sudden impulse told her to open it, to make sure that the head of the emperor was still inside. She knew that the fear was ridiculous—the weight had never left her—but still she needed to stare upon the imperious visage once more.

With her freezing fingers, she worked at the cinched cord and finally pried it open, so that the bronze face glared up at her from the ground. The emperor's stare seemed more triumphant, somehow, its vacant stare a haughty mask of rage. The Empire would not be trifled with, it seemed to say. She could not escape its soldiers.

She felt hopeless—lost—and it took the last of her resolve to heave the backpack to her shoulders once more.

But a twinkling of lights ahead gave her a final gasp of courage. At least there was a village nearby.

She fixed her eyes on it, prepared to trudge on. But not before giving one last look back.

There was some movement behind her, a glint of moon-lit metal, swinging low and limping along the ground. With horror, Samantha knew that it was Adam, and the trowel he kept sharper than a knife.

She began to sprint again. But this time, her legs were failing her, and no amount of resolve would get them to carry her faster. He would be on her soon. And so, instead of continuing to the village, she veered off to the left, into the rolling hills. She turned off her flashlight and looked for a place to hide.

There was a sudden dip in the ground before her, and then a rise, as if she was passing through some ancient, weed-grown moat. She proceeded along gropingly for a few paces farther and suddenly she became aware of an enormous shape ahead, rising sheer from the snow and grass.

What is this place? she wondered, as she reached the upright stone. It seemed to hum with the moonlight and with the wind that played across its surface. She felt its scratchy side. It was solid, colossal, and seemed to radiate the little warmth it had soaked in the day before. Nearby, another shape made the black sky blacker, and another, and another, towering up in a loose, arcing line into the darkened distance.

There were a dozen pillars, maybe more. Some were upright, others flat on the ground, and it was soon obvious that they made up a forest of monoliths grouped in a wide, loose ring upon the grassy expanse of the plain. She stumbled from one to another, delirious and exhausted, looking for one final refuge to make her last stand.

And suddenly, she realized where she was and spoke its name aloud.

"Avebury."

She knew it from Evan's video game, *Pillager of the Past*, and from her own research as well. It was older than centuries. Older than Cambridge and London, and older than Boudica too. It was five millennia old, at least, from when Britain had barely begun.

And could it protect her now? She flung herself down behind a towering slab, pressing against it and soaking in the stone's mysterious warmth. There was strange comfort to be found there, as if she was wrapped in the protection of some ancient force.

But then the moon emerged, big and full, and Samantha realized at once that she was not alone. Adam was entering the stone circle himself now, limping as he came. She saw the gleam of moonlight against his blade and held the head of the emperor closer.

"Okay, Samantha. Hand it over."

He stood in the middle of the large, loose circle, a dark shape in the moonlight. She could hear his ragged breath. His horrible scars—the ones she'd given him—shone slick and ugly across his face and throat. And he was exhausted. He seemed to stagger, even as he stood, delirious from his anger and the chase. But he was smiling also, knowing his victory was near.

"Let's make this easy. Just throw it to me and I'll let you go. It's your uncle I'm after. All I need is that head."

She didn't move, just pressed her face into the ground.

"You're honestly protecting him, Samantha? He's put you in danger. Again. Who does that to a kid your age? What kind of uncle is he?"

The comment struck home. Jay had indeed failed her. And it wasn't the first time.

"There's no one coming to help you, Samantha. I can wait you out."

Several minutes passed. She risked a look around the stone to see Adam with his back toward her, swaying with fatigue.

A band of silver paleness had broken above the horizon, so that the pillars in that direction stood up blackly against the light. And then the glow grew bright—much brighter than a winter's dawn.

A big orange car had entered the circle, the same one—Samantha knew at once—that had collided with her pursuer some hours before. Now it turned, its headlamps pointing directly at them so that the stones flashed white. Adam was caught in the brilliance as well and stood with his arm over his eyes as the car rolled to a stop, its beams still trained on the strange scene at the center of the monument.

Samantha took the chance, ducking from one stone to the next around the circle, toward the mysterious arrival. But she hesitated. Who was that, opening the car door and stepping outside? Adam couldn't take the force of the headlamps and turned instead to face the monumental stones.

"Who's there?" he cried out. "Who is that?"

There was no answer. Just the crunch of footsteps on the gravel.

And now dark, living shapes began to form on the stones of Avebury, like shadow puppets on a screen. There were two figures there, then four, then six, dancing from one stone to another, surrounding the wincing student.

Adam spun, taking in the scene around him. He was unnerved, suddenly on the defensive.

"Who's there?"

No answer still, just the sounds of the ancient countryside coming to life.

He took one last look behind him, weighing a final lunge for Samantha and her cargo. But half a dozen opponents were too many, even for someone like him. Finally, he raised his hands above his head, surrendering to the swarming shadows.

Even from Samantha's position, it was impossible to tell what was happening. Had a whole search party been formed? Had the Iceni mobilized to rescue her?

But Adam would not be there to find out.

He began to run, back the way he had come, loping across the chalk downs of Wessex. Samantha saw him slip on a patch of snow, then right himself. And at last he was gone, lost in the early morning gloom.

Only now did the car lights dim.

"Samantha?"

She recognized the voice at once and felt her heart well up.

It was Clare.

Samantha ran for her, and the professor wrapped her in a tight embrace.

"How did you know?" she managed. "How did find me here?"

"I got your voice message, Sam. I set off to find you at once."

"I mean, how did you know I'd be here? That I'd take the train to Swindon? That I'd come the rest of the way on foot."

Clare smiled.

"Because, Samantha Sutton, it's exactly what I would have done. You and I are very much alike."

It was the nicest compliment that Samantha had ever received. Only now did she look around for the others, whose shadows had danced upon the Avebury stones like a band of merry spirits, sending Adam scrambling away in fear. But there was no one to be found. Just three very large rabbits, clustered in the center of the monument, their six upright ears casting faint shadows in the early morning sun.

"Those aren't rabbits," she murmured.

"You're right," said the professor. "They're hares."

"For Boudica?" Samantha said, her voice barely a whisper.

"No," Clare said. "From her. To you."

Dear Samantha,

Odds are your uncle won't give even you this note. I don't think he likes me much after what's happened. Can't say I blame him! And if he does give it to you, I'm not sure you'll even read it. Can't say I'd blame you, either!

You'll be keen to know that Lord Catesby's park won't be built, after all. Not because the site's going to be listed—I don't think it will, after what's ~~been~~ happened. But the Emperor's money has all run out, my dad says, and the engineers may even take legal action.

Catesby's taken out all his rage on Oona Jessell. He's somehow already managed to get her sent down from Cambridge (or "expelled," I'd think you say in America). My dad saw her coming out of the Department after it happened. She looked something savage. I'd tell your uncle that he has another enemy, if I were you. Watch his back.

Anyway, I want to tell you how sorry I am, Samantha, and ~~how~~ how I hope we can one day be friends. And I'm selling my metal detector, so

# CHAPTER 21

**H**eathrow Airport was a clamor of restless voices, rising and falling and rising again in languages Samantha could not begin to identify. As she followed her uncle and brother into the vast, brightly lit departure lounge, it barely felt like England. And today, that was a sort of relief.

She found a seat and collapsed into it. She had had a chance to rest in Clare Barrows's Salisbury home, sitting by the cozy fire and writing in her notebook while her memory was still fresh. But her shoulders were still weary where her backpack had rubbed them raw two nights before, and it felt good to sit down. There was a long flight ahead of them, and then a busy week as she settled back into normal life. But Adam Quint was still out there, full of dark revenge, and Samantha had yet to get a good night's sleep.

She took out Graham's letter again, using all her remaining energy to focus on the positive. In some ways, they had won. The emperor's head was back with Clare and en route to its home in London, cleaned of all its mud and grime. With Catesby's finances run dry, no theme park would destroy the site of Wardy Hill, and Samantha was glad of it—even though the link to Boudica remained nothing more than local lore. And while Jay had not made any gains in recovering his reputation, he had not damaged it further. Samantha was to thank for that, though no thank-you had yet come.

She looked at him now in the seat beside her, pretending to listen to Evan as he rattled on about the video games that awaited him back at home. But Jay's mind was clearly elsewhere. Clare had refused to see him when she dropped Samantha off an hour before, bidding good-bye to her on the curb and leaving her to enter the airport alone. If Samantha knew her uncle, he had had a whole speech ready, full of confidence and charismatic charm. With no one to deliver it to, he seemed beaten, defeated. Older.

"Can I see your passport?" she asked him.

This had always cheered Jay up. Thumbing through the blue ragged book, full of stamps and sticker visas, she would pick one at random and he would tell her all about the teenage monk who had robbed him in Laos, the flash flood in Jordan's Petra, or the mud volcanoes of the Colombian coast. Today, though, Jay handed it to her in silence.

She flipped through it anyway, pulling out the boarding pass that Jay had tucked inside. But something about it struck her as odd. The destination did not match her own.

"Uncle Jay? You're not on our flight?"

"Wait, what?" asked Evan, shifting his crutches out of the way. "You're not going to California?"

Jay shook his head.

"No, guys. I'm off to see a friend. It's a lead on another job. Something to tide me over while my university makes up its mind."

But the place on the ticket had unnerved her.

"A job?" she asked. "There?"

Jay nodded. He seemed ashamed for not having told them, but even so, it was clear that he didn't want to talk about it. There were several awkward minutes of silence, then he took his passport back from her and stood.

"I should probably head to my gate," Jay said, leaning in to hug them both. "Safe travels, you two. Stay together. I'll try to see you soon."

With that he left them there in shocked silence. They watched as he showed his documents to an official, then trudged slowly down the hall.

"Don't worry about Uncle Jay," said Evan. "He never lets anything get to him."

That was usually true, she thought, and lately a big problem. But Samantha could sense her uncle's deep sadness all the way across the departure lounge.

And at last she felt her own tears rising. This wasn't how this project was supposed to end. Jay should be with Clare now, and a respected archaeologist once more. But he had ruined everything and Clare was gone. Jay was entirely alone.

A passing couple drove the point home. They were

obviously in love, their arms around each other as they made their way through the departure hall, wrapped in winter clothing. They were young and carefree, and as they handed their documents to the airport official, it seemed as if nothing in the world could stop them.

Jay and Clare were supposed to be like that, Samantha thought, boarding the plane together and off on their next adventure. They were supposed to be just as in love.

But something about the pair distracted her. The young woman's color seemed a little off, and her icy blue eyes seemed to suck some of the warmth from the room. The young man was tall and athletic, but his smile seemed more of a grimace than a grin, and the scars that raised in an $X$ on his throat and jaw seemed to glisten in the harsh, fluorescent light.

She jumped to her feet, knocking Evan's crutches to the ground.

She wanted to scream.

But Adam Quint and Oona Jessel were on Jay's flight, and there was nothing Samantha Sutton could do.

# AUTHOR'S NOTE

This book is a work of fiction. However, since it draws heavily on real archaeology done by real archaeologists at a real archaeological site, some explanation is needed.

It's hard not to be a little loose with Boudica's story, given how little is known about her. If—*if!*—the ancient historians are to be believed, she was a woman who lived most of her life in an already Romanized Britain, a member of one of its wealthiest native tribes and wife—then widow—of the Iceni king, whose deal with the Empire was meant to secure the future of his family.

When Boudica and her children fell victim to Rome's change of heart, and her protests were met with extreme violence, the rebellion she raised destroyed three of Rome's young colonies and almost caused the Empire to abandon the island altogether. When she was at last defeated, it was at the hands of a much smaller but much more professional Roman force, and—here's where my retelling differs—she died soon after from suicide or grief.

Now about that "if." Neither of the two classical historians who chronicled Boudica's life are exactly unassailable. The first, Tacitus, was five years old when the rebellion is said to have taken place. The other, Cassius Dio, would not be born for another hundred years. This begs the question: what survived of the actual story when these chronicles were written? And to what degree did the two historians shape the scraps of remembrance to their own persuasive needs? Was it a cautionary tale they were telling, about the price of betrayal or the consequences of female rule? Was it to serve as a warning for an Empire in trouble? Was the Warrior Queen story only propaganda? Was Boudica herself a complete invention?

We just don't know. And maybe we never will. These aren't questions well suited for archaeology—a science that does better with past peoples than it does with past persons or specific historical events. Yes, archaeologists have attributed various features and artifacts to the first-century British rebellion. Some claim that the ancient chronicles can be substantiated with physical evidence of the rampaging Iceni: a defaced Roman tombstone, the head of the Claudius statue from Camulodunum, and—most notably—thick layers of ash in each of the cities Boudica purportedly burnt to the ground. But, others feel this sort of work is archaeology in reverse: fitting artifacts to a story we think we know, rather than letting the data tell its own.

There are general, local associations between the Boudica narrative and Wardy Hill, but the one in this book is my invention. This is not to say that Wardy Hill isn't a noteworthy place. Situated at a strategic position on what once was an island at the edge of the Fens, the Iron Age enclosure seems to have been a place of refuge for a sizeable population into the Roman era. Notably, the residents of Wardy Hill seemed to have actively rejected Roman influence. Why? We don't know. But the lack of Roman goods is striking.

The results of Cambridge Archaeological Unit's 1991–1992 wintertime excavation are published in an excellent report entitled *Power and Island Communities: Excavations at the Wardy Hill Ringwork, Coveney, Ely.* I recommend it to anyone who would like to learn more about the site.

With a few exceptions, my fictional team's discoveries are based on those the report lays out. The Samian-ware pottery, scatterings of rings and jewelry, the high-status bucket stave, and cut-marked human bones were all excavated at Wardy in much the way I describe. I took some liberties with the Roman cavalry helmet, which was not excavated from Wardy but uncovered at Witcham Gravel, a few hundred yards to the southwest. Also, while a World War II pillbox still stands at Wardy Hill, it would not serve as a very good lab.

Those readers who have finished the book will know that I did—but didn't—stretch the truth with the statuary head of the Emperor Claudius, which is indeed thought by many to be the one described by Tacitus as plunder from Boudica's rebellion. In real life—I love this story—the head was found on a riverbank by young boys who thought it was a soccer ball. Realizing it was a statue of some kind, they took it home, painted it white, and stuck it on a post to display as decoration until its true history was discovered. Like the cavalry helmet, it now holds a place of honor in the British Museum's Hall of Roman Britain.

I haven't been completely fair to my alma mater. Though some of the attitudes and situations I describe are drawn from my own experience, Cambridge is an international and mostly modern institution. It's also a wonderful place to study archaeology. The faculty's teaching staff is kind and patient, and demonstrates a deep respect for all past peoples, regardless of period or region. Finally, any members of the House of Lords who happen to be associated with the Department have nothing in common with the one I have invented.

Sadly, metal detecting is the scourge I describe it to be. Under current English law the hobby is usually legal, and naive efforts to mitigate its harmful effects on the archaeological record have all been failures.

# ACKNOWLEDGMENTS

I am tremendously grateful for the help, encouragement, and great patience of my family, friends, colleagues, and mentors—most of whom, I'm lucky to say, fall into more than one of these categories.

Thanks first to my parents, Paul and Nancy Jacobs, for their careful readings of the manuscript and a lifetime of unquestioning support. Thanks also to my agent, Cathy Hemming, for her warmth, advice, and advocacy; to Steve Geck, my eerily insightful editor; and to Marissa Moss— travel buddy, talented illustrator, and gracious and hard-hitting role model. And thanks, too, to Jennifer Fosberry for her crucial, last-minute edits.

I'm awed by the generous counsel I've received from some of the world's foremost experts in British archaeology— including Francis Pryor, Chris Gosden, Paul Barford, and Christopher Evans. If any error or oversimplification has found its way into this book, it's my fault alone and likely contrary to their specific guidance.

Thanks also—and thank goodness—for the insights of Becca Smith, Katja Armstrong, Dan Bradley, and Richard Forsythe, whose expertise on regional dialects, the particulars of Cambridge's layout, Classical Latin, and the specifics of the National Rail Service has no doubt spared me from some massive, future embarrassment.

Final thanks to my emphatically joyful daughter, Ada, and to Lindsay, my staggeringly brilliant wife, who inspire me every day.

# ABOUT THE AUTHOR

Jordan Jacobs has loved archaeology for as long as he can remember. His childhood passion for mummies, castles, and Indiana Jones led to his participation in his first excavation at age thirteen in California's Sierra Nevada. After completing a high school archaeology program in the American Southwest, he followed his passion through his education at Stanford, Oxford, and Cambridge. Since then, Jacobs's work for the Smithsonian, the American Museum of Natural History, and UNESCO headquarters in Paris has focused on policy and the protection of archaeological sites in the developing world.

Jacobs's research and travel opportunities have taken him to almost fifty countries—from Cambodia's ancient palaces to Tunisia's Roman citadels, Guatemala's Mayan heartland, and the voodoo villages of Benin. He now works as Head of Cultural Policy at the Phoebe Hearst Museum of Anthropology at UC Berkeley.

If you liked *Samantha Sutton and the Winter of the Warrior Queen*, turn the page and check out these other great mysteries from Sourcebooks Jabberwocky.

# SAMANTHA SUTTON AND THE LABYRINTH OF LIES

## Jordan Jacobs

A legendary ghost, an ancient treasure, a mystery only Samantha Sutton can solve.

There's nothing twelve-year-old Samantha Sutton wants more than to become an adventure-seeking archaeologist like her brilliant Uncle Jay. Samantha's big dreams are finally coming true when Jay invites her along on a summer excavation exploring an ancient temple in the Peruvian Andes.

But this adventure isn't exactly what she thought it would be with her nosy older brother, Evan, and Jay's bossy colleagues monitoring her every move. On top of that, she has to deal with the local legend, El Loco: a ghostly madman who supposedly haunts the ruins. But when the project's most important finds go missing, it's up to Samantha to solve the mystery before Jay loses his job and the treasures of the temple are lost forever.

### PRAISE FOR *SAMANTHA SUTTON AND THE LABYRINTH OF LIES*:

"Readers will be focused on the mystery, pulled on by gripping suspense." —*Kirkus*

"Capable, passionate Sam is a rewarding heroine to follow." —*Publishers Weekly*

# MIRA'S DIARY: LOST IN PARIS

## Marissa Moss

*Who sends postcards anymore? I wondered when I saw it in the mailbox. Then I recognized the loopy handwriting and my stomach lurched, first in relief, then in boiling hot rage.*

When Mira receives a cryptic postcard from her missing mother, she sets off with her father and brother to find her in Paris. Only Mira doesn't know she's looking in the wrong century.

With an innocent touch to a gargoyle sculpture on the roof of Notre Dame, Mira is whisked into the past. There she learns her mother isn't just avoiding the family, she's in serious trouble. Following her mother's clues, Mira travels through time to help change history and bring her mother home.

### PRAISE FOR *MIRA'S DIARY: LOST IN PARIS*:

"Long after I finished this fast-paced and compelling novel, I thought about Mira. Would I be as determined in pursuit of truth and tolerance? Would you?" —Karen Cushman, Newbery Medal Winner

"Lost in Paris is a whirlwind, time-travelling tour of the city of lights—replete with fiery artists, evil beauties, creepy gargoyles and vibrant sketches...all my most favorite things." —Lisa Brown, bestselling author and illustrator of *How to Be* and *Sometimes*

# MIRA'S DIARY: HOME SWEET ROME

## Marissa Moss

*Your next time travel will be trickier because you'll need to disguise yourself. It's a dangerous time, Mira. So, be careful. I miss you terribly! Love, Mom*

As if traveling to a new country in search of her missing mother weren't difficult enough, Mira has to do it dressed as a boy. In a different century.

A new postcard from her time-traveling mother points Mira to 16th century Rome. But before she can rescue her mom, she must follow the clues left around the city to find Giordano Bruno, a famous thinker and mathematician, who discovered something so shocking that important Italian officials don't want it revealed. All the while avoiding the Watchers—time-traveling police who want Mira back in her own time.

It's another whirlwind adventure for Mira, and this time she is determined to bring her mother out of the past.

### PRAISE FOR *MIRA'S DIARY: HOME SWEET ROME*:

"An engrossing, diary-style blend of history, mystery, and time travel." —*Publishers Weekly*

"With an engaging story, accessible history, and a spunky heroine, *Mira's Diary* is an absorbing, fast-paced adventure." —*School Library Journal*